REVIVED

NEW YORK TIMES BEST SELLING AUTHOR
SAMANTHA TOWLE

OTHER CONTEMPORARY NOVELS BY SAMANTHA TOWLE

Revved

Trouble

THE STORM SERIES

The Mighty Storm
Wethering the Storm
Taming the Storm

PARANORMAL ROMANCES BY SAMANTHA TOWLE

The Bringer

THE ALEXANDRA JONES SERIES

First Bitten
Original Sin

Copyright © 2015 by Samantha Towle
All rights reserved.

Visit my website at www.samanthatowle.co.uk

Cover Designer: Najla Qamber Designs

Editor and Interior Designer: Jovana Shirley, Unforeseen Editing, www.unforeseenediting.com

No part of this book may be reproduced or transmitted in any form or by any means, electronic or mechanical, including photocopying, recording, or by any information storage and retrieval system without the written permission of the author, except for the use of brief quotations in a book review.

This book is a work of fiction. Names, characters, places, and incidents either are products of the author's imagination or are used fictitiously. Any resemblance to actual persons, living or dead, events, or locales is entirely coincidental.

ISBN-13: 978-1514757215

This is for all you Revved *fans and #CarrickCrushers out there.*

Prologue: India 1
Prologue: Leandro 7
Chapter One 11
Chapter Two 23
Chapter Three 31
Chapter Four 39
Chapter Five 47
Chapter Six 51
Chapter Seven 59
Chapter Eight 71
Chapter Nine 79
Chapter Ten 89
Chapter Eleven 101
Chapter Twelve 109
Chapter Thirteen 119
Chapter Fourteen 125
Chapter Fifteen 131
Chapter Sixteen 139
Chapter Seventeen 145
Chapter Eighteen 151
Chapter Nineteen 157
Chapter Twenty 163
Chapter Twenty-One 167
Chapter Twenty-Two 173
Chapter Twenty-Three 179
Chapter Twenty-Four 191
Chapter Twenty-Five 207
Chapter Twenty-Six 215
Chapter Twenty-Seven 221

Chapter Twenty-Eight	225
Chapter Twenty-Nine	231
Chapter Thirty	237
Chapter Thirty-One	243
Chapter Thirty-Two	251
Chapter Thirty-Three	257
Chapter Thirty-Four	263
Chapter Thirty-Five	271
Chapter Thirty-Six	279
Epilogue: Leandro	287
Epilogue: India	291
Acknowledgments	301
About the Author	303

INDIA

THIRTEEN YEARS AGO

✛ MANCHESTER, ENGLAND

TWO PINK LINES.

I check the instructions again.

Two pink lines…pregnant.

No. Oh God, no.

I can't be pregnant. I can't. I'm only seventeen. I live in a group home. I can't have a baby. I can barely look after myself.

It's okay, India. Paul will know what to do.

He's older, responsible. He'll fix this.

But no one can find out that I'm pregnant. If anyone finds out that Paul and I have been sleeping together, he'll be in trouble. Big trouble.

I'm just afraid to tell him. *What if he thinks I got pregnant on purpose?*

Kit. I need to tell Kit. He's my twin brother, my best friend. He'll know how to handle this.

But if Kit finds out about Paul and me, he'll kill Paul. My brother is really protective of me. And he might only be seventeen, but he's big for his age.

Oh God, what a mess.

There's a bang on the bathroom door at the group home I live in. There's no peace in this place.

"One minute!" I yell.

My hand shaking, I push the test back into its box, shove it into my jacket pocket, and zip it up. After washing my hands, I flush the toilet and unlock the door.

Zara, nosiest cow in the world, is on the other side. "You've been in there for ages. What were you doing?" She gives me a suspicious look.

"Same thing as you're going to do in here." Without another word, I walk past her.

I can't go to my room. I need to get out of here.

I need to talk to Paul.

He's not here today. He should be at home.

I'll go to his flat.

I should probably text him to say that I'm coming to see him. I always have to text him to let him know.

He worries that people might find out about us, so he says I should make sure that it's safe for me to go.

But nothing feels safe anymore.

I'm going to have a baby.

Leaving the group home, I artfully manage to dodge Kit.

I catch a bus for the short journey to Paul's flat.

I get off and walk on trembling legs to his place and go up the two flights of stairs to his door.

I ring the doorbell.

No answer. But I know he's here because his bicycle is outside in the hall.

I ring again but nothing.

Maybe he's in the shower and can't hear me.

I decide to try the door. He rarely locks it if he's in.

Handle turns.

I let myself inside and walk to the living room.

Not there.

Or the kitchen.

I walk past the bathroom. I can't hear the sound of running water.

Then, I hear voices. Plural. Coming from his bedroom.

And my heart sinks.

No. Please no.

Fear fills me like poison. I'm struggling to catch a breath. My body starts to shake, my heart banging against my rib cage.

Forcing myself to move, I stand outside his bedroom door. With a trembling hand, I reach out and turn the handle.

My sunken heart drops like a stone.

Paul is lying on his bed. He's naked with a woman astride him. A naked woman.

They're clearly having sex.

Jesus.

My hand clutches my stomach. The pain is so bad that it's spreading outward to the rest of my body.

Tears fill my eyes.

He instantly sees me standing there, and his face blanks. Shock and fear fill his features.

He grabs the woman by the arms, stopping her in her endeavors.

That's when she turns her face to me.

Then, I see she's not a woman at all.

She's a girl.

A girl I know. Cassie. She lives at the group home where I live.

And she's fourteen years old.

Bile rises in my throat.

I stumble out of the flat to the sound of Paul's shouting voice.

I run out of the building, heading straight for the bus stop, which is thankfully empty. I hide around the back of the bus shelter, so Paul can't see me.

I swipe the tears from my cheeks.

Cassie. She's only fourteen.

But wasn't I fifteen when Paul started sleeping with me? It seemed so romantic that a man wanted me then, but now, after seeing him with her…it seems wrong.

Why didn't I see it then? Why didn't I see what kind of man he is?

Now, I'm pregnant—with the man who works at my group home.

A man who likes to have sex with teenage girls.

I can't stop myself from throwing up.

When I reach the point of dry-heaving, I try to steady my breathing. My mind is going a mile a minute.

Moving away from the stench of my own vomit, I stand around to the side, still staying out of sight. Hand pressed to my stomach, I lean my back against the shelter. I slowly pull my phone from my pocket and speed-dial the only person in the world I have.

Kit answers on the first ring, "What's wrong?"

Twin intuition. Kit and I always know when there's a problem with the other.

"I'm in trouble." Tears tumble down my cheeks.

"What kind of trouble?"

"I-I…I'm pregnant."

Silence.

But I can hear him breathing down the line.

"Kit?"

"Where are you?" Disappointment laces his voice.

It slices me wide open.

A sob escapes me. I take a deep breath. "I'm at a bus stop."

"Where?"

I hold my breath before speaking next, "The one near…Paul's flat."

More silence.

He doesn't need to say anything. I hear it in that silence.

That's how Kit deals with things. He doesn't rage or shout. His silence is his anger, and it speaks volumes.

"I'm coming to get you now." There's a barely restrained edge in his voice.

"Don't be angry with me, Kit. *Please*," I sob.

"I'm not angry with you, India." His voice is marginally softer.

But he always calls me Indy. He only calls me India when he's angry with me.

"I'm angry with that motherfucker. No, I'm fucking beyond angry. I'm livid. I'm gonna kill that motherfucking pervert!"

"Kit…no! Please!"

"I'm coming now, India. And don't you fucking move from where you are. I mean it."

Then, he's gone, and I'm left clutching the phone in my hand. Feeling like my life is over, I pray to God to fix this.

LEANDRO

ONE YEAR AGO

 SAO PAULO, BRAZIL

CLOSING MY EYES, I recite the words of my hero, the great Ayrton Senna, in my head, as I always do before each race.

"Being second is to be the first of the ones who lose."

Right before I climb into my car, I pray it works for me this time.

I can't lose.

I have to win this race.

My points are down, but I am on poll today. But still, that pain-in-my-ass Carrick Ryan could beat me again if I don't pull it out of the bag today.

I can fucking do this.

I'm Leandro Silva, for fuck's sake.

I'm the man who men want to be.

Pulling on my helmet, I slide in the cockpit.

Focus is everything right now.

My life is fucking great. And I can make it even better if I take the gold home today.

Brazil will love me even more if I win today.

My mechanic hands me my steering wheel. I fix it in place.

I'm ready to go.

I give a nod to let my mechanics know that I am ready. The voices in my ears start talking.

I pull out into the lane and begin my warm up lap.

Then, I'm in starting position, along with the other drivers.

My engine is revving, and I am more than ready.

Red…

Red…

Red…

Red…

Red…

Go!

I slam down hard on the accelerator and start moving alongside all the other cars, gaining traction.

Soon enough, I'm in the lead. Ryan is hot on my tail, but I keep this up, and I'm golden. I'm in for a win for sure.

Winning in my home country…nothing better. Well, apart from winning the championship.

I reach a corner. I steer through it.

What the fuck? She's sticking. I can't turn.

Fuck! I tug at the steering wheel, trying to turn, but she won't give, and the corner is coming up too fast.

Panicked voices are in my ears. They know something is wrong, but I can't speak, too focused on what is happening right now.

Come on, baby. Turn.

No matter what I do, the steering wheel is stuck, and I'm not going to turn in time.

Oh God.

I know there's nothing I can do.

This is it. I'm fucked.

The wall comes at me fast. I close my eyes.

The impact is as hard as I expected. I feel my body shatter.

Pain…excruciating.

REVIVED

My skin…hot.
Smoke in my lungs.
Can't breathe…
Blackness.

LEANDRO

✚ LONDON, ENGLAND

YOU EVER HAVE THE KNOWLEDGE of why you are somewhere, but you're not really sure if it is the right place to be?

That's how I feel while sitting in the waiting room of my new therapist, Dr. India Harris.

Well, I say new because this is the first time I'm meeting with her.

How the fuck did it come to this? When did I turn into this version of myself? A man who needs to see a therapist.

Of course I know the answer to that question.

The day of my accident. The day I nearly died.

Well, technically, I did die, but the doctors managed to resuscitate me.

Shame.

Sometimes, I wonder if it would have been better if they hadn't. Now, I am less than half the man I used to be. A pussified version of myself, who can't climb into a regular car, let alone my race car.

I can't drive. And without that, I am nothing.

Now, I have to see a goddamn therapist as my last-ditch attempt to get me back into a car.

So, I'm here to see Dr. Harris because she's apparently one of the best.

She'll *fix* me.

Part of me is intrigued to see if that is even possible because I know how truly fucked up I am. And it is going to take a fucking miracle worker to bring back the Leandro Silva of before.

The Leandro the world wonders what the hell has happened to.

Am I here by choice? No.

My team is making me. Well, *making me* sounds harsh. They didn't drag me here, kicking and screaming. I'm under contract, so I'm currently being paid to do nothing.

I sit on my ass and drink and fuck women.

I don't work for my money.

At the last meeting, I was told, in no uncertain terms, that if I didn't pull my head out of my ass and start racing again, my contract would not be renewed.

It makes sense. Who would want to spend millions of pounds on a racing driver who can't race?

My mother would happily never have me race again.

But my colleagues and friends think it's time I sort my shit out.

Particularly, my friend—a person who, twelve months ago, I would never have thought I would call a friend—Carrick Ryan. Once my rival, he's now, surprisingly, my closest friend.

After my accident, he and his then girlfriend and now wife, Andi, came to visit me in the hospital back home in Brazil.

Every time they were back in Brazil to visit Andi's mother or to attend a race for Carrick, which was regularly, they would come see me.

Then, Carrick and I started talking on the phone.

When I realized he wasn't the dick I thought he was, we became friends.

Dr. Harris is Andi's therapist. She recommended the doctor to me. Andi has been seeing her to deal with her fears over Carrick's racing, which are related to her father

REVIVED

dying in a race when she was a small child. Her dad died in front of her. It royally screwed her up.

Both Andi and Carrick assure me that Dr. Harris will be able to help me.

Hence, why my ass is in this chair in the waiting room.

Impatient, I glance at the clock, tapping my fingers on the arm of the chair.

My appointment was due to start five minutes ago.

I hate waiting.

I'll wait five more minutes, and then I'm out of here.

My eyes move to the magazines on the table. A sports mag is peeking out from under the fashion mags. Leaning forward, I pull it out, instantly wishing I hadn't.

On the cover of the magazine is a picture of me with the caption, *What the Bad Side of Formula 1 Looks Like*.

Nice.

So, now, I'm the bad side of Formula 1. Good to know.

I already know what the media say about me. How I've turned from a great racer into a drunk and a whore.

They're not wrong on the whore part. Well, *whore* is a bit harsh. I don't charge for my services. And I wouldn't say I'm a drunk. I just like to drink—a lot.

I shouldn't read the article. I know this, but the sadistic part of me has me turning those pages.

Finding the article, eyes scanning the text, I pick out the usual shit.

> *Why is Silva no longer racing? Physically, he's healthy. Is it mental problems? Fear over racing because of his accident? Is that why he drinks—drowning his misery in alcohol? Such a shame to see a once great driver fall from grace so dramatically.*

Frustration and rage grip my chest like a vise.

Fuck this. I don't need this shit.

Even though I can't race, it's not like I actually need to.

I don't need to race. I just need to drink and fuck. That's all I need now. All I will ever need.

Liar.

I'm a liar and a chickenshit. And that's why I'm sitting in the waiting room to see a therapist.

Maybe I am beyond help.

Tossing the magazine back onto the table, I get to my feet, ready to leave this place, just as the door opens, revealing the epitome of what I could really do with screwing right now.

My eyes trail up the tanned, toned legs to the fitted pencil skirt that I would happily hitch up to see the magnificent pussy that I bet lies beneath. A pale-pink blouse is tucked into that skirt, covering what looks like a fantastically sized pair of tits. Silky blonde hair sits on her shoulders. Hair that I would enjoy getting my hands all tangled in while I fuck those bright red lips of hers, enjoying seeing that lipstick smeared all over my cock.

My dick pulses in my jeans, more than ready to proposition her with the offer.

"Mr. Silva." She steps forward. "I'm Dr. Harris. But please call me India."

She's Dr. Harris?

This hitch-your-skirt-up-and-let-me-fuck-you-right-now woman is my new therapist.

Well, that's just fucking great. It's not like I can bang my therapist.

I put my cock on hold and give her my best smile, the one that always has panties dropping to the floor, as I say, "And you can call me Leandro."

"Leandro. Okay."

I see a definite flush in her cheeks. The same flush I see in all women who want to fuck me.

Stop it. She's your therapist.

Not yet she isn't. This is only my first session to see if we like each other.

We might not.

Who am I kidding? I definitely like her. Well, I would like her right up until I came, and then I wouldn't want to see her again.

Do I really want to screw up getting help from a brilliant therapist for the sake of a fuck that I can get with someone else later?

"I apologize that I'm a little late for our appointment."

"No problem." I follow her into her office.

Standard therapist's office, all neutral colors and calm feel to it. Not that I have been in a therapist's office before.

"Please take a seat." She gestures to a comfy-looking seat as she sits down in one a few feet in front of me with a coffee table separating us. "Would you like a drink before we start?"

"No, I'm fine. Thank you," I say with my eyes glued on her legs, which she's just crossed.

She clears her throat, dragging my eyes up to hers.

Reaching forward, she picks up a manila folder, setting it on her lap. "So, this is our introductory meeting. This will help me get to know a little about you and what you need help with. It will let you get to know me and see if we're a good fit together, if you think I can help you."

We'd definitely be a good fit. Her naked, me inside her.

I think we'd fit just perfectly.

"I'll make notes, if that's okay with you? Some therapists like to tape the sessions, but I prefer pen and paper."

"Fine. Whatever." I give her a small smile, so I don't come off like the asshole I am.

She returns my smile, eyes on mine.

I feel that smile all the way down to my cock.

She looks away, down at the folder. Opening it up, she picks up a pen from the table and holds it, poised over the paper before her. "So, let's start with the reason you're here?"

Tell her why I'm here.

I'm here because my life is fucked. Fucked because of one accident.

I don't want to sound like a whiny-ass pussy to anyone, but I know, to get better, I have to fess up my shit to this woman.

"I was in an accident." My voice is monotone.

She nods as she begins writing.

"On the track. I'm a racing driver."

"Did your accident result in major injuries?" Her eyes meet with mine. She's looking at me like she doesn't know, and her words sure as hell sound like she doesn't know.

I thought the world knew everything about me.

Maybe not her.

The knowledge relaxes me a little, and from out of nowhere, I find myself wanting to tell this woman everything.

My biggest fears. My regrets. The self-loathing I feel at my own weaknesses.

"Yes." I take a deep breath. "Both my legs were broken. My wrist was shattered. I had numerous broken ribs. But those injuries were the easy part." I give a sardonic smile. "The worst were…a burst fracture in my lower vertebrae and a subdural hematoma." I tap a finger to my head where the scar lies hidden beneath my overgrown hair. "I was on the operating table with my head wide open when my heart stopped beating." I take a deep breath. "I was technically dead for about a minute."

"And how does that feel, knowing that you died?"

I lift a shoulder in a half shrug, like it doesn't matter. It does matter.

"I don't know. But I do know how it doesn't make me feel."

"And how is that?"

"Alive. I know that it should make me feel more alive now than ever. But I don't."

"Why?"

"Because I can't race. Without racing, I'm nothing."

"Are you sure that's true?"

"If I wasn't, I wouldn't be here."

Eyes leaving me, she stares at the words she's written. "You haven't raced since the accident?"

"No."

"Are you physically able to drive a car? Your injuries haven't hindered that?"

"No, they haven't. I spent a year going through rehabilitation, making sure I could get back in a car." *And now, I can't because I'm a fucking coward.*

"So, it's not your body keeping you from racing. It's your mind."

"I wouldn't fucking be here if it wasn't." I don't mean to curse or snap at her, but I can't help it. And I won't apologize for it either, because I'm an asshole.

Her eyes meet with mine, her gaze steady. "How about traveling as a passenger in a car? How do you find that?"

"I manage." *Just.*

"The same level of anxiety as when you've attempted to drive?"

"No. Slightly less. Not as bad."

"Do you suffer from anxiety attacks?"

I frown. "Only when I try to drive a car," I mutter quietly.

Admitting that I have anxiety attacks is not easy for me.

She scribbles on the paper again. The scratch of the pen is driving me to distraction. That, and her fucking legs and her tits, which are rising up and down with each breath she takes.

I don't want to talk anymore. I just want to fuck her and not think about any of my shit. Bury myself so deep inside her body until she's all I can think about and feel and see.

"Now that you're no longer racing, how do you spend your time?"

I let out a hard laugh. "You want the glossy version or the real version?"

"The truth. I only ever want you to tell me the truth here. If you don't feel you can do that right now, that's fine. But no lies. I can't help you if you lie to me."

"Okay." I blow out a breath. "How do I spend my days? Regretting the day before, missing my life from before the accident, and nursing a hangover. Then, I go out to a bar, get drunk, and hook up with a woman. Take her to a hotel, her place, an alleyway, bar restroom—anywhere really, and I fuck her. Then, I do the exact same the next day and the day after."

That's the first time I've laid my life bare like that to anyone.

And she doesn't flinch. I suppose she must hear all kinds of shit.

"Still think you can help me?" I give her a challenging look.

"Yes." She gives me a steady stare. "You drink to cover the way you're feeling. I'm sure you don't need me to tell you that it's a bad idea. The alcohol—are you addicted?"

"Straight to the point." I laugh, but it's hollow, even to my own ears.

It's been so long since I laughed for real that I can't remember the sound.

She uncrosses her legs. My attention is immediately brought to them. She has great fucking legs. And she's wearing panty hose. I wonder if there's a garter belt under that skirt.

"I'm sorry if that offends you, but it's how I do things. I might ask you things that make you uncomfortable. You don't have to answer, but it will help me help you if you do."

"No."

"You're sure?"

"I'm sure. I'm not a drunk."

"The thought of not drinking again—how does that make you feel?"

I think about it for a moment. "It doesn't make me feel anything." Not that anything makes me feel anymore.

"Still, I'd recommend seeing someone about the drinking. I know a great group that deals with substance—"

"I'm not an alcoholic," I bite. "I might have problems, but that's not one of them."

She carefully eyes me.

"Okay. We'll shelf that...for now." She puts her pen down on the paper on her lap and looks at me.

Her red lips are slightly parted, and all I can think of doing is smearing that lipstick all over her mouth as I kiss it.

"Our time is nearly up. The first session is always short. The next time, we'll have a full hour to talk."

I know what I'd rather do in sixty minutes with her, and it doesn't involve a lot of talking.

But she's the best, and I need to get better.

"Is there anything else you want to talk about before we end this session? Anything you feel I should know?"

I want to fuck you. "No. Actually, yes." I scratch my nose. "I have to be back on the track by January, mid-January at the very latest, to allow me to prepare for the start of the Prix in March."

She puts her notepad and pen on the table as she glances at the calendar on the wall, which is currently on the month of November. "That gives us three months. Three and a half, at a push."

"Impossible?" The weak part of me wants her to say yes, so my coward has a way out. I fight against it.

"No. I like a challenge." Her lips lift into a soft smile, making me smile. "But this means intensive treatment. I'll need to see you at least three times a week. Are you up for that?"

I flex my fingers from the fist they were curled into. "I'm up for it."

"Good." She presses her hands together in a clap and rises from her seat. "Sadie, my receptionist, will be in touch with you tomorrow to schedule your appointments. We book them in batches for intensive treatments."

"Okay."

"So, I'll see you in a few days, Leandro, and we can get started on getting you back on that racetrack."

I follow her to the door, watching her ass sway as she moves. She's heading to a different door than the one I entered.

"This is the exit door," she explains. "I always have my patients leave through this door than the one they came in as I usually have another patient waiting to see me. Most people prefer anonymity—as I imagine you would."

She holds the door open for me, allowing me to pass through.

I turn to face her. "This can't get into the press," I tell her.

From the other side, she smiles at me. "Anything you tell me never leaves this room. You're safe here."

I give her a nod. "Okay. Well, I'll see you in a few days."

Turning, I hear the door close behind me, and I jog down the stairs. I let myself out the door at the bottom that takes me out to the street.

Breathing in the crisp, cool air, I run a hand through my hair.

Then, I pull my cell from my pocket and dial.

I don't even give him a chance to speak. I just hear the answering click before I start talking, "Why the fuck didn't you tell me that she looked like *that?*" I growl down the phone at Carrick.

"Hello to you, too. And who looks like what?" There's laughter in his voice.

Bastard.

"You know exactly who I'm talking about—Dr. Harris, dickface," My cock starts to harden at the mere thought of her.

Jesus. What the hell am I now? A teenager getting a boner over an attractive woman.

Who am I kidding? She's not attractive. She's gorgeous.

"I have no clue what you're talking about."

"Stop being a cock. You know exactly what I'm talking about. You might be pussy-whipped and have Andi vision, but you know a hot chick when you see one. You could have warned me."

"Sorry, but the thought didn't even cross my mind. Yeah, she's decent looking, but she's not my type. I never thought you'd want to bang her. Actually, scrap that. You'll screw anything at the moment, so really, my warning was there when I told you she was a woman."

"Funny, dickhead."

"I love it when you talk dirty to me."

"Fuck off."

He laughs loudly. "Wanting to fuck Dr. Harris aside, how did it go? She's good, right? She's helped Andi a lot."

"Yeah, she's good, I suppose."

"So, she thinks she can help you?"

"That's what she says." *That is, if I don't fuck her first and screw it up.*

INDIA

✠ LONDON, ENGLAND

Relieved to be home, I open my front door, pizza boxes in hand.

"I'm home," I call out.

"In the kitchen," Kit calls back.

Kicking off my heels, I head to the kitchen.

Kit and the love of my life, Jett—my baby boy who's not a baby anymore—are sitting around the table, playing a card game.

"Hey, honey." I kiss the top of Jett's head as I place the pizzas on the table.

"Hey, Mum. You had a good day?" He smiles up at me.

That smile, those blue eyes. They make the longest days worth it.

"Yeah. Good, long."

"You work too hard."

Affectionately ruffling his hair, I see that Kit has a beer on the table and Jett has a Coke. I grab myself a wine glass from the cupboard and fill it with a white I opened yesterday. The pizza boxes are already open and being devoured before I make it back to the table with my glass of wine and some paper napkins in hand.

I toss a napkin over to Kit and hand one to Jett. I take the seat next to him and grab a slice before they're gone.

Kit can eat a pizza by himself, and Jett's not far off from being able to do so either.

At twelve years old, he has so much of my brother and me in him—and, thankfully, nothing of his father. Not that I'd love him any less if he did. I'm just glad there isn't any of that man in him.

Jett is a Harris through and through. He has our blond hair and blue eyes and Kit's build. I'm five-six, and my son is already taller than me. I think he's going to reach Kit's six-three, and I wouldn't be surprised if Jett surpasses that.

My brother is a handsome bastard, and he knows it. Jett is his double, so I foresee a lot of broken hearts in his future. Kit leaves a trail of them in his wake. I'm trying to teach Jett to treat women with more respect than my brother does.

Kit's job exposes him to a lot of beautiful women. He's a model.

When Jett was a few months old, Kit started modeling part-time to make more money when he wasn't working seasonal construction jobs. His money helped me pay the bills. From the compensation I had received from the courts after what had happened with Jett's father, I didn't have a lot leftover after paying for the house and using the rest to put myself through school while I also worked part-time in a supermarket.

I owe my brother everything. He's sacrificed so much for Jett and me.

As time has gone on, Kit's gotten larger campaigns, some that take him out of the country, but we always make it work to ensure one of us is here for Jett. If a job doesn't fit with our schedules, Kit doesn't take it. He's in the position now where he can pick and choose his jobs.

Putting my slice down on the napkin, I take a drink of my much-needed wine.

After my session with Leandro Silva—which was definitely enlightening and very interesting—I took a frantic call from Sarah, another one of my patients. She's having a really tough time at the moment.

Three years ago, Sarah broke things off with her boyfriend. He stalked her for months, and one night, he broke into her home while she was sleeping and raped her in her bed.

He went to prison for his crime. But he's now out on parole after serving only half of his sentence, and she's struggling to cope with that fact.

I've been treating Sarah since the rape, and she was reaching a good place in her life and finally moving forward. So, his release, which was a shock to her, has set her back miles.

She's afraid to leave her home, in fear of seeing him. She's terrified that he might come get her again even though a restraining order is in place. She has that fear, and I understand it.

It took me an hour to talk her down on the phone, and I had to promise that I would go to her house first thing in the morning for a face-to-face appointment. With my appointment calendar full, I will have to come in an hour earlier. But there aren't many things I wouldn't do for my patients.

"How'd the new patient go today?" Kit asks me.

Besides the odd bits, like if I'm taking on a new patient, I don't talk to Kit or Jett about my patients or tell them who they are.

"It was fine."

"Do you think you can help him or her?" Jett asks me.

I smile at him. "Yes, I'm sure I can."

It's a good thing I don't tell them who my patients are, or Jett would have a meltdown. He's obsessed with Formula 1.

If he found out that I was treating Leandro Silva—let alone that I had been treating Andressa Ryan, the wife of Carrick Ryan—he would bug me until I let him meet them.

Leandro Silva is a whole other ballgame though.

Of course I'd known he was handsome, but seeing him in the flesh exposed me to the actual beauty of him, and it knocked me off-balance for a moment. Then, I kicked myself into professional mode. I'm nothing but professional.

But just hearing about his accident, how he'd almost died, what he was going through now...

Don't get me wrong. I hear all manner of heartbreaking stories of what people have endured, but listening to him struck a chord with me in a way that not many people do.

"So, how was school today?" I ask Jett.

He flickers a look at Kit, who smiles at him and nods.

"Am I missing something here?" I look between the pair of them.

"I got picked for the team." Jett gives me a shy grin.

"You did? That's amazing news!" I wrap my arms around him, hugging him. Leaning back, I look at his face. "I thought they were going to pick the team next week?"

"They brought it forward."

Aside from being a Formula 1 nut, my son also loves football. And he's been picked for the school team.

"We need to celebrate!" I exclaim. "We'll go out this weekend, do something."

"Sounds great. Anyway, I've got to go finish my homework. I have to keep my grades up, or I'll be kicked off the team before I even get started."

I'm about to protest about him finishing his dinner when I see that he's already eaten half of the pizza and is taking another slice with him.

Getting up, he kisses my cheek.

"I'll come up and see you before bed." I affectionately pat his cheek.

I eat my own slice of pizza, which has cooled considerably.

Kit gets up from the table and gets another beer from the fridge. He brings the bottle of wine, topping my glass off.

"Thanks." I smile at him, and then it fades a little. "Why didn't Jett call me to tell me he'd made the team?"

"He wanted to wait until he saw you."

"Right." I blow out a breath. "I wish I'd been home earlier to hear about it." I feel a little deflated, hating that I'm not always here for this stuff and that Kit is.

From the day I found out I was pregnant, Kit took care of me. The day Jett was born, Kit became the father figure in his life, and he's been here ever since.

I will forever be indebted to him for that.

When Jett was a baby, I knew I wanted to give him everything in life that Kit and I never had. So, I made the decision to go to college, then university. Being a single mother didn't make that easy, so between Kit and me, we've raised him, and as the years have gone on, the daily demands of my job have meant that Kit's around for the important school stuff, more than I am,

"So, are you coming to celebrate with us this weekend, or do you have a hot date?" I tease my brother.

He's a serial dater. Actually, *dater* is probably being generous. He can barely stick with the same girl for longer than a day. Not that I'm anyone to judge. I haven't had a serious relationship, in…well, *ever*. And I've never been in love. Not the real kind.

My extensive psychological training could tell you exactly why Kit and I are the way we are when it comes to relationships, but I'd rather not delve into my own psyche, or my brothers for that matter.

"I don't date, Indy. You know that." He gives me a cheeky grin.

"Maybe you should try it and get a steady girlfriend?"

"Like you and Dr. Dull?" He takes a sip of beer.

I frown at him.

Dr. Dull—I mean, *Dan* is the guy I'm currently dating. I've been seeing him for two months. Kit doesn't think much of him.

"I really wish you wouldn't call him that." I sigh. "Jett calls him that now because of you."

"Jett calls him that because Dan is dull as fuck."

"Jett hasn't met him, so he has no clue that Dan is dull—I mean, if he is dull or not!" I bite.

Laughter bursts from Kit.

"And he's not! He's not dull at all," I say, defensively folding my arms. "He's quite interesting in fact."

"Oh, yeah?" Kit's brow lifts. "Then, tell me one interesting fact about him."

Shit.

Come on, India. There's got to be something interesting about Dan…

"He, erm…he's, um…"

With his satisfactory win, Kit's smirk deepens as his arms fold over his chest, leaning back in his chair.

Kit will not win this.

Dan is not dull. He's nice. Good. Safe.

"He likes…watching *Breaking Bad*." I give a satisfactory look, picking up my slice of pizza and taking a bite.

"Wow. Jesus, I was so wrong about him, Indy. The guy lives on the edge."

I flip him the bird. "Stop being an arse."

Kit chuckles. "You can do better than him."

"Dan's nice to me."

"So is the postman."

"The postman? What the hell are you talking about?" I exclaim, puzzled.

"I'm talking about you playing it safe with Dr. Dull. I get it, Indy. I do. You were burned badly, but it was a long time ago. And I want you to be happy. You're not happy with dating dull fucks like Dan."

"I appreciate your concern, but I'm happy as I am."

"You're safe and comfortable."

"And what's wrong with safe and comfortable?" I frown.

"It's boring."

"Yeah, well, look what happened to me the last time I chased excitement."

"I know." He blows out a breath, like he's breathing out the past. "But that was thirteen years ago. You're a different person now. And you can do way better than Dr. Dull, Indy. You deserve better."

I don't know why, but a flash of Leandro Silva's face passes through my mind.

Brushing it aside, I stare at my brother. My heart swells for him even though he's irritating me with his interference in my love life, but I know he does it because he cares about me.

"I know you're only looking out for me. But what I have with Dan works—"

"What you have is boredom." He grins, back to playful.

I give him the middle finger again.

"Anyway, what about you?" I lean forward, wrapping my hands around my glass.

He's fine with commenting on the men I date, but at least I date. What he does barely constitutes as dating.

He's never had a steady girlfriend. Sometimes, a part of me worries that's because of Jett and me.

"What about me?" He tips his bottle back, taking a drink.

"Why haven't you settled down?"

"Have you seen me? There's too much good here not to share it."

My brother is a good-looking bastard, and he knows it. But he's also a great person with an amazing heart, and I just wish he'd share that with someone.

"I think you should try dating just one girl. Try it out. See how you get on. What about that model you went out with last week? Tanya? She seemed nice."

"She was nice. And we didn't go out, Indy. We went to her place. We got naked. I stayed for three hours. I came. Came again. Then, I came home."

"Ugh, Kit! Jesus Christ! Way too much info for me, thanks." I know he's done it as deflection, so I won't keep pushing.

Chuckling, he puts his bottle down on the table. "So, will Dr. Dull be joining us this weekend to celebrate Jett getting on the team?"

"No. I'm not ready for Jett to meet him yet."

Kit raises a knowing eyebrow.

"Soon." *Maybe.* I'm just not really sure if Dan is the guy I'll be introducing Jett too. "But I want it to just the three of us, a family celebration."

"Family night. Sounds good to me." Leaning over the table, he clinks his bottle on my glass.

three

LEANDRO

✚ LONDON, ENGLAND

I AWAKE WITH A START. The sound of crushing metal resounding in my ears, heat on my body from the flames, smoke clogging my lungs.

Panic crashes into me.

Rapid blinks bring my eyes to the white ceiling before moving them down the walls.

I'm in a bed.

Eyes casting around the room, I see I'm in what looks like a hotel room.

As I drag my hands over my face, a sturdy pounding takes over my head, and the taste of last night's alcohol is apparent on my sandpaper tongue.

This is not an unusual start to the day for me.

My life.

My craptastic life.

Rolling over, I see the littering of condom wrappers on the bedside table, which tells of a good night.

Yet I don't feel good.

After seeing the hot doctor yesterday, I couldn't get the thought of fucking her out of my mind. I was restless and horny. Instead of going home after my appointment, I went to a bar. Clearly, I got wasted and hooked up with whoever is lying next to me.

I stealthily climb out of bed, so not to wake the body next to me. I pull on my clothes, slip my feet into my shoes, retrieve my wallet, keys, and phone from the desk, and shove them in my pocket.

Then, I quietly leave the room.

Shitty thing to do? Yes.

But I'm not exactly a stand-up guy nowadays, and I'm just not in the mood for the morning-after conversation that would no doubt ensue.

I take the elevator down and make my way over to the reception desk.

Paying for the room, I leave the hotel for the morning air and hail a taxi.

It doesn't take long to get home. I pay the driver and let myself in my house.

The silence echoes through me.

I pick up the mail from the mat and dump it on the hallway table without looking at it. I walk to the kitchen and see the house phone blinking a few messages at me.

Probably my mother. She's been calling regularly since I moved back to London, and she'll want to know how my first session with Dr. Harris went.

What do I say? Well, I wanted to fuck the doctor, but of course, I couldn't, so I instead went out, got wasted, and fucked a random woman.

Not what my mother would want to hear.

She had wanted me to stay in Brazil. But I couldn't. I felt too smothered there with my family fussing around me, wanting to help.

I thought that coming back here would fix things... fix me.

It hasn't.

Needing to wash the night off of me, I head upstairs and take a shower. I let the hot spray beat on my face to the point of pain, just needing to feel something...anything.

Toweling off, I brush my teeth, staring at myself in the mirror.

The beard covering my face hides who I am…who I used to be.

Flashes of last night flicker through my mind.

The alcohol flowing. The girl all but riding my cock in the bar. Then, riding it for real in the hotel room.

The thoughts should make me feel good.

They don't.

They make me feel empty.

Going into my bedroom, I get some black jogging pants and a plain black T-shirt.

Slipping my cell in my pocket, I head downstairs. In the silence, I go to the kitchen and turn on the coffee machine.

Stepping away from the counter, I bend at the waist and rest my folded arms on the counter, and lay my head on them, letting the noise of the coffee machine abuse my head and rattle through the emptiness in my hollow chest.

My senses breathing in the smell of coffee, I grab a cup and pour some out.

Strong and black.

Turning, I press my back against the counter and stare at a picture on the wall.

It's a signed picture of Ayrton Senna that my father got for me when I was a child.

I should have died. I would have died a legend.

Not the man I am now.

A washed-up has-been.

I can't be *him* anymore. This weak fucking version of myself.

I have to race again.

I have to get back in a car.

I have to do this.

I can do this.

I've been driving all my life.

Putting my coffee down, I push my feet into my sneakers and head for the internal door to the garage.

I stall when I reach the door.

I haven't been in here since before the accident.

My hand starts to shake.

I'm being ridiculous.

Clenching my fist, I force the tension away.

I open the door.

A strong wave of stale air hits me. Breathing through it, I reach for the light switch, turning it on.

And there she sits.

My car. A blue '67 Chevrolet Camaro Pro Touring Coupe.

She was for sale in the local garage near my home back in Brazil, and I had my eye on her for ages. My father bought her for me when I turned eighteen. I had her shipped over when I moved to London. She goes everywhere with me.

I can do this. All I have to do is go over there, push the key in the ignition, and turn her over.

Forcing my fears away, I move my feet to my car.

Unlocking it, I open the door.

She still smells the same, aside from the stale dank air escaping her.

Deep breath, I climb inside.

I shut the door behind me with a clank.

Trapped. Fire.

Squeezing my eyes shut, I ignore the fear in my head.

"I can do this," I say to myself.

Breathing in through my nose, I lift the keys. It's not until I try to push the key in the ignition that I realize how badly my hand is shaking again.

"Fuck," the word hisses out through my teeth. "I can do this. Nothing is going to happen to me. Lightning doesn't strike twice. Now, stop being a pussy, Silva, and drive the fucking car."

I slide the key in, and before my fear talks me out of it, I turn the engine on.

She chugs and sputters for a few seconds. In those seconds, a voice in my mind prays that she won't start.

If she doesn't work, then I can't drive her.
Not my fault then. I wouldn't be chickening out.

She rumbles to life, and the radio comes on loud.

With the feel of the engine vibrating and the music playing, my head explodes. Images of the accident assault my senses.

I can smell the smoke.

Taste the blood in my mouth.

Feel my chest compressing.

I can't breathe.

My fingers scramble to turn the engine off.

Opening the door, I fall from the car onto my knees. I gasp for air.

"Fuck!" I cry out, gripping my head in frustration. "Fuck! Fuck! Fuck!" I slam my fist onto the floor, not caring about the pain that shoots through my hand.

Then, I really lose it.

Getting to my feet, I grab a baseball bat that's propped up against the wall, and I start to smash the hell out of my car.

My vision is red, and I beat my frustrations and pain and fears out on the car, hitting the metal and glass over and over. But no matter how many times I hit it, I don't feel any better.

Staggering back, I see the damage I've done.

She's wrecked.

Like me.

The car that my father bought for me, all I have left of him, and I destroyed her.

Grief lances through me.

What the fuck is wrong with me?

I stagger back into my house, heading for my office.

I see all my trophies lined there, taunting me.

Then, I realize the bat is still in my hand.

With rage still burning in my veins, I take the bat to my trophies, wiping out what's left of my career, smashing them to pieces until nothing is left but carnage.

The bat falls from my shaking hands.

I don't feel better. I feel worse, if possible.

I hate myself.

I drop to my knees, among the mess I created. My head in my hands, I grip my hair, and for the first time since the accident, I cry.

I don't know how long I stay there for.

Drying my face with the back of my hand, I get up and walk over to my desk.

Sitting in my chair, I open the bottom drawer, pulling out the bottle of whiskey I keep in there.

I unscrew the cap and take a long drink. Then, another. And another.

Then, without thought, I pull my cell from my pocket, and dial Dr. Harris before I realize what I'm doing.

"Dr. Harris's office."

It's her receptionist.

"Is it possible to speak with Dr. Harris?" My voice sounds scratchy.

"Dr. Harris is currently in an appointment. Who is calling?"

I grit my teeth. "Leandro Silva."

"Mr. Silva, I can have Dr. Harris call you back. Or if it's an emergency—"

"It's not an emergency." I take another drink from the bottle.

"Should I have her call you?"

"No. Just forget it."

"Are you sure? Because—"

"I'm sure," I cut her off. "I'll see her at my appointment tomorrow." Then, I hang up the phone.

Why the hell did I call her?

Frustrated, I toss my cell on the desk and down some more whiskey.

It's too quiet in here.

The silence in the room feels almost as painful as the noise in my head.

Reaching for my phone, I turn on the music to drown it out.

Fingers curled around the bottle, I drop my head to the desk, as the sound of Ed Sheeran's "Bloodstream" kicks in.

INDIA

✢ LONDON, ENGLAND

"*LEANDRO SILVA CALLED. He sounded on edge, told me not to bother telling you he called, but I knew you would want to know.*"

Sadie's words ring in my head. They've been bothering me ever since she said them to me yesterday.

I tried calling Leandro back as soon as she gave me the message, but I got his voice mail. He didn't call back.

Now, he's late for his appointment. Forty minutes late.

I've been treating him for only a week now—three sessions, four including his initial session—and so far, he's talked around everything but his actual problem, no matter how much I try to steer him to it. I didn't want to push him in the initial, I wanted to let him lead the pace, but if he wants to be back in his racing car by January, then I'm going to have to take some decisive action and push him forward.

But this, not turning up for his appointment, just isn't going to cut it.

I tap my fingernails on my desk, debating on what to do. Then, my office phone rings.

I snatch it up.

"Leandro Silva is here for his appointment," Sadie says down the line.

I try to ignore the actual level of relief I feel, which is more than I usually do in these cases. "Send him in."

Ten seconds later, the door opens, and a disheveled-looking Leandro walks in my office before closing the door behind him. His clothes are rumpled, like he slept in them. His overgrown black hair is messy, like he just fell out of bed and ran his hands through it.

But even still, he looks handsome.

As my eyes move down from his face, I see something red on his shirt, near the top button.

I immediately think blood. But when I narrow my vision on it, I see it's not blood at all.

It's lipstick. Red lipstick.

I curl my fingers into my palms, nails biting my skin. "Are you okay?" I ask. My voice sounds tight.

What the hell is wrong with me?

I will myself to relax.

He rolls up his shirtsleeves, revealing strong tanned forearms dusted with black hairs. "I'm fine."

He's hovering by the door he just closed, seemingly unsure of what to do, so I get up from my desk and move to the seating area.

There's no apology for his lateness, and I don't prompt it, no matter how much I want to.

"Can I get you anything?" I ask before sitting.

"No."

He still hasn't sat down.

"Are you going to sit down?"

He glances at the chair like he didn't even know it was there.

With a nod, he walks over and sits down.

Leaning forward, forearms on his thighs, he clasps his hands together.

That's when I smell it—alcohol. The smell is strong on him. And I can smell perfume. Cheap perfume.

They bother me equally in measure.

But I ignore the perfume issue before I start questioning my own issues with it, and I focus on the alcohol.

"Leandro, I'm going to ask you a question, and I want an honest answer."

His eyes flicker up to mine.

"Are you drunk right now?" I should have worded that differently. I don't know why I seem to keep losing my footing with him.

But I will not treat someone while they're under the influence of alcohol or illegal substances.

Annoyance flashes through his eyes, and then they narrow on me. "No." His jaw is tight.

"I can smell it on you—the alcohol. I will not treat you while you're drunk or high." I scoot forward in my seat, my back straight, and I'm sitting on the edge, my hands curling around it.

"I'm not drunk or high," he grinds out the words. His hands are clasped so tightly together that his knuckles are white. "If you smell alcohol on me, it's because I was drinking last night. Clearly, it was way too much because I woke up in a hotel room and realized I was late for my appointment with you. So, I pulled on last night's clothes because they were all I had to wear, and I came straight here. I haven't even showered."

Yes, I can tell.

I bite my tongue so hard that I'm pretty sure I draw blood.

I exhale a calming breath. "You could have called and rescheduled your appointment. It wouldn't have been a problem."

My statement seems to throw him. His face blanks, like the thought didn't even occur to him.

Then, his expression hardens. "I didn't want to miss my appointment today."

"But it's okay to be late for it?" I shouldn't have said that. I don't know why I did.

I clear my throat. I go for a change of tactic. "Why didn't you want to miss your appointment?"

His eyes move to the wall behind me. He's silent for a moment. Then, he looks back to me. "Because I want to get past this. I want to be the man I used to be."

"You know that there's nothing wrong with the man you are now. Barring your coping mechanisms, the vices, you're still the same man you were."

"No, I'm not." His voice is a low growl. He looks away.

"Well, Leandro, if you want to change, get back to the man you used to be, then you need to make the effort here. And this"—I gesture a hand to him—"isn't making the effort."

His dark eyes flash back to mine. His jaw is tight, looking like it might shatter. "I came, didn't I?"

"Yes." I nod. "But forty minutes late."

His gaze narrows. Then, he moves his eyes to my empty hands. "Don't you need to make notes or something?" He juts his chin in my direction.

"No, I don't need to make notes. The appointment will be short, as you have only twenty minutes left. I'll remember all we talk about in that time. Don't worry."

His brows pull together, a furrow appearing between them. "You're not going to see me for the full hour?"

"No, I can't. I have other patients who have scheduled appointments, who need my help, too."

"For fuck's sake!" he growls. Leaning forward, he rests his elbows on his thighs and drives his fingers into his black hair.

I let the silence settle between us, leaving him to talk when he's ready.

"I had a…bad day yesterday." His voice is low, nearing a whisper.

"Bad in what way?"

He lifts those black eyes to mine, and I see a world of pain in them.

"Bad, as in...I tried to drive my car."

"And how did that go?"

He lets out a bitter-sounding laugh. "It didn't. I choked like a little bitch. Then, I got out of my car and smashed the hell out of her with a baseball bat."

"How did that make you feel?"

"Smashing my car up? Good, while I was doing it. Then, afterward...I felt like shit, so I went inside and smashed up all my racing trophies."

"And did smashing up your trophies make you feel better?"

"No."

"Why do you think you did it—smashing up your car and trophies?"

"Because I didn't want constant reminders of who I used to be. And who I am now."

He has a clear perception of why he behaves as he does. That gives me a lot of hope for his recovery.

"And who are you now?"

"A shell of the man I was." His shoulders drop. "I'm the guy who can't face the failure that he is, so I did the same as always whenever I feel like that. I went out to a bar and got trashed. Then, I woke up in a hotel room with two women in bed with me and little recollection of the night before."

Getting up from my seat, I grab my water bottle from my desk. I'm covering. It's really bothering me, knowing that he had sex with not only one woman, but two.

Why is this affecting me in this way?

It shouldn't. And it can't.

I push my feelings aside and sit back down. "Sorry. My throat is dry today," I explain in way of my water departure.

He's closely watching me with those dark eyes of his.

"You're not a failure, Leandro. You suffered a terrible accident. What you're feeling is normal."

"I don't…" He blows out a breath. "I don't feel normal. I feel weak." His words are whispered, his voice broken.

I feel his pain wrap around me in a way that I'm not familiar with.

"You're not weak, Leandro. You're human." My voice sounds different, even to my own ears. I always soften my tone with my patients, but there's something else in my voice that I can't place.

His eyes lift to mine, and something unexpected moves through my chest.

Compassion.

It's compassion. I feel it all the time for my patients.

Before I can question myself, I quickly glance from him to the clock.

Clearing my throat, I say, "I'm really sorry that I can't extend our session right now, but I also don't want to leave this until our next session. I think talking more today could really help. Can you come back at six p.m., and we'll talk more then? How does that sound to you?"

I see the first flicker of a genuine smile on his face.

"That would be great. Thank you."

His sincerity touches me like fingers brushing over my skin.

Crap! I was supposed to have dinner with Dan after work before his shift at the hospital. We've both been working a lot, and his shifts have meant that we haven't been able to see each other much over the last two weeks.

I have to call him and let him know that I'll be seeing a patient, so I can't make it.

"Okay." I get up from my seat and walk toward the exit door. "So, I'll see you back here at six."

After he walks toward me, I open the door, and Leandro's arm accidentally brushes mine. Electricity sparks up my arm with an intensity that I've never felt before. My lungs feel compressed.

Lifting my eyes to his face, I see he's already looking at me.

His eyes are fathomless. Depthless. Eyes I could fall into.

I feel caught off guard.

My face is warm, and I know my cheeks are red. Catching myself, I look away and wrap my hand around my arm, willing the feel of his touch to dissipate.

"Sadie won't be here when you arrive. She'll have left for the day, so just come straight into my office. I'll be here." Maintaining professionalism, I force my eyes back to his.

I can't get a read on him.

He's smiling, but what that smile means, I'm not sure.

Does he know he affected me just now?

There's a dimple etched deep in his cheek. It only works to increase his handsomeness.

I feel a ripple in my chest.

You're his therapist.

I take a step back.

"I'll see you at six, India." He turns and begins walking down the stairs.

Closing the door, I realize that's the first time he's called me by my first name, and hearing him say it with his sexy Brazilian accent...well, let's just say the feeling it leaves me with is amazing.

And that's not good.

It's not good at all.

five

LEANDRO

✚ LONDON, ENGLAND

I FELT SOMETHING when my arm brushed India's. Something intense.

A simple brush of our arms, and exhilaration rushed through me.

The thing is, when touching women, I haven't felt anything since the accident. No connection. Nothing. I fuck to forget, not because I want those women.

And I'm pretty sure India felt our connection, too. I saw the way her cheeks flushed and how she curled her hand around her arm where we'd touched.

I affect her.

I wasn't sure if I did, but now, I'm pretty damn sure that I do.

I like her. But I don't want to fuck this up because I really think she can help me. After last night, I need her help more than I realized.

It's almost six p.m., and I'm on my way back to India's office.

India. I love the sound of her name each time I say it.

And I love how her voice sounds when saying my name.

I wonder how it will sound as it screams from her lips while I'm fucking her.

I can't fuck her.

Balancing the coffees I just picked up from Starbucks with the takeout sandwiches, I push through the door into her reception area.

It's empty, as she said it would be.

It'll be just her and me here. I don't know if that's a good idea, to be honest. I don't know if I can trust myself not to make a move.

Jesus, I'm a grown man. I can control myself around her.

I give a knock on her door before letting myself in.

She's sitting at her desk, talking on the phone. She smiles those red lips at me, and I feel my cock stir to life.

Down, boy.

The smile still on her face, she lifts a finger, letting me know that she'll be a minute.

I give a nod and then put the coffees and the bag containing the sandwiches down on the table. I take a seat.

"Sounds good. Okay. See you later. Love you."

Love you?

She's definitely not married, as there's no ring.

Does she have a boyfriend?

Of course she has a boyfriend. Look at her.

Hanging up her phone, she gets up from her chair and walks over to where I'm sitting. She takes her seat across from me. "Sorry about that."

"No worries. I brought coffee and a couple of sandwiches in case you haven't eaten."

Her eyes flicker with surprise, like I'm the first guy to ever bring her food.

"I haven't eaten. That was really thoughtful of you, Leandro. Thank you. But please let me reimburse you for the coffee and sandwich."

She makes to get up, but I stop her with my words. "No. My treat." I wave her off.

She pauses for a moment and then lowers her butt back into the seat. "Okay. Thank you."

Reaching over the coffee table separating us, I hand her one of the coffees, and in the exchange, I make sure that my fingers brush hers.

Why I do that, I have no clue.

Okay, I do have a clue. I want to see her react to me again.

My eyes search her face for a reaction, but I get nothing this time.

Feeling a bit deflated, I pick up my own coffee and rest back in the chair.

"I got you a black coffee," I tell her. "I wasn't sure if you took milk or sugar." I reach into my pocket and pull out some tiny milk capsules and sugar sachets.

"Black is perfect." She smiles, the cup by her lips. Then, she takes a sip.

She drinks black coffee and wears red lipstick.

She's fucking perfect.

"So, I was thinking"—she puts the coffee back down—"about how we should approach your treatment going forward."

"I'm listening."

"Well, am I right in thinking that you feel that to get your life back, you need to be able to race?"

"I don't feel. I know," I say with surety.

"Okay. So, of course, you need to talk about the accident, get those feelings out there for you to deal with them. Clearly, bottling them up isn't working for you. I thought, while we're doing that, we can work on getting you back in a car."

All my muscles stiffen up, and she notices.

"Baby steps," she says softly. "What I mean is, I was thinking we could go outside, sit in my car, and do our session in there."

I lift a brow. "Your methods are a little strange. Anyone ever tell you that?"

"Yes. Right before they tell me that my methods really helped them."

A smile edges her lips, and it's sexy as fuck.

"Confident?" I tease.

"Confidence is surety, and I'm sure this will help."

"Okay." I pick up my coffee and get to my feet. "Lead the way."

I give a sweeping hand gesture as she gets to her feet.

"Let me just grab my car keys," she says.

I watch her walk away from me, over to her desk, where she leans overs to retrieve her keys. The fabric of her fitted pencil skirt stretches over her ass.

She has an amazing ass.

God, the things I could do to that ass while she's bent over that desk.

My cock starts to stir in my pants. I have to quickly rearrange myself before she turns back around to me.

"Should I bring the sandwiches as well?" I ask.

"Of course." She smiles up at me, as she bends to retrieve her coffee from the table.

Snatching up the bag containing the sandwiches, I wait for her to round the coffee table, then, I follow her out of the office and to her car.

INDIA

✣ LONDON, ENGLAND

THE MOMENT WE'RE SEATED IN MY CAR, I wonder if I've made a mistake, putting myself in such close proximity to Leandro.

I can smell the sandalwood in his aftershave along with his own unique scent, and it's doing things to me.

The man is like a walking sexual conductor.

It's unnerving.

Because a man has never affected me in this way before.

I haven't ever felt as physically attracted to a man as I do Leandro.

I'm his therapist.

The reminder hits me like a blast of cold water in the face, and my libido. I need to put a stop to my feelings and thoughts—right now.

"Nice car," he comments from the passenger seat.

"Thank you."

I have to have a cool car with a car-obsessed son. Jett picked it out. He saw it at the showroom, and it was love at first sight for him, so of course, I had to buy it.

There isn't anything I wouldn't do for my son, including taking out a twenty-thousand-pound loan to buy a fifteen-year-old Aston Martin that had seventy-five-thousand miles on the clock. I have to admit, it is a stunning car and awesome to drive. I feel like a movie star when I drive it.

I almost tell Leandro that it was Jett who talked me into buying it, but I stop myself. I don't share my private life with patients.

"A 2000 Aston Martin DB7 Vantage, right?"

"Right." I smile. "You seem surprised I have this car."

He blinks back at me, his shoulder lifting in a half shrug. "I guess I just expected you to have a…I don't know, an Audi or a Toyota. This doesn't fit with your…image."

"You mean, the image that you have of me."

Something passes through his eyes that I can't discern.

"I guess." He looks away. "So, are you into cars?"

"No. But someone close to me is. I was talked into buying this. It's pretty, and it gets me from A to B, so I'm happy." I let out a light laugh.

He laughs, and it's rich and deep. "That sounds like something I would expect you, a woman, to say."

"Well, I'm glad I tick off at least one of your stereotypical boxes."

He turns to look at me. His stare is direct and intense. "You tick more than one box."

I feel a tremor deep inside. I swallow down.

I tear my eyes from his. "What sandwiches did you bring?"

There's a slight pause before he answers, "I played it safe." He reaches into the bag and pulls them out. "Ham or turkey?"

"Turkey, please."

He hands it over. I make sure not to touch his fingers, like when he handed me the coffee earlier. I felt like I had an electrical surge pulsing up my finger. It took everything in me to maintain my composure.

I unwrap the sandwich and take a bite. I have to hold back a moan. I haven't eaten all day, and right now, this sandwich tastes like heaven.

Putting the sandwich on my lap, I pick up my coffee from the cup holder in my car, and I catch Leandro looking away from me.

Was he watching me?

I scratch the thought from my mind and focus on my job, which is helping him.

Taking a sip of coffee, I keep the cup in my hand. "How does this feel, being here in my car?"

"Fine." He shrugs. "It's stationary, and I'm in the passenger seat."

"How is traveling in a car as a passenger? Better or worse?"

Pressing his cup to his lips, he appears to think my question over. "Well, I avoid being in cars as much as possible, which is easy while living in the city since I can travel pretty much anywhere by the Tube. But when I do have to be a passenger…I'm anxious."

"Because?"

"I'm not in control." He takes a breath, setting his coffee on his thigh. His fingers curl around the cup. "I have to be in control in all aspects of my life. That's what frustrates me about all of this."

"Not being in control?"

"Mmhmm."

"So, you try to take control back in the only way you can at the moment, and that's in a destructive manner in your life."

I can feel his eyes on me, so I turn in my seat to look at him. It's important to maintain eye contact with a patient—only, being in the car isn't easy.

"You mean, the drinking and the women?"

Lifting a shoulder, I say, "Do you think those are positive things in your life?"

"I drank and had women before the accident."

"But I'm guessing, before, you did those things for enjoyment, not to cover your pain."

He looks out the window, away from me. "Do you always have to be right?" His tone is light, so I know I haven't pushed him too far. He brings his eyes back to me.

"It's part of my job," I say in a teasing manner. "But, in all seriousness, just because I think something doesn't make it right. It's what you think that counts."

"I guess." He takes another sip of coffee.

"So, it's easier sitting in the passenger seat. If I asked you to sit in the driver's seat with the engine off, would that be possible?"

"Do I have a choice?"

There's no humor in his voice, so I tread back carefully.

"You always have a choice, Leandro," I say in a soft voice. "Nothing has to happen that you don't feel comfortable with. You ever think I'm pushing you too hard, tell me. We'll stop and reevaluate."

"I was teasing, India, but good to know where you stand. And it's fine. Let's do it. Nothing can happen to me in a parked car, right?"

"Right." I smile, my eyes meeting with his.

"So…"

"So?"

"Are you going to crawl over my lap to swap seats, or are we getting out of the car?" He grins at me and my face flushes.

Crawling over his lap…

"We're getting out of the car."

We pass at the back of my car, and surprisingly, he's in the car before me.

I shut my door with a soft clunk. "How does this feel?" I ask him, assessing his face.

"Fine, I guess. I feel…stupid."

"Stupid?"

"Yeah." He rests his forearms on the steering wheel. "I'm a grown-ass man who needs help getting into a car."

"No, you're a grown-ass man recovering from a serious accident that nearly took your life." I take a deep breath and go for the plunge with my assessment. "Leandro, have you heard of post-traumatic stress disorder?"

"Yes. People who come back from war have it."

"Yes, but it's not only military personnel who suffer from PTSD. People who have survived a traumatic experience, like you did, can also suffer from PTSD."

He turns his face to me. "You think I have PTSD?" He points a finger at himself.

"A mild form, yes."

He faces forward, staring out the windshield. He's silent for a long time.

"Does knowing that bother you?" I ask breaking the silence. "I'm not putting a label on what your issue is, Leandro. I'm just giving you something to work from. Understanding your problem is half of the battle to beating it."

"You sound like a psychology textbook."

"You read many of them?" I smile.

Meeting my eyes, he returns that smile, and it momentarily lightens his dark eyes.

"Oh, yes, all the time. I have a stack on my bedside table. *Idiot's Guide to Psychology*."

"That's my favorite."

He laughs. It's a rich deep sound, and I feel it all the way down to my toes. I scrunch them up in my shoes.

"Right. Give me your keys." He thrusts his hand out at me.

"You want my keys?"

"Yes." His stare on me is direct, but his face is relaxed.

"Why?"

"Because I'm going to see if I can start this engine without freaking out like a pussy again."

"You sure you're ready for this? It was only last night when you tried—"

"I'm sure."

His hand is still held out, so I retrieve my keys from my jacket pocket and hand them to him. It's impossible to avoid touching him this time, but I make it quick and brief while ensuring I avoid eye contact with him, so he can't see the effect his touch has on me.

Facing forward, he starts to flex his hands out, and he takes a deep breath.

"Just take your time. You feel stressed or panicky at any point, just stop and take deep breaths."

"I got this." He grins at me.

"And don't worry if you lose it again. I'm insured."

"Is that an invitation to smash your car up?" He laughs.

"Sure. Why not? It's about time I got a new one." My lip lifts at the corner in a half smile.

He laughs again. I really like hearing him laugh. It makes me feel like we're taking positive steps forward, and it's not at all about the way his laugh makes me feel inside.

One more deep breath, he punches the key into the ignition and turns it over without a moment's hesitation.

I watch his eyes close as my car rumbles to life.

His hands are wrapped around the steering wheel, his knuckles white from his tight grip.

"How do you feel?" I ask softly.

"Better than I did last night." He opens one eye and looks at me, a touch of a smile on his lips.

"Damn, so I won't get a new car out of this."

He chuckles, and I can feel the tension already leaving his body.

He closes his eyes again. Hands still on the steering wheel, he rests his head back against the seat and blows out a breath.

We sit like that for a long moment. Leandro acclimating himself to his environment. Me watching him, assessing if a panic attack might be about to happen.

But his breathing seems even, and his grip on the steering wheel has relaxed a little.

"When I woke up in the hospital, I know I should have felt relieved to be alive. And I guess a part of me did. But a bigger part of me wished I'd died in that crash...because I knew, right then and there, that I wouldn't be able to get back in a car. And if I wasn't racing, then I might as well be dead." Opening his eyes, he tilts his head my way and stares at me. "I know you probably don't understand that, but racing is my whole life. It's all I ever wanted to do, all I was ever good at. Losing it...it's killing me slowly."

"You'll get it back," I tell him with surety. Then, I do something I never, ever do. I make him a promise. "I'll help you get it back. I promise you." Before I can stop myself, I lay my hand on his arm.

"Thank you." His words are soft as he looks back out the windshield where small droplets of rain have started to appear.

And I retract my burning hand, knowing I need to find my professional balance here.

SEVEN

LEANDRO

✢ LONDON, ENGLAND

My phone buzzes in my pocket. Pulling it out, I see it's Carrick.

"I'm in the taxi and on my way. I'm just running late. I had a meeting earlier at Lissa." Lissa is my team headquarters. Tilting the phone away from my mouth, I give the driver the address to the restaurant.

Over this last month, I've been working a lot with her at getting used to being back inside a car. India has been taking me out on drives. First, we started with me sitting in the back and then moved up to me sitting in the passenger seat. I haven't driven yet, but I no longer freak out at being in a car or the sound of the engine running.

Sounds lame considering what I do for a living, but I have to take it slow. Those are India's words. She says if I rush it, I might end up hindering myself and risk an anxiety attack, taking myself back steps.

I don't want that.

To a degree, this whole baby-steps shit is frustrating because I want nothing more than to be able to drive a car. But I trust her, and it's clearly working as I don't feel like I'm going to lose my shit in this taxi right now or panic like a little bitch when I sit behind the wheel of a car, like I would have done before she started helping me.

"Just checking that you didn't forget." Carrick chuckles.

"Like I would."

"Yeah, sure. Just like you didn't forget the last time."

"I'm never going to live that down, am I?"

I forgot because I was drunk and holed up in some chick's apartment, fucking the night away. I'd met her at the supermarket where I was buying a bottle of whiskey. We'd ended up taking it back to her place, drinking it, and—well, you know the rest.

I felt like a complete shit because I'd let my friends down.

"No, because Andressa had to explain to the date she brought for you that you hadn't stood her up."

"Because I hadn't known she was bringing a date for me."

Even if I'd known she brought me a date, it probably wouldn't have changed the way that day and night went. Dates want more than one night.

Then, it dawns on me why he's actually ringing.

"Please tell me that Andi hasn't brought another date for me tonight?"

Silence.

And his silence speaks volumes.

"Oh god," I groan. "She has, hasn't she?" I groan. "There's no way you'd be checking up on me like a woman if she hadn't. Andi made you call me, right?"

"Maybe."

"God, you're so pussy-whipped."

"There's a lot to be said for being whipped."

"You're a dick. And if I didn't platonically love your wife, then I'd be calling her a pain in my ass right now."

"She just wants you to be happy."

"Jesus, why didn't she learn from the first time she set me up? Dates and me don't go together."

The first dinner we had together when I moved back to London, Andi brought along a date for me. Her hairdresser. Granted, the date didn't go too badly because I ended up taking the hairdresser back to her place and fucking her. Problem was, that was all it was—a fuck. Sadly, she wanted more and didn't take my rejection too well. Andi had to find a new hairdresser.

So, God knows why she's insistent on constantly trying to set me up with people she knows.

"You really need to get your woman under control."

Carrick laughs. "Ha! If it were possible, I'd have done it ages ago. So, can I tell Andressa that you'll be here soon and that you're over the fucking moon that she's brought you a date?"

"Is the date hot?"

"If you like that type."

"What type?"

"Yoga instructors."

Hmm…

"They're seriously bendy, right? Then, yeah, tell Andi I'm over the fucking moon, and I'm skipping over fucking rainbows that she's brought along a yoga instructor as a date for me. I'll see you in ten, dickface." Then, I hang up the phone.

Resting my head back on the seat, I blow out a breath, rubbing my clean-shaven chin.

I got rid of the beard. I even had my hair cut.

I thought it was about time. And it will show India that I am really trying to clean myself up.

Okay, so pep talk, Silva…

I will not have sex with the bendy yoga instructor—unless she is absolutely clear on the fact that it is a one-time thing. Then, fucking her will be fine.

Unless she's dog ugly, of course.

And I will not get drunk. I'll fuck the bendy yoga instructor because I actually want to, because there's chemistry, and not because I am wasted or want to forget myself in her body.

If only India could hear me now, she'd be so proud. She'd be proud that I'm not going to screw somebody.

I laugh in my head at that thought.

Since India started treating me, my drinking has slowed down to a stop, and the random hook-ups are also nonexistent. I haven't had sex since that night with those two women that caused me to run late for my appointment with India the next day.

It's not been easy, but working on my issues with India is giving me purpose, something I didn't have before. My goal is to work toward getting back in a car, driving it, and then eventually racing.

One step at a time, no matter how long it takes.

Well, aside from being about to enter the last year of my contract. That kind of puts a time cap on it.

The taxi pulls up outside the restaurant. I pay the driver and climb out.

It's started to rain, so I quickly make my way inside. The maître d' approaches me. She instantly recognizes me. I've gotten very familiar with the look people get in their eyes when they recognize who I am.

"My friends are already here. I'm joining Carrick Ryan."

If she recognizes me, then she definitely knows who Carrick is.

"I'll take you to your table." She gives me a coquettish smile.

It's impossible for me not to return it. I'm a flirty bastard by nature.

As I follow behind the maître d', I check out her ass.

Nice. Curvy. An ass you could grab ahold of while you fucked her.

But it's nowhere near as good an ass as India's.

"You're late," Andi says as I approach the table, giving me a chastising look, but there's a smile on her lips, so I know she's not as mad as she might like to make out.

As I reach the table, I let my eyes flicker over to the yoga instructor.

Dark hair. Pretty face. Big tits.

"Sorry." I lean down and kiss both of Andi's cheeks. "You look lovely, as always."

"Oi, dickface. Hands off my wife."

"Good to see you, too, Ryan." I smirk at him.

Grinning at me, he stands, and we do that handshake and half hug that us men like to do.

"Been a while. You doing okay?" he quietly asks me.

I meet his eyes, giving him a nod. "I'm doing good."

"Leandro, this is Katrina," Andi says.

Turning to Katrina, I smile at her, properly looking her over, as I move around the table where, of course, I've been strategically seated next to her.

She has a strappy red dress on, and her ample cleavage is spilling out of it.

I put my hand out to shake hers. "Nice to meet you, Katrina. I'm Leandro."

She slips her hand into mine, and I kiss her cheeks, but I feel nothing. No spark or connection.

A strange sense of relief settles inside me.

I'm relieved that I don't have a connection with the hot woman? What the hell is wrong with me?

India. That's what's wrong with me.

She's the only person I feel that spark with, and she's the only woman I can't have.

Story of my fucking life at the moment.

Every time I touch India, I feel something that I haven't ever felt with a woman, even before the accident. Sure, I've sparked and connected with women in the past, but what I feel every time I touch India is pure exhilaration. Like I'm about to start the greatest race of my life.

"I know who you are. And call me Kat." She gives me a flirty smile, just like the maître d' did moments before.

"What can I get you to drink?" a waitress asks, appearing at our table.

I glance at the table and see what everyone's drinking. Carrick's on the whiskey, like usual, Andi has a beer, and Katrina has a glass of red wine.

I want to keep my mind clear tonight, so I'm not going to drink. "I'll just have a lemonade with a slice of lime."

"Are you driving tonight?" Kat asks me.

"No." I pretend not to see the smile on Andi's face. I know she thinks I drink too much.

I did drink too much.

Kat turns in her seat to me, pressing her knee right up against my thigh. "So, why aren't you drinking?" she asks, like it's a given that I should be drinking. That's probably because of what she's read and heard about me recently.

Something uncomfortable moves in my chest.

"I just like to keep a clear mind when in the company of such beautiful women." I turn my charm on to stop her from asking any more questions that I'm not in the mood to answer.

"What's everyone having?" Andi says, opening her menu.

I flicker an appreciative look to her, to which she smiles.

I'm not an alcoholic because coming off the drink hasn't been too hard. But I was using it as a crutch, and until I know I can drink for the enjoyment again, I'm staying off it. I just don't want to have to explain myself to a complete stranger.

I open my menu, noting the fact that Kat hasn't moved her leg from against mine. Then, I see her hand drop into her lap, and she starts to inch it toward my leg.

Okay. She moves fast.

Not that I have a problem with fast. I'm just not going to go there with her.

No chemistry, no fucking.

Her fingertips have just made it to my thigh when the waitress returns with my drink, so Kat retracts her hand, placing it on the table.

When I lift my eyes, I catch Carrick grinning at me.

I give him a fuck-off look, to which he chuckles.

"I've decided." Carrick slaps his menu shut. "What are you having, babe?" he asks Andi.

"I can't decide."

"What about the veal?"

Smiling, she shakes her head, and he laughs, clearly sharing a private joke. Taking her hand in his, he kisses it.

I feel a small pang in my chest at the realization that I might never have that with someone.

"Hey, Carrick, look. Dr. Harris is here."

Andi's words have my eyes snapping up from the table.

Turning his head in the direction where Andi is looking, Carrick says, "Oh, yeah."

My eyes search her out, but a pillar is blocking my view, and I can't see her from where I'm seated.

"Who's Dr. Harris?" Kat asks.

"She's my therapist," Andi answers with ease.

The Andi before India would have had a problem answering that question. She was secretive and kept things to herself—her words, not mine—but since India has being treating her, Andi is more open, less afraid to tell people things about herself.

"I've had—sometimes still have—worries over Carrick's racing, and she's helps me deal with it," Andi explains to Kat.

I slide a glance at Carrick, and the fucker is grinning at me.

I know it's not because he'll say anything about me seeing India, and neither will Andi.

Then, about two seconds later, I see the reason for his grin when India comes into view, and so does the man she's with.

She's on a date?

I feel like I've just been punched in the chest.

Is this the guy she was on the phone with the other week? The one she said, "I love you," to?

The guy looks like a dick. Sure, I can't see him properly from here, but he's definitely not good enough for her.

No man could be.

She's amazing.

And she looks beautiful tonight. She always looks gorgeous, but tonight, seeing her out of her work clothes, makes her look different.

Her hair is down, like usual, the blonde ends brushing her shoulders, and her lips are painted red.

But she's wearing a pretty white dress. It's fitted over the bust and waist and flares out at the bottom.

She looks like a fucking angel.

"I'm gonna go over and say hello." Andi rises from her seat.

I watch as she walks over to India. I see the real smile that India gives Andi and feel the envy at the hug she receives from India. And I stare unabashed as India introduces Andi to the dickhead she's with.

I sip my lemonade as Andi turns, pointing to where we're sitting. India's blue eyes meet with me, and I feel a jolt go down my spine, careening straight for my dick.

Andi says something to her, and then they're moving toward us.

How do I handle this?

Do I pretend not to know her?

I don't want Kat to know I'm seeing a therapist. I don't know the chick, and she could tell someone or sell it to the press. I don't want that shit spattered all over the news.

Leandro Silva Seeing a Shrink.

Yeah, no, thanks.

Then, India's standing by our table with the dickhead, and all rational thought leaves my mind.

I have to force myself not to stare. So, I give the dickhead a quick once-over.

Gray suit. Floppy blond hair. He looks like he just fell out of a Hugh Grant movie.

Prick.

"Dr. Harris, it's nice to see you again." Carrick is on his feet, greeting her.

He kisses her cheek, and I feel the urge to punch him.

"I'm still just India." She laughs.

The sound greets my dick like a sweet kiss from her red lips.

"Yeah, never could get used to calling you by your first name."

I decide to take decisive action—or should I call it, playing games?

Standing from the table, I reach a hand over it and say to India, "Leandro Silva. Nice to meet you."

As she brings her eyes to mine, there's no flicker of surprise, so maybe she expected me to act like I didn't know her.

It kind of pisses me off that she was expecting it.

She slides her hand into mine, and I feel like she's burned me.

"India Harris. It's nice to meet you, Leandro."

Our eyes lock.

She looks away first and looks straight at Kat.

Is that jealousy or disapproval in her eyes?

I hope for jealousy.

Her lips press together, the way they do when I tell her about something or someone I've done that she thinks is a bad choice for me.

Definitely disapproval then.

The knowledge bothers the fuck out of me.

A hand in Kat's direction, I say to India, "This is Kat—" *Fuck, I don't know her surname.*

"Kat Whisker." She stands up beside me, reaching a hand out to India.

Kat Whisker?

I have to hold back a laugh, and it's hard going. I can see that India has humor dancing in her eyes.

She would never laugh though. She's too kind to laugh at someone in that way.

Carrick's not so obvious or kind because the bastard laughs, which he quickly turns into a cough. Andi shoots a look at him.

Kat doesn't seem to notice as she's too busy eyeing India while shaking her hand.

"This is Dr. Daniel Walker," India introduces the prick to everyone.

And, of course, he's a doctor. I bet the asshole works with sick kids or something.

"Please, just call me Dan."

He smiles at us, and I want to punch him.

"Dan's an ER doctor," India tells us. She sounds proud.

I feel a stab of jealousy, which is ridiculous.

Why would I be jealous?

"An ER doctor with a rare night off." He smiles at India, his hand moving to rest on her lower back.

Now, all I can think about it ripping his hand off the small of her back and crushing it until he gets the message never to touch her again.

"Leandro's a Formula One driver, like Carrick." Kat slips her hand through my arm, curling her fingers over my bicep. "I'm sure you must have heard of him."

"Leandro Silva, of course." Dan clicks his fingers. He turns to Carrick. "And you're Carrick Ryan. Great to meet you both. I don't get a chance to watch much racing, but when I do, you two are always my firm favorites."

Ass-licker.

He shakes my hand first. I make sure to give a firm squeeze. If he notices, he doesn't let on.

"Well, we should leave you to it and get to our table." India indicates to the waitress, who's been hovering this whole time.

"Why don't you join us?" Andi says.

I feel Kat's hand tighten on my arm.

"That'd be okay, wouldn't it?" Andi asks the waitress. She looks back to India. "If you want to join us, of course."

India looks to Dan.

He smiles. "Of course. As long as you don't mind us crashing your party."

I feel like raising my hand and saying that I mind.

I mind a fucking lot.

I don't want to sit here and watch them fawn all over each other. Not that there's been much fawning.

"Of course not," the waitress replies.

Clicking her fingers, she gets the attention of a waiter, who brings over two more chairs and two place settings for them.

By now, I've managed to extract Kat's hand from my arm, and I'm sitting back in my seat.

We've all had to move around a bit, so Kat is practically sitting on my lap, and somehow, India has ended up in the chair next to me.

Well, this is going to be a fun night.

How the fuck did I end up on a couples night with my shrink?

Maybe I should have that drink now.

eight

INDIA

✈ LONDON, ENGLAND

I KNEW I SHOULD HAVE WRITTEN THIS NIGHT OFF.

First, my car broke down on my way out shopping to buy a new pair of stockings, as I hadn't realized I had run out, and I was stuck waiting for the RAC to come fix my car. They couldn't, so it's currently at the garage.

Then, my heel snapped while I was at the shop, buying the stockings, so I had to go and buy a new pair of shoes. That wasn't too bad, as I ended up also buying the ones I'm wearing now as well as the new dress I'm wearing.

Then, after getting caught in the rain and having to hail a taxi home, I'd just run a bath when a patient called. Of course I took the call, and by the time I was done, my bath was cold. So, I had to take a shower.

Then, my hair straightener wouldn't work, and to round it off, I broke my favorite lipstick.

It's been a shithole of a day, so of course, I would see Leandro Silva here on a date.

It's good that he's dating, and he's clearly not drinking, judging from the lemonade he just ordered.

But his date is a bit handsy. I have a full show of her hand on his thigh, inching its way up. He has to keep stopping when she gets too high. Really, he should just tell her to knock it off. I mean, of course, it's not bothering me.

I just don't think you should grope someone in public at dinner.

An image of Leandro's hand sliding up my thigh flashes through my mind, and I feel myself grow hot.

I take a drink of my wine to cool off.

Just focus on your food and the pleasant conversation and Dan sitting next to me.

Not the man on my left.

Or his handsy date.

Kat Whisker.

The laugh I held back earlier slips out, which I quickly cover with a cough. Dan glances at me and then goes back to talking to Carrick.

I can feel Leandro's eyes on me, but I won't look at him.

But then again, maybe not looking at him is even more obvious.

I'll just casually look at him, like a normal person would.

I glance in his direction to find him already staring at me.

Why is he staring at me? And why do I have to find him so damn attractive?

It's not helping that he's all looking seriously dapper, and his beard is gone.

I wonder if he shaved his beard off for his date with handsy Kat.

It's not like I can even ask him. He made it clear that he doesn't want people to know we know each other. That's understandable. I am his therapist after all, and Leandro has a public persona to keep up even if it has been sketchy as of late.

I smile at him and try to think of something that a person who doesn't know him would say. "How's your dinner?"

Wow, that was awesome, India.

A grin edges his lips. "It's okay. The steak is a bit overdone for my liking. I prefer it *rare*." His eyes flash with the emphasis on the last word.

Okay. Deep breath. I take another sip of my wine.

"How's yours?" His deep accented voice seems closer.

As I turn my head, I see that he's leaning in my direction.

I glance down at my salmon, which I've hardly touched. "It's good."

When I meet his eyes again, he's smiling at me.

My ear pricks up when I hear Dan ask Carrick, "So, how do you guys know India?"

I glance at Andi, gauging her response. She has loosened up so much since I first met her. She's more open, but whether she'll want Dan to know I was treating her is another story.

"India helped me deal with some issues I had with Carrick's racing."

Okay, she's fine with it, which is good.

I smile at her.

"So, is she as good as they say?"

"Better," Leandro says, surprising me.

The whole table turns to him.

His face doesn't even flicker. "Andi raved about her, and the change in her was noticeable, even to me."

I give Andi a warm smile.

"So, have you used your connections to take Jett to the Prix?" Dan says jovially. He knows what a Formula 1 nut Jett is.

"Who's Jett?" That's Leandro again.

"India's son," Dan answers casually.

He doesn't know that Leandro is a patient.

I don't discuss my private life with my patients.

I can feel my face heating.

"I didn't realize you had a son," Andi says.

"India's fiercely protective of him," Dan comments. "I haven't even met him, and we've been dating for two months."

I can hear the issue in his voice, and it makes me uncomfortable.

I know it bothers Dan that he hasn't met Jett yet, but I don't introduce men to my son, not unless I'm serious about them. And I haven't been serious about anyone ever before. So, introducing someone to Jett would mean I really see a future with the guy, and I'm not sure if Dan is that person.

"How old is your son?" Andi asks with a lift to her voice. Probably to take away from the discomfort of Dan's comment.

I try to curb my need to protect my life from people. "He's twelve."

"Twelve?" Leandro exclaims from beside me.

I know for a fact that my cheeks are bright red right now.

I really want to kick Dan in the shin, hard, for bringing Jett up.

"What I mean is, you don't look old enough to have a twelve-year-old," Leandro says, his voice sounding different.

I swallow past a breath. "I was young when I had him." I force bright into my voice and my eyes to look at him.

What I see staring back makes my breath catch and sends shivers hurtling through my body, all the way down to my toes.

The way he's looking at me is like he's seeing me in a whole new light.

Not just as his therapist, but as a woman.

And it thrills me to my very core.

"I can't believe you never told me that you know Carrick Ryan."

We're outside my front door, and Dan has his arms around me.

He's driven me home from dinner. Andi was trying to talk us into drinks afterward, but in all honesty, I didn't want to hang around and watch Kat feel up Leandro.

It was bugging me.

It shouldn't have because I'm seeing Dan, and I'm Leandro's therapist. But I don't lie to myself, and being attracted to the guy is a problem.

One that I need to control.

Because I can't stop treating him.

I should. Finding a patient attractive is never a good thing. But I've never found myself in this situation before.

What reason would I give to stop treating him?

Oh, I kind of find you insanely attractive, so I can't treat you anymore.

I don't think so.

I just need to pull up my big girl panties and repeatedly remind myself that he's my patient.

And I'm also in Dan's arms right now, arguing with myself over another man.

I'm scoring major points tonight.

Right, no more Leandro thoughts.

"Andi's a patient, and I only know Carrick through her. And you're not a big Formula One fan, so I didn't think it'd matter if I told you or not."

"It doesn't." He brushes my nose with his. "But the guy is a legend, as is Leandro Silva. Though I hear he's not racing anymore after his accident."

"Hmm…"

"So, dinner was nice."

"It was."

He brushes his lips over mine in that soft way of his.

It's nice. Just, sometimes, I wish he'd go wild with me. Push me up against the door and ravage me.

Not kiss me like he thinks I'm going to break.

Feeling oddly frustrated, I deepen the kiss, slipping my tongue into his mouth. Pressing my body up against his, I moan into his mouth.

His fingers gently slide into my hair.

But I don't want him to be gentle.

I push him up against the outside wall of my house. Splaying my hands on his chest, I kiss him harder. Nipping his lip with my teeth, I let my hand lower to his erection that's digging into my hip. I start to rub him through the fabric.

Then, I lower the zipper of his trousers, but he catches my hand, stopping me.

"India."

Embarrassment floods my face at his blatant rejection. I pull my hand away and take a step back from him, looking at anything but him. "God, I'm so sorry."

I don't know why I did that. We haven't even had sex yet. I wanted to take it slow, and it's been a long time since I've had sex with any man.

What was I planning on doing? Have sex with him in my doorway?

It's not like I'd take him inside and have sex with him while my son is sleeping in the next room, and my brother is down the hall. Then, there's the fact that Jett hasn't met him, and Kit has met him only once.

What has gotten into me?

"I should go inside." My eyes are currently on my feet, which start to move toward my front door.

"No, India, wait." He catches my arm, pulling me back to him.

He slides his hands around my waist. I reluctantly look him in the face.

"I'm sorry," he says earnestly. "You just caught me off guard. I guess I wasn't expecting it. We haven't had sex, and you haven't made any move in that direction until now."

I stare down at my feet, unable to look at him a moment longer. "I guess...I just got caught up in the moment."

"India, look at me, please."

Reluctantly, I lift my eyes to his.

His hand cups my cheek, caressing it with his thumb. "I like that you got caught up in the moment, and I'm more than happy to move on to that next stage of our relationship, but only if you're really ready."

"I don't know. I guess...maybe." I shrug.

For an educated woman, I'm just full of articulation tonight, aren't I?

"India, I want what you want. There's no pressure here."

Frustration builds in my mind, buzzing in my ears, and I instantly see my problem here.

I want him to want what *he* wants. Not want what *I* want. I need him to be more assertive. Tell me that he wants me, and the rest be damned. Press me up against this wall, and kiss the hell out of me. Tell me how much he needs to be inside me. That he can't breathe without me.

I need passion from him.

I bet Leandro isn't this considerate or gentle with the women he has sex with. I bet he's full of passion. I bet he just tells them straight that he wants them.

Not that I'd want to be one of Leandro's one-night conquests. Like Kat bloody Whisker.

Ugh! Shit! Fuckity fuck, I'm bringing Leandro into this again!

No more Leandro thoughts.

"Just...think about it, and let me know, okay?" Dan says.

I have to bite back my frustration. "Yeah, sure."

He gently presses his lips to mine. I quickly break away, not wanting to kiss him right now, and I step toward the door, getting my keys from my clutch.

"I'll call you tomorrow," he says.

"Speak to you then."

I close the door behind me and lock it. Then, I lean up against it, my heart beating hard in my chest, and I know it's not beating that way because of Dan, but because of thoughts of a certain Brazilian race car driver.

LEANDRO

✚ LONDON, ENGLAND

WALKING TOWARD THE TUBE STATION, my head is completely up my ass. I just had a meeting with the team bosses at some fancy restaurant where the dishes were so small I came out still hungry.

The meeting was pointless because I had nothing new to tell them.

I'm still in therapy, and I'm still not driving yet.

They said the same as before. I don't return next year, and I'm out.

I can't be pissed at them. They're running a business and currently paying for a driver who doesn't drive.

If anything, they're being good to me. I know it's out of loyalty and respect. But that can only go so far.

I'm well aware that the season is fast approaching. It's the end of November. Racing season starts in March.

I need to be back in my car and soon, or my career will be over for good.

A flash of blonde hair catches my attention. It instantly makes me think of India.

Not that that's a rarity at the moment. Currently, she's all I think about.

Seeing her last night with the prick she's dating drove me insane. It took everything in me not to reach over and strangle the guy.

Knowing he gets to put his hands on her…

I clench my fists at the thought.

Seriously though, what does she see in the guy? Sure, he's a doctor, but he's boring as hell.

I was just glad to be seated away from him, so I didn't have to make conversation with the tool. Though it was fun to watch Carrick being tortured from having to listen to him.

That's what he gets for being complicit in setting me up with Kat.

Jesus, that woman was like an octopus. Her hands were everywhere.

Don't get me wrong. I don't mind having my junk felt up but not in full view of everyone—especially not when the one woman I do actually want to have her hand on my cock is sitting next to me.

After last night, if it hadn't been clear to me before, then it was abundantly clear to me then that I want to have sex with India.

Repeatedly.

I just need to figure out how to make that happen and how to make Dan the dickhead, disappear.

God, I can't believe she's dating that boring asshole. I don't care that he's a doctor, and he saves lives. She deserves better than him.

You?

No. She deserves better than me, but I'm a selfish bastard, and when I want something, I take it.

I push open the door to the Tube station, and I walk straight into India—literally.

"Oops. Sorry," she says.

She has her eyes down, hand searching in her bag. When she lifts her eyes to me, I see the surprise flicker through them.

Then, she smiles widely. "Leandro."

My eyes quickly graze over her body. She's dressed down in skinny jeans and a T-shirt with a fitted black leather jacket. It makes her look younger.

And my cock instantly stands to attention.

I step a little closer, getting into her space. "India. Last night, and now, this morning. If I didn't know better, I would think the universe is trying to put us together."

Her eyes flicker nervously to the side. Following her gaze, I see a boy standing beside her, curiously looking at me.

I immediately know it's her son. He has the exact same blue eyes as her.

She clears her throat, in that way she does when she's uncomfortable. It's surprising how quickly I've become accustomed to her little ways.

"Leandro, this is my son, Jett." She takes a step away from me, revealing more of him.

I remember her saying last night that he's twelve. This kid is tall for his age. I'm six foot, and he's only about half a foot shorter than me.

His head tilts to the side, his eyes sparking with excitement.

"You're Leandro Silva." He sounds flabbergasted.

She said he's a big Formula 1 fan.

"I am." I smile.

"Holy crap!" He flicks his eyes to India. "You know Leandro Silva? How do you know Leandro Silva? And why didn't you tell me that you know Leandro Silva?" The kid's voice is raising a decibel higher. He might be tall, but his voice hasn't broken yet, and his high pitch is raising some attention.

I pull the ball cap I'm wearing down lower over my eyes. I don't mind a little attention, but right now, I don't want people intruding while I have her here.

"Jett, please don't say crap. And could you lower your voice a little? People are starting to stare." India laughs softly.

His eyes scan quickly around. "Sorry." His eyes come back to me. "I'm just a huge fan. *Huge.*" He emphasizes with his hands.

"It's okay." I smile at him again.

I glance back to India. She's chewing on her lip, looking a little more than disconcerted.

Yes, it turns me on. Her lip-chewing and nervousness are doing it for me. But then again, pretty much everything she does turns me on.

We're in this awkward pause where none of us knows quite exactly what to say. Jett is staring at me in awe, and his mouth keeps opening and closing like he has a hundred questions to ask but no clue where to start.

I decide to fill the gap.

"Did you take the Tube?" That is clearly the dumbest thing I could ask, considering they were exiting the station.

Smooth, Silva, real smooth.

A smile spreads onto India's face. "My car is in the garage," she tells me. "So, we're slaves to public transport."

Another awkward pause.

Putting her hand on Jett's arm, she says, "Well, we should get going—"

"No!" Jett says loudly. His face instantly goes bright red. "I mean, we're going for coffee. Well, I'm having hot chocolate 'cause I'm clearly too young for coffee. But do you want to come with us and have coffee? Or tea? Hot chocolate? Whatever you drink really..." He trails off, looking uncomfortable.

Chuckling, I part my lips to speak, but I don't get a chance.

"I'm sure Leandro has better things to do than have coffee with us, Jett."

Do I?

I glance at her. There's something in her eyes that I can't quite discern, but it looks an awful lot like uncertainty.

I look back to Jett and smile. "Actually, I can't think of anything I'd rather do right now."

Okay, I'm turning the charm on, but I do actually mean that. There's nowhere else I'd rather be right now than with her. And meeting her kid is an added bonus.

I slide my eyes back to India, locking them with hers. "I'd love to have coffee with you."

A smile warms her eyes.

"We were just going to Starbucks. Is that okay with you?"

Anywhere with you, is okay with me. "Perfect."

I walk with them toward Starbucks. India begins walking in front of us while Jett is talking incessantly to me about my past races. I listen to him talk, answer his questions, and force myself not to stare at India's magnificent ass in those tight jeans. Seems like it'd be disrespectful to ogle her in front of her kid.

Stepping in front when we reach Starbucks, I open the door for her.

"Thanks." She doesn't meet my eyes when she speaks, but I see the flush on her face.

Jett walks through, still talking to me about racing, and I follow him in.

"You two take a seat. I'll go get the drinks," I tell them. "Hot chocolate for you, Jett?" I check. "And a black coffee for you, India?"

"You know how my mum takes her coffee?" Jett's voice punches through the air.

And I see the smile on India's face freeze.

When I look at Jett, I see he's got a big-ass grin on his face.

Kid is quick.

But I'm quicker.

"I brought her coffee once. It stuck with me. I have a great memory." I tap a finger to my head. "You want anything to go with that hot chocolate?"

Glancing past me at the food on display, he says, "A blueberry muffin would be great, please."

"We'll go find somewhere to sit," India says, still looking a little flustered.

I join the small queue, watching when they take a seat at the back of the coffee shop.

I place the order, getting myself a black coffee, and try to ignore the stare from the server, hoping she doesn't recognize me.

I manage to get my order without issue, and I carry everything over to the table. Putting the tray down, I hand Jett his drink and muffin.

"Thanks," he mumbles. Instantly, he takes a bite of muffin.

"Thank you." India smiles at me as I put her coffee on the table in front of her.

She wraps her hands around the cup, like she needs the warmth.

"So, Mum says she met you at dinner last night. You were there with a patient of hers who is a friend of yours."

I slide my eyes to India before looking back to Jett. I nod and say, "I was."

"Is it another Formula One driver?"

"Jett!" she chastises lightly in only that way a mother can.

I laugh at his directness.

"Stop prying," she says to him.

"You don't ask, you don't find out." He shrugs, taking another bite of his muffin.

"Jett has got a point," I say, which earns me a frown from India, causing me to chuckle. "And it would be wrong of me to talk about it as it's my friend's private business," I tell Jett. "But to answer your question, no, she is not a driver."

"She? Someone you're dating then?"

"Jett!" India's voice is louder now, and she's red in the face.

It makes me laugh again. I love to see her flustered.

"I'm so sorry," India says to me. "He's not usually this nosy."

"Yes, I am," Jett replies.

India shoots a look at him.

I'm still laughing.

I like this kid.

"No, I'm not dating her. She's married to my friend," I answer.

"And that's enough of those questions," India cuts him off when he opens his mouth again.

"Fine," he huffs, turning in his seat to look at her. "But I have to ask because you don't tell me anything—like the fact that you met Leandro Silva last night."

"I've hardly had the chance," she responds, sounding exasperated. "You were sleeping when I got home."

"You couldn't have told me at breakfast?"

I'm watching them with fascination. India is always so calm and in control in our sessions, but right now, she's at the mercy of her twelve-year-old kid, who's close to breaking her in front of my eyes.

I'm tempted to ask him his secret on how to do it.

"Okay!" She throws her hands up in the air. "Fine. I'm sorry, Jett. I could have told you this morning."

"Notice that she said *could*, not *should*," he says to me, grinning.

He clearly loves winding her up.

India makes a frustrated sound before picking up her coffee, and she blows on it, like she always does before taking a sip.

"I'm just teasing, Mum." He nudges her shoulder with his.

"You were driving me nuts is what you were doing." She chuckles good-naturedly.

"So"—Jett turns his full attention back to me—"you bought Mum coffee at dinner?"

"What?"

"You met at dinner last night, but you said you knew how she took her coffee 'cause you'd gotten it once for her."

Shit.

This kid is way too observant. He doesn't miss a trick. I'd be impressed—if it wasn't me he was currently putting on the spot.

"After dinner," India chimes in. "There was no coffee at the restaurant, so we all went to a coffee shop, and Leandro bought my coffee."

"Why didn't Dr. Dull get you the coffee?"

I almost choke on my own coffee. *Dr. Dull?* I knew I liked this kid.

"Jett! I really wish you wouldn't call him that. I swear to God, Kit…" she mutters.

Who's Kit?

Jett must read my mind because he says, "Kit's my uncle, Mum's twin brother. He calls Dan, Dr. Dull, and Mum hates it."

"I can see why."

And I mean her brother naming Dan, Dr. Dull. It couldn't be more fitting.

I think I'm going to like her brother as well.

India's eyes hit mine, her brows rising, and I don't elaborate on my meaning of what I just said.

"So, you like racing?" I say to Jett, turning my attention to him.

"I love it."

"Just Formula One or any kind of racing?"

"Formula One mainly, but I like karting, too."

"Have you ever been to the Prix?"

"No." He gives a sad shake of his head. "Mum says the tickets are too expensive."

"They are too expensive." I smile lightly, sliding my eyes to hers, and I catch her looking at me with a weird expression on her face.

"Well, I can get you tickets to the Prix at Silverstone—"

"Yes!" He excitedly bangs his hands on the table.

"But only if it's okay with your mother."

Turning to India, he gives her an expectant look.

She lets out a breath. "It's okay with me." She raises her hands in defeat, but she has a smile on her face.

I like seeing her smile, and making her son happy has to score me some brownie points. Then, an idea comes to me.

"I was just thinking…as the Prix is a long ways off—and again, only as long as your mom is okay with it—I'm attending a Karting Championship tomorrow. I have to present an award, a favor for a friend. You're both more than welcome to come along."

"Are you serious?" Jett's eyes nearly bug out of his head.

"I'm serious." I smile.

"Mum?" He gives her another expectant look.

Looking at me, she shakes her head, but I know she's not mad as a smile teases her lips.

"Tomorrow where?" she asks me.

"Shenington Airfield in Banbury. About an hour's drive away."

"Can we go? Please! Please!" Jett pleads, his hands pressed together in front of him.

She stares at him for a long moment. I can see her mind working.

"I don't know, honey. I don't have my car, and Kit's working tomorrow, so I can't borrow his—"

"You don't need your car. I'll take you both."

"You're driving there?" she asks, her voice careful.

Always the therapist.

"I have a driver taking me. I'm rich and lazy." I give a laugh, but it sounds weak even to my own ears.

Of course she knows why I'm not driving, but I don't want to look lame in front of her son.

But then, he's a Formula 1 fan, so he's probably heard stories about me.

"If I were you, I wouldn't drive myself around either," Jett says, leaning back in his chair. "I'd have a chauffeur and save my driving for the tracks."

He's either oblivious or a good kid.

Going by who his mother is, I'm going to go with good kid.

Sitting forward, he wraps his arm around her shoulders. "So, can we go, Mum? Please…"

She looks at me, and I shrug my shoulders, smiling. Leaning back in my chair, I grab my coffee and take a sip.

Releasing her, he says, "You have to say yes as this will be the biggest thing to ever happen to me in my life. And do you know how many levels of cool I'll climb at school if I say I spent the day with Leandro Silva?"

"Are you sure it'll be no trouble?" India asks me.

A day spent with you?

"No trouble at all."

"So, is that a yes?" Jett checks with India.

"It's a yes."

"Yes!" He fist-bumps the air before planting a kiss on India's cheek.

Then, he's on his phone, probably texting his friends or updating his Facebook status.

I glance at India and find her already watching me.

Thank you, she mouths to me.

It gives me this warm feeling in my chest, like it's something secret she's giving just to me.

You're welcome, I mouth back.

INDIA

✚ BANBURY, ENGLAND

THIS IS A BAD IDEA.

I really shouldn't be here, but it's not like I could say no when Leandro Silva, one of Jett's heroes, was there, offering him tickets to go watch a karting championship race. Jett's face was all lit up, and I would be Devil Mother if I'd said no, but I would be Mother of the Year if I said yes. Who could turn down the chance to be Mother of the Year, right?

And it's not like I could explain to Jett that it would be unethical of me to take the tickets and spend the day with Leandro because he's my patient.

But then, technically, I didn't take the tickets. Jett did. Leandro gave them to him, and Jett gave the spare ticket to me.

So, that's my rationalization on the situation, and I'm sticking with it.

How I ended up in the back of the car with Leandro and Jett in the front with the driver and with control of the stereo though is beyond me.

But I really need to put my work head on because Leandro is being even more charming than usual, and he looks so bloody hot in his jeans and black shirt. And those depthless eyes of his every time they meet with mine...I swear, they are sucking me in. And his accent...sweet baby

Jesus, his accent. I feel the need to cross my legs every time he speaks in general, but sitting here with him, isolated in the back of this car because Jett put up the bloody privacy glass, without my work head on...it's not good.

And so very good.

I need to say something to fill the quiet tension.

"Thank you for inviting Jett today," I say. It was the only thing I could think of to say.

"You already said that. Five minutes ago. And when I first picked you up."

"Did I?"

I make the mistake of looking at him.

Fly trapped in web.

"You did." His voice is soft and alluring.

I have to force myself to look away. I fix my gaze on the scenery outside my window.

"India, are you okay? You seem nervous."

My eyes swing back to him. "Nervous? I'm not nervous." My voice comes out high-pitched and saying, *I'm totally nervous.*

"No?" He tilts his head to the side, and some of those soft black strands fall into his eyes.

My fingers itch to brush them away. Maybe run into his hair and feel it, see if it's as soft as I think it will be.

I'm his therapist. And I'm dating Dan.

I sit on my hands. "Okay, maybe I'm a little nervous."

"Why?" He moistens his lips with his tongue.

If I didn't know better, I'd think he did that to torture me.

Finding my mouth dry, I lick my own lips for moisture. "Because...I'm your therapist." I lower my voice to a whisper even though I know Jett can't hear me up front.

"And?"

"And..." I frown. "It's unethical of me to be socializing with you."

"It's unethical of you to spend time with me?"

"In a non-therapist-patient capacity, yes."

"And that's the only reason you're nervous right now?" His eyes bore into mine.

No, it's not the only reason. I'm mostly nervous because I have the strongest urge to kiss you right now and find out if you taste as amazing as I think you will. And if Jett weren't sitting in the front of this car right now, I'd have a hard time stopping myself from doing so.

Jesus, what is wrong with me? Why can I control my thoughts while with him at the office but not here?

"Of course it is. What other reason would there be?" I have to force my voice to sound even, and it's seriously hard going.

"No reason." He looks away from me.

I stare down at my hands.

From the moment he met me, I've seen Leandro look at me in a sexual way, but I know that's because he uses sex as a defense mechanism.

He looked at me the way he would any other woman he deemed attractive—as a temporary means of escapism.

But, lately, the way he's been looking at me is different.

I don't know how to explain it, but he's no longer looking at me like I'm just another object for him to screw.

He's looking at me like he actually wants *me*.

And it scares the crap out of me.

Because I want him, too.

"So, why don't you treat this like a therapy session, if it's bothering you so much?" His words come from nowhere, and his tone is biting. He sounds pissed off. "I can talk to you about the usual shit—you know, how my life sucks—if that'll make you feel better about being here with me."

"You're blowing it out of context, Leandro."

"Am I, Dr. Harris?"

Not since out first initial meeting has he called me Dr. Harris. He always calls me India.

And hearing him calling me Dr. Harris scratches over my skin like unwelcome nails.

"You said being here with me is unethical, so I'm trying to make it ethical for you."

I blow out a breath. "What do you want me to say?"

"Isn't that usually my line?"

"Jesus, Leandro!" I snap, my anger getting the better of me. "What is it that you want from me here?"

He glances my way, his black eyes looking through me, his jaw set. "Nothing." He turns his face away from me. "I am sorry I put you in a difficult position by giving Jett the tickets. I should have thought about it. It's not like you could say no to him once I'd made the offer."

He's right…and wrong. The mother in me couldn't say no, but the doctor should have. Jett would have been angry, but he'd have gotten over it.

I put myself in this position.

Maybe because a part of me wants to be here with Leandro.

And now, I've offended him, and I don't know how to take it back.

"Look, I'm sorry." I reach out and touch his arm. The instant I do, I know it's a mistake because the connection I always feel around him increases tenfold.

All the air is sucked out of the car, leaving me breathless. I can feel the heat of his body through the shirt beneath my palm, setting my skin ablaze.

I can't take my eyes off of him. He's so beautiful.

His hand comes to mine. His index finger lightly traces up my skin until it reaches my wrist. His fingers circle it until his hand is holding me.

His eyes move down to my mouth. I see them flare to life.

"India…" he says my name on a breath.

I almost come undone.

Almost.

Coming to my senses, remembering who I am, who we are and where we are, I pull away from him and turn to face the window.

I hear him exhale loudly. He sounds frustrated.

I close my eyes on the sound, and my hand wraps around the one that now feels like it has a permanent imprint of him on it.

We haven't spoken since *the* moment, and you could cut the tension between us with a knife right now.

I can't believe how close I came to kissing him.

How did I go from being his therapist to this…what exactly?

A man I want to kiss…and more.

He's a patient, for God's sake! What the hell am I thinking?

Would I have actually let it happen? Would I have kissed him?

The fact that I don't know the clear answer to those questions is a clear sign that I should be running far from him.

The sign for Shenington Airfield comes into view. I breathe a quiet sigh of relief.

I just need to get through today. Then, I can get back to just seeing him in a professional capacity, and I'll be okay.

It's just that seeing him at dinner on Friday night, bumping into him yesterday and having coffee, seeing how great he was with Jett, and spending today with him…it's just confusing me.

And it's not like Leandro has any real feelings for me.

He has sex with different women all the time. Maybe not so much lately. But he was a player long before the accident.

The driver pulls up into the parking area.

Jett climbs out. The driver opens my door, and I climb out with Leandro getting out behind me.

"This place is awesome!" Jett comes around the car to me, excitement on his face.

I love seeing him happy like this.

"This way." Leandro gestures.

I follow behind while Jett walks with him, asking him questions about today's race.

I can see people staring at him. He doesn't seem to notice, but then he must be used to people staring at him.

I sometimes forget how well known he is. When it's just him and me talking in my office, he's just Leandro.

Out here, he's a world-renowned Formula 1 driver.

Going through the paddock area, we reach a section where a guy is at the door. He greets Leandro, shaking his hand. Then, he opens the door, and Leandro ushers Jett and me through first before coming in behind us.

Not many people are in here. Looks to be a private viewing area that opens up onto the karting track.

"Leandro fucking Silva!"

I turn at the sound of the male voice, not loving the fact that he just cursed in front of Jett.

Good-looking, brown hair, nice smile. I recognize him but can't place him.

"Carter, how are you doing?" Leandro greets him, smiling.

They do that manly handshake-hug thing that men do.

"I'm good. How are you doing after the accident? I know this shit's tough—"

"I'm fine," Leandro cuts him off, the tone in his voice instantly harder.

Carter stares at him for a moment, his brow furrowed. Then, his face relaxes. "Well, I'm glad to hear it. But if you do need to talk, you know where I am. We need to get together more often anyway. And thanks for doing this today. The kids will love seeing you here."

"No problem," Leandro says with a dismissive wave of his hand.

I see Carter's eyes go to me and Jett, standing behind Leandro.

"Carter, this is my friend India Harris, and her son, Jett. Jett's a big Formula One fan. India, Jett, this is Carter Simmons."

Carter Simmons. I knew I recognized him.

I remember his accident. Leandro and Carter used to drive for the same team, the one Leandro still drives for.

Carter had an accident in his first year. His left arm was partially severed in the accident, leaving him with limited movement in it. It was his first and last year. I remember it being a big thing in the news as he was a promising young English driver. Everyone had had high hopes for him.

Tragic that his career was cut short before it had barely begun.

"Big racing fan, huh?" Carter says to Jett. "Well, you're with a racing legend today. That's gotta be pretty awesome."

"It is." Jett grins in Leandro's direction.

"You like to race yourself?"

"I go karting when I can."

"You any good?"

Jett shrugs. "I'm okay."

Carter smiles. "I have a feeling you're probably better than okay. You should come down sometime and try the tracks out."

"That'd be awesome." Jett beams.

"Cool. Well, can I get you guys anything to drink?" Carter asks.

"I'd love a black coffee," I say on a shiver.

I'm wrapped up warm in jeans, a jumper, and a warm jacket, but the chill is still creeping in.

"Black coffee. Silva, you want anything?"

"Same as India."

"Cool. Well, why don't you come and give me a hand in getting the drinks, Jett? Then, I can introduce you to the lads racing today."

Jett looks at me, checking that it's okay to go, and I give him a reassuring smile.

I watch him leave with Carter.

"You want to sit down?" Leandro gestures to some chairs near the viewing area.

"Sure."

I walk over and take a seat, and Leandro sits in the seat beside me.

I'm so aware of him right now, and I really wish I weren't.

"So, Jett seems to be enjoying himself so far," Leandro says.

"He's in his element here." I smile.

I watch as he leans forward, putting his arms on the railing. He looks out at the karts warming up on the track. A sigh that sounds an awful lot like longing comes from him.

"You really miss it." It's not a question. I already know he does.

He turns his head to me, resting his cheek on his arm. "How can I miss something with a physical ache and be absolutely terrified of it at the same time?"

"Usually, the things we love most are the things that terrify us."

He stares at me for a long moment before turning to look back out at the track.

"How did you get into racing?" I lean forward, putting my arms next to his on the railing.

"My dad was a world champion rally driver. Racing was always a given for me. I started in rally, but my interest in Formula One was always stronger. I wanted to go in that direction, and he fully supported me."

"He must be proud of you."

"He was." He gives a sad smile. "He died a long time ago. Just after my first year in Formula One. Heart attack."

My chest squeezes for him, for his loss. "I'm sorry."

"It was a long time ago." He shrugs.

I wish he wouldn't do that. Brush things off like they don't matter.

When I look at him, he's already staring at me.

"What?" I ask self-consciously.

"I had a question, but I'm afraid to ask. I don't want to cross that ethical line."

I give him a look. "I said I was sorry for that comment. But it is strictly true. Socializing with you isn't ethical."

"Says who?"

"The Health and Care Professions Council."

"Ah, what do they know?" He chuckles.

Too much. They'd be frowning, waving my practice license in my face, if they could see me right now.

"So, that question?" I'm treading dangerous water here, but I feel like I owe him a little of myself. And part of me wants to tell him.

"Jett's father…where is he?"

My body freezes stiff. I have to force myself to swallow down.

"He isn't around."

"Were you married?"

"That's two questions." I smile, so I don't come off as a bitch.

"Fair enough." He shrugs, not pushing it.

The fact that he does that makes me answer, "No, we weren't married. I was young and naive. But out of that naïveté, I got the best thing in my life."

"He's a great kid."

"He is." I smile.

"Okay, I have one last question."

I give him a look, which makes him laugh.

"Sure. Why not?" I lift my hands in defeat. In all honesty, I'm enjoying talking to him like this.

"The guy you're dating. Seriously, you could do better than him."

I frown at the conversation taking an unexpected turn, my hackles instantly rising. "Well, I could say the same for you."

"What do you mean by that?" His tone sounds about as defensive as mine.

"Kat Whisker. I mean, really?" I have to resist the urge to roll my eyes. "You can do better than her, Leandro."

Where did that come from? I really shouldn't have said that.

"Is this you speaking as my therapist?" His tone is suddenly so even that I can't get a read on it.

Am I speaking as his therapist?

I already know the answer to this, and it's making my skin prickle with unease. No matter what I say now, I'll be shooting myself in the foot.

I take a deep breath and put my professional head on. "I shouldn't have said that. I spoke out of turn."

"Why do you do that?" he growls, forcing my eyes to his.

"Do what?"

"Put on the professional shit when faced with a question you're afraid to answer."

"I'm not afraid to answer," I bite.

"So, answer truthfully then." He challenges me with his tone and his eyes. "What you said about Kat—was that said as my therapist or my friend?"

I chew my lip, delaying my answer. Then, through gritted teeth, I mutter, "As your friend...I guess."

I try to ignore the smile of satisfaction on his face, but it bugs me, which is why I can't stop myself from saying, "And what about what you said about Dan not being good enough for me? Were you saying that as my friend?"

He stares at me for a long moment. "No, India, I definitely wasn't saying that as your friend."

eleven

LEANDRO

✚ BANBURY, ENGLAND

"No, India, I definitely wasn't saying that as your friend."

Smart move, Silva. Why didn't I just tell her that I want to strip her naked and fuck her until neither of us can walk?

God, I am a total fucking idiot.

She didn't say much after that, and I was relieved when Jett and Carter reappeared a few minutes later.

India is all about professionalism. If me telling her that I didn't think her boyfriend was good enough for her didn't spell out that I wanted her, then my awesome line did.

Even though I'm fairly sure that India wants me, too, she's gun-shy. She's afraid to cross that arbitrary line.

I need to be careful how I approach this. I don't want to push her away by being too forward because I could end up losing her if I do.

And I really don't want to lose her from my life.

The race is over. I've presented the trophy to the winner. Both Jett and India seem like they've had a good day. Well, I know Jett has. The kid is full of enthusiasm. Can't stop talking about the karting as we walk back to the car.

"And Carter said I could come down anytime, Mum. Isn't that awesome?"

"It's great, sweetheart."

"So, when can I come?"

"Well, we can sort something out between your Uncle Kit and me and arrange a day to come down."

"Cool. I'm hungry. Can we grab something to eat?"

"You're always hungry," India teases him.

"I'm a growing man."

"Boy…you're still a boy. And you'll always be a baby to me." She wraps her arms around him, planting a kiss on his cheek.

"Mum! You're ruining my street cred."

"Sorry." She grins, ruffling his hair.

"We can grab dinner on the way back, if you would like?" I'm expecting a look of horror from India, knowing that I am crossing that line of hers again, considering how much I have pushed things already today.

So, I'm totally taken by surprise when she says, "Sure. That'd be great."

"Cool. I know this nice place I can take us."

We climb back into the car.

Taking the front seat, Jett immediately takes control of the stereo.

I've never really spent time around kids, but I like Jett. He's a cool kid.

And he likes racing, which makes conversations easy with him.

I've just clipped my seat belt in when India leans close and says, "You looked surprised when I said yes to dinner."

She's so close that I can smell the intoxicating scent of her perfume.

"I was surprised. I thought I might have been crossing your ethical line." Lips pressed together, I lift my shoulder in a half shrug.

A light smile on her lips, she shifts back to her side of the car. "I've already crossed the line today. What's a little further going to hurt?"

I'll cross any line she wants me to. Cross it so far that the fucking line she adheres to will be invisible to her.

"It won't hurt at all." I smile to myself, looking out the window.

We end up stopping to eat at a country pub on the way back to London.

"Should we invite your driver to eat with us?" India asks.

The question makes me grin.

"He's not *my* driver, India. I pay the company he works for to drive me when I need it. He hasn't driven me before."

"Thanks for the thorough explanation. But I still feel bad about us going to eat and leaving him out here."

"So, ask him." I chuckle.

I watch her round the car and go talk to the driver as I walk toward the pub with Jett.

"She has a thing for strays," Jett says to me. "Something to do with her job I think."

"The driver's a stray?" I laugh.

"Nah, but she just can't bear the thought of anyone ever feeling bad or being left out."

"Not a bad trait to have," I say to him.

He stares up at me. "Do you like my mum?"

"Do I like her?"

"Do you want to date her? Because if you do, I'd be totally cool with it—obviously."

Chuckling, I shake my head. "It's...complicated."

"Because of Dan? They're not serious, so no problem there."

Yeah, there is Dan. But he's just more of a minor irritant than a complication.

No, the complication is, she's my therapist. And it's not a problem for me, but it will be for India.

Stopping by the pub door, I look over at India, watching as she makes her way back to us.

"But you do like her?"

I look down at him. "Yeah…I do."

"Cool 'cause I'm pretty sure she likes you, too."

I don't chance to question him further because India reaches us.

"He didn't want to join us. He's eaten already," she tells us.

"Just the three of us then." I pull open the door to the pub, allowing India and Jett through first.

The pub isn't busy. Just a few locals by the looks of it. We grab a table by the window in the back. A waitress comes over, handing us some menus, and she takes our drink order.

"I'm just going to the ladies' room," India tells us.

I have to force myself not to watch her walk away. It's harder than you'd think.

The waitress brings over our drinks.

Lemonade for me. I take a sip and then say to Jett, "So, Jett, you enjoyed karting?"

"Loved it. I mean, I've really enjoyed karting when I've been with my friends and Uncle Kit, but I never really thought about doing it beyond fun—you know, racing seriously like those lads were today."

"Karting is where a lot of Formula One drivers start out," I tell him.

"Is that where you started?" he asks me.

"No, I started in rally driving before moving on to Formula One. My dad was a rally champion." I'm surprised at how easily I can talk with Jett. I've not had much experience around kids. But he does seem mature for his age. "Carrick Ryan started out karting."

"I think I did know that. He was karting champion at one point, right?"

"Yes, he was. Look, if you're interested in getting into karting a bit more, I can help. There's Carter's place where you can kart, but there are more local places around you as well. Carrick will know a lot, and I know he'd be happy to help."

I haven't asked him yet, but I know he would.

"I forgot you were friends with Carrick Ryan. Weren't you guys, like, rivals once upon a time?" He leans forward with interest.

"We still are, to a degree." I laugh. I think Carrick and I will always have rivalry, but now, it's in good humor, whereas we were complete shits to each other before. "We're good friends now though. Carrick and his wife, Andi, were around a lot after I had my accident. They didn't have to be—we weren't even friends then—and it showed me the type of people they were."

"He seems cool."

"He is. Just don't tell him I said so. I'd never hear the end of it."

Jett laughs before taking a drink of his Coke through the straw. "I think I do want to get involved in karting. Do a bit, and see if I'm any good."

"Cool. Then, I'll help. As long as your mom is okay with it."

"She will be," he says confidently. "So, your accident was pretty bad, huh? I was watching on TV when it happened. You died for a while, right?"

How is it that kids just have this way of asking questions that make them hurt less?

"It was bad, and yes, I died for a short while."

"Must be weird, dying like that, and then being brought back to life," he muses, chewing on his straw. "When you died, did you see a white light and stuff, like people say?"

"No light." I shake my head. "Honestly, I don't remember anything about it. Just the crash and then nothing until I woke up in the hospital."

There's a short pause and then he asks, "Do you think you'll ever race again?"

I take a drink before answering him, "I want to race again. And I'm trying to get to that point."

"I really hope you do. I missed watching you race on TV this last season."

"Well, hopefully, you'll watch me next year, and this time, in the stands at Silverstone."

"That'd be amazing." He smiles.

"What are you boys talking about?" India asks, arriving back at the table.

"About me going karting. Leandro said he'd help me get into it, as long as it was okay with you."

India shoots me a look. I see the motherly worry in her eyes.

"It's safe, low speeds," I assure her.

"You really want to get into karting?" she asks Jett.

"Yeah, I think I really do." He smiles at her.

"I'm not saying no, but it's an expensive sport, Jett. You need to be serious about it."

"It's not that expensive, and it's not like I want you to buy me a kart. I'll just rent one."

Is money a problem for India? She has a good job, but London is an expensive place to live, and she is a lone parent.

She stares at him for a long moment. I can see her mind working. It makes me want to help her, take care of her.

"Okay, we'll figure it out. But no taking up any of Leandro's time. He's a busy man."

Guess that's me being dismissed from helping.

India and her fucking rules of ethics are pissing me off. I'm getting whiplash from her today. One minute, she's okay with things, and the next, she's backing right off.

It's like one step forward and two massive steps back with her.

An idea sparks to mind.

Well, I might not be able to help Jett with karting, but there is one thing I can do for him.

Twelve

INDIA

✦ LONDON, ENGLAND

"ARE YOU OKAY?" I glance at Leandro.

He blows out a staggered breath through clenched teeth. "Yes…no…yes."

"You don't have to do this. Not yet. Not if it feels too soon."

He looks at me. "Time is creeping up on me. It's the middle of December now. I need to be back in the cockpit in a few weeks, a month max, or I'll never race again. I have to be able to drive a standard car before getting into a race car. I'm sick of being a mental cripple, India. I have to do this." He gives me a stare that screams desperation and determination.

The desperation concerns me. "I just don't want you to rush yourself, Leandro, and set yourself back weeks. You've been making excellent progress."

"And that progress needs to speed up now—rapidly. It's now or never, India."

"Okay." I nod, accepting his wishes. "Just take deep breaths. Might feel the need to rush, but you don't need to rush this particular moment. And remember, I'm here with you. You're not alone."

He gives me an appreciative soft smile, and then he fixes his eyes on his hands gripping the steering wheel.

We're in my car, which I got back fixed and working better than before, even though it cost me a pretty penny. Leandro is adamant about wanting to drive it. As he was my last appointment of the day, I drove us to a large car park that I knew would be quiet at this time of day. I thought it would be safer here, in case he froze up at the wheel.

"I can do this."

"You can do this," I assure him. "You've driven cars that go speeds I can't even imagine. You lived through a crash that could have been fatal. You're a survivor. You can do this."

I touch his arm to reassure him, ignoring the pang of energy I feel at the contact with him.

"I can do this," he repeats.

Eyes focused on the windshield, he grits his teeth and blows out a breath between them. Then, he slips the gearstick into first, and we start to slowly move forward.

I don't say anything. I just leave him to it. He knows I'm here, if he needs me, but this is something he needs to do himself.

Then, he's moving a bit faster, moving up through the gears. I intently watch him, seeing the tension leaving his body.

"You're doing it," I say softly.

"I'm doing it." I can hear the tremor of relief in his voice.

"How are you feeling?"

"Good." He exhales, a smile in his voice. "I'm feeling…really fucking good."

After a few minutes of him easing us around the car park, I ask him, "Do you think you could go out into traffic and drive?"

He glances at me. There's no apprehension on his face. "Yes."

"Why don't you drive yourself home then? Save me from driving you there." I smile.

"Only if you will come in for a drink with me, to celebrate me finally getting back behind the wheel."

His eyes are on the road as he pulls out of the car park and onto the street.

I stare at his side profile. "I probably shouldn't."

"That ethical line again, huh? So, it is against the rules for a therapist to toast a big success with her patient?"

"When you put it that way, then no, I guess not. But only one drink, and a small one. I have to drive myself home."

"One small drink it is."

I feel him pressing down on the gas, propelling us forward into the thick of traffic.

Leandro drives us into Mayfair. He pulls my car into a parking space in front of an integral garage to a gorgeous-looking house. He turns the engine off and looks at me. There's a light in his eyes.

"You did it." I smile at him.

"Yes, I did it."

I feel the sudden urge to hug him in this momentous moment, and I guess he's thinking the same thing because he's suddenly leaning over the console and wrapping his arms around me, pulling me to him.

Shock freezes me in place. That, and his smell. *God, he smells good.*

"Thank you," he whispers into my hair.

The feel of his breath brushing through my strands, whispering onto my skin, has my arms sliding around him, hugging him back.

"It was all you." *Is that my voice that sounds all breathy?*

He pulls back a touch but doesn't let go. He's staring into my eyes, and I feel a tremble deep inside me.

"No." He softly shakes his head. "I couldn't have done it without you."

I can't speak. His eyes are moving over my face, settling on my mouth.

Oh God.

I think he's going to kiss me.

I want him to kiss me.

With gargantuan strength, I pull out of his hold and clear my throat. "So, is this your house?" I gesture to the house through the windshield, my eyes pinned on it.

I can't look at him. I don't dare look at him.

"It is." His voice sounds rougher than normal.

I hear the click of his door opening, pushing me into action. I climb out of my car. He's waiting for me at his side of the car. I walk to him on unsteady legs. My heart is beating a mile a minute.

Using the remote sensor, he locks my car and hands me the keys. His fingers graze over mine, making me shiver.

What am I thinking? I'm his therapist.

He's just grateful for me helping him. He's confusing that with wanting me.

Clenching my keys in my fist, I drop them in my bag.

"Thanks for trusting me to drive your car." He smiles at me as he walks to his front door.

"You don't have to thank me. There was never any doubt in my mind that you could do it," I say from behind him. "So, how did it feel, driving out on the roads?"

He unlocks the door and turns on the hall light.

"Once I got past the initial apprehension, I started to feel okay. I am not saying I wasn't having thoughts about the accident, but I pushed them aside and got on with it. That was when I remembered that feeling I always got when I drove. It felt good. But I know it'll be a whole different ball game when I take a car out on the track."

I step inside his house and close the door behind me. "Baby steps." I offer him a gentle smile. "And if you need any support out on the track, let me know. I can be there."

He takes a step closer to me. My heart starts to thrum in my chest.

"You'd do that?"

"Yes." *My voice has gone all breathy again. He's your patient, India.* "I mean, of course, it's all part of the therapy service." I straighten up, changing the tone of my voice.

"Of course it is." A frown crosses his face like a dark shadow. He turns from me and begins walking down the hall. "What would you like to drink?" His tone sounds hard.

Feeling off-balance and confused, I kick my heels off and follow him. As I walk, I ask, "What do you have?"

"I don't have much alcohol in here anymore since I cut back, but I do have a bottle of champagne."

"Champagne works for me."

I walk into his kitchen. It's modern, all glossy white cabinets and silver countertops.

"Wow. This is a nice kitchen."

"Thanks." He takes his jacket off, hanging it over the back of a stool at the breakfast island. Then, he moves across the kitchen and gets a bottle from the fridge. "Do you like to cook?"

"Not really. I just like kitchens. They're my thing. I want to have a kitchen just like yours and have someone cook for me. Then, I could just sit here all day, eating amazing food, while staring at my pretty kitchen." I grin at him, and he returns it.

I remove my jacket and take a seat on a stool at the breakfast island, and set my jacket on my lap.

Leandro puts two champagne glasses down in front of me. He holds up the bottle as he unwraps the foil from the champagne.

Bollinger. Very nice.

He pops the cork with ease.

"I'm impressed," I say at his cork-popping abilities.

"Years of practice on the podium." He pours out the champagne into the glasses.

"And you'll have many more years of it, too."

He picks up his glass. "Here's to hoping."

I pick up my glass and chink it against his. "You will. I'm sure of it." I take a sip of my champagne. *Delicious.*

"You know, this is my first drink in weeks." He leans his hip against the counter.

"I shouldn't be encouraging your drinking."

He lets out a deep chuckle. "I'm not an alcoholic, India. I just used it as a tool to make me feel better."

"But it didn't."

"No…but I do feel better now. Because of you."

That makes me smile. "Leandro, all I've done is listen and guide."

"No." He shakes his head. "You have done so much more than that." He puts his glass down, eyes fixed on me.

My belly starts doing flips. I look away.

"Are you hungry?" he asks. "I can make you something to eat."

"As appetizing as that sounds, I have to get home. It's my turn to make dinner tonight. I can't leave Jett starving."

I finish off my champagne, fully aware that he's watching me.

"Thank you for the drink." I slide off the stool.

My legs feel wobbly, and it's not because of the champagne. It's because of the beautiful man standing before me. I pull my jacket on.

"Sorry to drink and run." I turn and head out of the kitchen.

"Don't apologize. You have a son to get home to."

He's behind me as I walk down the hall to the front door. I'm fully aware of his nearness, and his delicious scent. He's driving me to distraction.

I really need to get out of here before I do something stupid.

I slip my feet into my heels and turn to him. He's a lot closer than I expected.

"Well, I guess I'll see you in a few days." I tuck my hair behind my ear.

"You will."

We're staring at each other, and I'm pretty sure I just looked at his mouth.

Time for me to go.

"Okay...well..." I fumble for the handle behind me.

He leans into me. I close my eyes, my lips parting on a breath...

Then, I hear the door click open.

I blink my eyelids apart. He's watching me, a hint of amusement on his face.

Oh god.

Embarrassment floods me.

"I'll see you in a few days," I mumble, then, I'm out of there, lickety-split.

"Good night, India," he calls from behind me.

Flustered, I get my keys from my bag and climb into my car.

He's standing in his doorway, watching me.

I start the engine and slam the car into reverse. He lifts a hand in good-bye, so I throw a quick wave at him and peel out of there.

Oh my God, I'm mortified!

I really thought he was going to kiss me. And worse, I was going to let him.

This is all just getting out of hand, and I'm spending way too much time with him outside of our sessions.

I need to rein this in and get back to what we are. Therapist and patient.

By the time I'm parking beside Kit's car on our tiny drive twenty minutes later, I'm calm and thinking more rationally.

I'm the therapist. Nothing can or will ever happen with Leandro.

I need to get his handsome face out of my head and ignore the way he makes me feel when I'm around him—like a hot mess of sexual frustration—and look at him as I do all my other patients.

I let myself in the house. "I'm home," I call out.

No answer.

I drop my bag in the hall and kick off my shoes before wandering through to the kitchen. Through the window, I see our garage door is open. We have an old garage in the back garden as our house opens up onto a wide alleyway. We don't use the garage for parking, just for storing junk.

I open the back door and go barefoot into the garden. I can hear Jett's excited voice in there, talking to Kit.

"Hey, what are you doing out here?" I poke my head inside the garage.

Then, I see it.

"Is that what I think it is?" I step inside the garage. "Is that a...kart?"

Jett grins at me. "It is. It's brand-new, top of the range."

"And where did it come from?"

I'm not stupid. I know how much these things cost. Mainly because I looked at the prices of them online last night after Jett had told me he wanted to start karting. They cost around two thousand pounds.

"It arrived about an hour ago," Kit tells me.

"And who bought it? Please don't tell me you got it for him," I narrow my eyes at Kit.

He's been known to make impulsive purchases for Jett in the past.

"Not me." He holds his hands up in protest, but has a shit-eating grin plastered all over his face. "But I'm thinking that Brazilian race car driver has a thing for my sister."

"What?" The word comes out strangled.

"Oh, he totally does. He told me yesterday that he likes you," Jett announces.

"I'm sorry. What?" I snap my gaze to Jett.

"Yesterday, I asked Leandro if he likes you, and he said it was complicated, but yes, he does."

What?

Kit lets out a deep laugh. "Well, I'm figuring he likes you an awful lot as he's just dropped a couple of grand on a kart for your son, all to impress you."

"Leandro bought this?" I choke out. I know he has, but I just needed to say the words out loud.

"That's what the delivery paper says." Kit thrusts it into my hand.

I stare down at it in disbelief. My head feels like it's about to explode.

I can't believe he did this.

"He bought Jett a kart. I just can't…I mean…why?" I look at Kit, like he has the answer.

"I think it's pretty obvious why, Indy." He raises a brow, giving me a knowing look.

I take a step back. I feel like I can't breathe. "This…isn't right. I mean, I just…can't…" My eyes come to Jett's. "You're not keeping it." I jab a finger at the offending kart, and immediately feel a stab in my heart at the crestfallen look on Jett's face.

This is all Leandro's fault! How dare he buy my son a kart without even talking to me about it! Not that I would have let him buy him one even if he had.

What the hell was he thinking!

Anger flares in my gut like a volcanic explosion.

My hand curling around the delivery note, I swivel on my heel and march out of there. "I'll be back in half an hour. Start dinner for me," I call to them.

"Where are you going?" Kit calls after me.

"To shove this delivery note up a certain race car driver's arse!" I stomp back into the house, put my heels back on, grab my car keys, and slam my way out of there and into my car, heading straight back to the place where I just came from.

LEANDRO

✦ LONDON, ENGLAND

I'VE JUST GOTTEN OUT OF THE SHOWER when I hear the doorbell ringing along with hammering on my front door.

Grabbing a pair of pajama bottoms, I quickly pull them on and jog downstairs.

"Okay, I'm coming. I'm coming!" I call out to the incessant banger and doorbell ringer.

I check through the peephole to see who it is.

India. And she doesn't look happy.

Fuck. The kart must have been delivered today.

My conversation with Carrick a few days prior flashes through my mind.

"Ryan, I need to buy a kart. Best place to get one?"

"Why? Are you thinking of taking a step back in your career?"

"Funny. It's not for me."

"Who's it for?"

"A friend."

"Does that friend happen to be a certain therapist we both know?"

"You stalking me, Ryan?"

He lets out a laugh. "Doesn't take a genius to figure it out. The good doctor tells us that she's got a kid who is obsessed with Formula One. You take him to watch a karting race. The next day, I'm getting a call from you, asking about the best place to buy a kart. Actually, it does take a genius. Fuck, I'm good at this shit."

"You're a prick."

"A good-looking prick though. Admit it."

"You're an ugly bastard. Now, tell me where to get this fucking kart."

"Look, in all seriousness, do you think it's a good idea to buy her kid a kart? You might want to fuck her, but she is your therapist. And it's an extravagant gift."

"I'm buying it for Jett, not her. And it's not an extravagant gift."

"Said like a true rich kid. And trust me, nothing says, 'I want to fuck you,' like buying a woman's kid a two-thousand-pound kart."

"Look, are you gonna help me get the kart or not?"

"You know I'll help. One thing though, can I be there when it's delivered, so I can see her reaction?"

Buying it was the wrong thing to do.

I fucking hate it when Ryan's right.

I can't admit I was wrong about it now though. I have to see this through to the end.

Manning up, I unlock the door and pull it open.

God, she looks gorgeous. Her cheeks are flushed from the cold. The breeze is blowing her hair into her face. She pushes it back with her hand.

Her gaze immediately falls on my bare chest. Her pupils dilate, her eyes filling with obvious lust.

She wants me.

I have to hold back the smug grin I feel.

"You're wet," she says, sounding breathless.

Well, I am kind of hoping you are wet, too, baby, and that is why you are here.

"I was in the shower."

"Oh. Right…" Her eyes are still fixed on my chest.

And even though I'd be quite happy to let her stare at me all day, I need to know if she's here to yell at me for buying the kart, or if by some miracle she's here to thank me for it.

I'm really, really hoping for the latter.

"India, did you need me for something?"

She seems to come back to her senses. "Oh, yeah, I did—I mean, I do!" Her eyes flick up to mine, the lust gone, replaced with fire and ire. "What's the meaning of this?" She thrusts a piece of paper in my face.

She looks even more beautiful when she's angry.

"What's the meaning of what?" I ask, taking the paper from her, I look at it.

It's a delivery note for the kart.

"The kart, Leandro. Why would you buy my son a kart?"

Here we go…

"Because Jett said he wanted to get involved in the sport. Having his own kart will make that easier for him."

She looks at me, eyes wide. "Do you not see how wildly inappropriate buying a kart for my son is?"

I fold my arms over my chest. "No. I really don't see the problem here."

"You don't see the problem here?" She screeches, gesturing wildly with her hands. "I'm your bloody therapist! That's the problem!"

I glance around, making sure there was no one to hear that. Last thing I want is my private business to be spread about.

"Clearly, you're pissed off, but I'd prefer it if you didn't shout my business in the street." My voice is low, angry. Now, I'm pissed off.

A flash of guilt passes over her face. "I shouldn't have said that…I'm…sorry." She looks contrite.

"Come inside. We can talk in here." I stand aside, letting her in, and I close the door behind her.

Then, we're both facing each other in my partially lit hallway. She leans against one wall, arms folded over her chest, and I lean against the other.

"Look, I know you were trying to do a nice thing, Leandro...but I'm your therapist. It would be wrong of me to accept your gift."

I can tell that some of her anger has dissipated, but it's still there, simmering beneath that hot skin of hers.

Part of me wants to make her angry again. I like angry India. She is sexy as hell.

"I didn't buy it for you. I bought it for Jett."

"And Jett is my son. It would be"—she runs her hand through her hair, letting out a sigh—"unethical to keep it."

That word explodes in my head. "Jesus Christ! I'm so fucking sick of hearing that word! It was a gift, India. Accept it. Don't. I really don't care. But stop throwing the unethical-therapist bullshit in my face! You say this, me buying a gift, is unethical. That barely scratches the surface of the unethical things I want to do to you."

I hear her sharp intake of breath. It is like a soft palm over my cock.

Her eyes fill with lust again, her full red lips parting.

God, I want to kiss her. Fuck her...

I move off the wall, taking a step toward her. "Right now, I want to get down on my knees, pull off your panties, and show you just how unethical my tongue can be."

"Y-you can't say things like that to me," she stammers.

"No?" I cock my head to the side as I take another step toward her. "So, you don't want me to make you come with my unethical tongue or fuck you with my unethically hard cock? Because it is hard, India. Really fucking hard because of you...for you." I palm my dick through my pajama pants.

Her eyes go to my hand, watching me touch myself. "N-no." Her voice sounds weak, inefficient.

I know she doesn't mean it.

"Liar." I take another step. "You want me as much as I want you. You're just afraid to admit it because of the bullshit reasons you've built up in your head."

She says nothing.

I take her silence as an invitation.

I move forward the final step and press my body against hers. *She feels amazing.*

She's trembling. It gives me a sense of tremendous power.

I trace my fingers over her cheek. "You're so fucking beautiful, India. *Eu quero você.*"

She closes her eyes, and I don't hesitate another second. I take what I want and capture her mouth with mine.

Her lips part over mine on a breathy moan, and I take advantage to kiss her deeper, sliding my tongue against hers.

She's not touching me yet, but I don't care. She's kissing me back, and right now, that's all that matters.

I slip my hands around her tiny waist, pulling her into me, as I press my leg between hers.

She parts her legs on a groan, accepting me, and her arms come around my neck. She kisses me back, hard. And that's when the kiss gets wet and crazy.

Hands on her ass, I lift her off the floor, pressing her back into the wall.

My cock is rock-hard and nestled up against her heat. I can feel her wetness through my pajama pants, and it's driving me fucking wild.

I kiss her recklessly, like I've wanted to since the moment I met her.

Her fingers have threaded up into my hair, and she's tugging on it as she sucks on my tongue.

I can't wait to feel these lips around my cock.

And she tastes fucking amazing, sweet. But I bet her pussy tastes even sweeter.

I need to taste her. Then, I'm going to spend the rest of the night buried inside her.

"I'm going to fuck you all night long, India."

I feel her body freeze. Then, "Stop," she pants, her hand pressed against my chest. "We have to stop."

What? No.

She pushes against me as she loosens her legs from around my waist, giving me no choice but to release her, letting her feet drop to the floor.

Sliding along the wall, she backs away from me, putting an unwelcome distance between us.

Her lips are swollen from my kiss, her red lipstick smeared. Her hair is all ruffled, chest flushed with desire. I've never seen a more beautiful sight. And it's being dampened by the fact that I know she's leaving before we've even begun.

I've never felt more frustrated or at a loss for what to do.

"India—"

"No, Leandro. I'm a doctor…a therapist. I made an oath—*shit*…" Her eyes fill with tears.

The sight actually rips into me.

"India…please…" I reach for her, but she steps back.

"No." She takes a deep breath. "This"—she lifts a hand between us—"can't happen…ever again."

Then, she's fleeing from my house, getting in her car. Ignoring my pleas for her to stay, she drives away from me.

And I stand here wondering if I had never spoken a word, broken the moment, whether she would have let it go all the way, if she would have let me have her.

Fourteen

INDIA

✢ LONDON, ENGLAND

OH GOD.

I cover my face with my hands.
What have I done?
How could I let that happen?

But he was all wet from the shower, he smelled so good, his chest was bare, showing a sexy smattering of dark hair, and he had a six-pack and the V.
The V!
And he spoke to me in Portuguese.
Portuguese!
How the hell was I supposed to resist that?

It takes me the whole drive home to calm down and a lot of willpower to not turn around and go back there to let him finish what he started. In a daze, I'm still not myself when I get home.

Kit knows something is wrong with me.

Jett's not talking to me because I said the kart has to go back.

And I kissed Leandro Silva.
I kissed a patient.
Oh God.

I let my head drop with a thud on the kitchen table. I hear Kit's soft laugh as he enters the kitchen.

"Wine?" he asks.

"Whiskey," I reply.

"Uh-oh. Must be bad if you're breaking out the whiskey."

I lift my head to see him pulling our emergency bottle of Jack from the cupboard along with two glasses.

Sitting on the chair across from mine, he pours whiskey in the two glasses and pushes one over to me. I pick it up and immediately down it, relishing the burn in my throat.

He laughs. Picking up the bottle, he pours me another. "You want to talk about it?"

I meet his gaze. "I messed up, Kit. Big time."

"The last time you said that to me, you were pregnant with Jett, and that turned out okay." He points to the ceiling, gesturing to Jett's room situated above the kitchen. "More than okay, despite the bumpy road that came with it."

He's referring to Jett's father. The only thing I have to be thankful to that man for is the beautiful boy upstairs.

"Don't you mean, mountainous hazard road that came with it?"

He lets out a low chuckle. "Look, whatever it is, Indy, it can't be anything worse than what we've already been through. And you know you can tell me anything. No judgment."

"I kissed Leandro Silva. Well, I let him kiss me, and then I kissed him back."

"And the problem is...Dr. Dull?" he asks, lifting his glass to his lips.

"No. Well, yes. But no."

Shit. Dan! I can't believe I didn't even think of him in all of this. That tells me one thing. I need to end things with Dan.

Kit stares at me for a long moment, and then I see it click in his eyes.

He lowers his glass to the table. "He's your patient." It isn't a question.

But I answer with a resounding groan and drop my head to the table.

His hands find my head, one pressed on each side. He lifts my head from the table, forcing me to look at him. "I'll take that as a yes."

Freeing my head from his hands, I sit up, pressing my back against the chair. I blow out a breath. "Yes."

I see the concern furrow his brow.

"This isn't good, Indy."

"I know that!" I snap but instantly regret it. "I'm sorry," I tell him.

He nods. "What does this mean?"

"It means that, if the Health and Care Professions Council find out, I'll lose my license. And if he brought up malpractice...I could, at the very least, be sued. Worst case...I'd go to prison."

"Would Leandro tell them?"

"I don't think so...but I broke the rules. Not just the rules. My oath as a therapist, Kit. I should tell the HCPC myself, confess now."

"And lose everything you've worked for over a kiss with a man who was fully aware of everything he was doing?"

"It's not that simple." I put my head in my hands. "I'm just like him..." I lift my head, my eyes meeting Kit's. "I'm exactly like Paul."

His eyes flare with anger. "You are nothing like that piece of shit. You were fifteen when he started a...physical relationship with you. You were a minor. A foster kid. Needy and vulnerable. And he was your fucking caregiver. You are none of those things to Leandro Silva. He is a grown man from a good background, with an established career."

I slowly shake my head. "He might be all those things, but if he was a hundred percent okay, then I wouldn't have been treating him."

"None of us are ever a hundred percent okay, Indy. You know that. Can you tell me what you were treating him for?"

I trace my fingers over the wood patterns on the table. "You know I can't."

"I think you've already broken the rules when it comes to Leandro Silva, so telling me won't hurt. It might actually help."

I take a deep breath. I can trust Kit. I know I can. I hate to break trust with a patient, but I need help. "After his accident...he's been suffering from PTSD. He can't get back in a car to drive. He's unable to race. I've been helping him with that."

"Okay..." He nods. "Any substance abuse?"

"He drank, but he stopped easily enough. He was drinking to forget, and he was using sex with random women to make himself feel better."

"He sounds like pretty much every celebrity out there right now." He chuckles.

"It's not funny, Kit."

"No, it's not. But he's not broken in the worst sense of the word. He suffered a terrible accident that stopped him from doing what he loved, and he needed help finding his way back to it."

"And I've been that help. He's built a reliance on me, and he is mistaking that for something else. Because of my own feelings for him, I let it happen."

"You're always so hard on yourself, Indy. By the sound of things, he's fully capable of making his own decisions. You haven't taken advantage."

I give him a look, telling him exactly what I think of that statement. "It's wrong, Kit." I rub my eyes with the heels of my hands.

"If you weren't his therapist and he was still the same man with the same problems, then it wouldn't be wrong."

"No, but I am, and it is. God, I wish it were that simple."

"Life is only as hard as you make it. And don't go throwing your career away over one kiss with a man who knew full well what he was doing."

I pick my glass up and get up from the table. "Thanks, Kit. For listening…and helping." I kiss the top of his head as I pass him. "I'm gonna head upstairs. Take a shower, and think things over. I need to process everything."

"Don't be too hard on yourself, Indy. You're only human."

"But I'm a therapist, and I know better."

Cradling my glass to my chest, I head upstairs. I look in on Jett as I pass his room. I see him sleeping in bed, his TV still on. I go in and turn off his TV. Kissing his forehead, I close his door behind me.

I go into my bedroom and sit on the edge of the bed.

I need to call Dan, break things off with him. I hate that I've deceived him like this. He's a good man, but clearly, he's not the man for me. I think I've always known deep down. But I just wanted a good guy, a safe guy.

Not a hotheaded racing driver.

God, why do I always want the wrong man?

Finishing off my drink for Dutch courage, I dial Dan's number.

He picks up on the second ring. "Hey, you."

I feel sick at the sound of his voice. "Hey."

"How are you doing?"

"Good. Look, Dan, are you okay to talk?"

"Hang on…" I hear a door open and then close. "Go ahead. Is everything okay?"

"Not really."

"India?"

"I can't see you anymore."

"Are you being serious?"

"I'm sorry."

He blows out a breath. "Why?"

"I just—"

"If you're going to say that it's not you, it's me, you might as well just hang up the phone now."

Tears spring to my eyes. "I like you, Dan. I do. I just don't feel the spark that I should…and I…I have feelings for someone else. I'm really sorry."

His silence is painful.

"And have you fucked this someone else?" he finally bites out.

His words surprise me because I've never heard him speak this way before.

"No, of course not! He kissed me, but I stopped it. Then, I came home and called you."

"Who is it?"

"I…that doesn't matter. I'm just so sorry."

"Yeah, well, you should be. Good-bye, India."

The line goes dead.

I fall back onto the bed, covering my face with my hands.

When did my life become such a mess?

The moment I met Leandro Silva.

I can't go on like this, driving myself crazy. And I can't keep treating him, not after tonight.

There's only one thing I can do.

I'm going to have to refer him to another therapist and cut him from my life—permanently.

I curl my arm around my stomach, pressing against the ache the thought leaves inside me.

fifteen

LEANDRO

✛ LONDON, ENGLAND

"You okay in there?"

My hands are gripped around the wheel. I move my eyes to Carrick, who's standing outside the car, by the driver's door.

Giving a nod to him, I slide down the visor on my helmet with a click. "I'm fine."

"I'm in your ear. Talk to me if you need to." He taps his finger to the earpiece he's wearing that will connect us while I'm out on the track.

I give another nod, not taking my eyes off the road ahead.

With his hand, he taps the roof of the car and moves away to stand in the pit to watch me.

We're at Silverstone. I'm driving Carrick's Bugatti Veyron Super Sport. This will be my first time back on a track since the accident

Since I drove India's car, I've had the growing urge to get back out here.

I had rented a car the very next morning, as I wanted to keep driving. My car is still fucked, after I smashed her up, so I had a garage take my car to fix her.

For the last few days, I've been driving around on my own for hours at a time, building my confidence. Driving on my own was a risk but a huge achievement for me.

I had taken the car out on the highway to feel some speed but it didn't feel enough and that was when I knew it was time to get back on the track.

Even though I made the decision to do this, I still felt afraid at the thought.

I wanted to call India, but I couldn't.

So, I called Carrick, and here we are.

Truth is, I could have used any car. I just needed someone here with me.

I really wanted that someone to be India, but I haven't spoken to her since the kiss on Wednesday. It's Saturday now.

I'm trying to give her space, let her come to me. I was hoping she would have come to me before now. The days passing aren't leaving the best feeling in my gut, but I know that charging in there with my guns blazing, demanding she talk to me, won't help shit.

India needs to be approached with thought and caution.

I have my appointment with her on Monday morning, so if I haven't heard from her before then, then that will be the day we talk.

And we will definitely talk. If not more.

I know for sure she wants me now, so there's no stopping me. She can deny it and say it can't happen, but it will.

The chemistry between us is off the charts. I've never felt anything like it before, and I don't intend on walking away from it. I've felt her body under my hands. Seen the way she responds to me. There's no stopping that kind of desire, no matter how hard she might try.

I turn the engine on, and rev it. The car vibrates beneath me. Tremors run up my arms. My heart starts to beat like a motherfucker. My mouth dries.

I blink against the onslaught of fear coming for me.

The barrier coming toward me.

Smoke. I can smell it in my nose. Taste it on my sandpaper tongue.

Feel the pain in my bones.

Stop.

That was the past.

Lightning doesn't strike twice.

Unless you're a seriously unlucky fucker.

A laugh escapes me.

"You okay?" Carrick's voice comes in my ear.

"Yes. Just realizing what a sick fuck I am."

"I could've told you that years ago." He chuckles. "You good?"

I blow out a breath. "Yes."

My arms are still shaking down to my hands. I grip the steering wheel, willing myself to calm down.

It's a good job I'm not taking out my Formula 1 car. I knew I wouldn't be up for that just yet. I need to get used to being back out here, and being in control of a car at high speeds and being comfortable with it again. Carrick's Bugatti is a good car to do it in.

I'm going to take this car around the track, like I've done a million times before. Nothing is going to happen to me.

Deep breath, in and out.

I realize that my hands are no longer shaking.

I feel a sense of self-satisfaction bleeding into my veins.

Control. That's what it is about.

I just need to take hold of my fear and manage it. If I'm good at one thing, it's control. I thrive on it. It's like a fucking aphrodisiac for me.

I shift the stick into first.

Breathe.

One…two…three…

Easing off the clutch, I hit the accelerator and take off.

I'm at a hundred kilometers in no time.

This car can move.

One sixty.

My heart is starting to pound against my ribs.

Fear and adrenaline.

I can see the wall approaching with the corner I need to take.

My hands start to shake. Sweat trickles down my face.

Don't lose it now, Silva.

Think of anything but the accident.

India.

The way she tastes. Her perfect mouth. How she felt wrapped around me while I kissed her.

Easing my foot onto the brake, I take the corner. Back on the straight, I ease the accelerator back down, pushing the speed up a little further.

Creeping back to a hundred.

One forty.

One sixty.

Two hundred.

The sound of metal crushing splinters in my ears, sounding so fucking real.

I hit the brakes.

It's not real. It's not real.

It's just in my mind.

Think of India.

What she'll look like naked. How she'll feel when I fuck her.

I press back on the accelerator, taking the car back to two hundred.

More. I need to take her higher.

I can do this.

I press down a little more.

Two twenty.

My heart is pounding, and I can't calm it.

So, stop fighting it, and use the adrenaline to push yourself further.

Imagine fucking India. That this car is her body. How hard I'm going to ride her. How high I'm going to take her.

Two sixty.

Bend her every which way I can. Fuck her hard and fast against every surface in my house.

Three hundred.

My head between her legs, tasting her, making her scream my name.

Three twenty.

India on her knees at my feet with my cock between those bee-stung lips of hers.

Three forty.

Coming inside her. On her tits. On her face. Marking every part of her with my cum.

Three fifty.

I'm fucking doing it.

Parting my lips, I blow out a breath, sweat dripping past them, into my mouth.

"Three fifty! You've fucking done it!" Carrick's elated voice comes in my ear. "So, does this mean you're back, Silva?"

I pull in a deep breath, slowly blowing it out. "Yeah." I grin. "I'm definitely back."

I burn up five more laps before coming back in.

Carrick is waiting for me, a shit-eating grin on his face.

Getting out of the car, I pull my helmet off and then my balaclava before running a hand over my sweat-soaked hair.

"You looked good out there," he says.

"I fucking felt good." Shutting the car door, I round to his side.

"You think next time you can get in an F1 car?"

Putting my helmet down, I strip my coveralls down to the waist, my T-shirt clinging to my skin. I'm hot from the adrenaline still pumping around my body. "Yes, I think so." As I say it, I feel doubt, so I quickly quash it.

"Next week?" Carrick asks.

"No, tomorrow. I don't want to fuck around. I want to get back in and get back training." I can barely keep still. My body is pumped.

"About time. I haven't had any decent competition for a while."

"I'll be kicking your ass out there next season." I laugh as I toss the keys to his car back to him. "What are you doing now?" I ask him. "You want to grab a beer?"

I feel like I need to do something. Going home right now just doesn't seem like an option.

What I really want to do is fuck, but I'm not screwing some random to relieve an itch.

The only one I want to scratch this itch with is India.

"I can't. I need to go home and change. We're having dinner with my dad. Why don't you join us?"

"No, but thanks." I wave him off, hiding my disappointment.

Owen Ryan is not my favorite person. Not that I'd ever tell Carrick this, but I think his dad is a total jackass.

"You got something better to do? Or someone?" He grins, raising his eyebrow.

Carrick knows about me kissing India. I don't usually talk about my personal life, but I know I can trust Carrick.

"Nope."

"You still haven't heard from her?"

"No. I'm giving her time to come around."

"You think she will?"

"Yeah," I say, grinning. "I know she will."

"Well, keep me updated." He starts to back away, heading for his Bugatti. "Let me know when you've finally nailed the good doctor."

Laughing, I shake my head at him.

I pick up my helmet and head out to the parking lot to my rental car. I toss my helmet on the backseat and head home to take a shower. I park my rental Mercedes in the driveway and head inside. Picking the mail up from the mat, I head to the kitchen. I toss the mail on the counter, and then I notice that the top letter has India's office stamp on it.

I tear the envelope open. My heart suddenly has an uneven rhythm.

My eyes scan the letter.

Dear Mr. Silva,

I feel that I can no longer treat you effectively. I have included a referral for another therapist.

I wish you all the best for the future.

Sincerely,

Dr. India Harris

My hand tightens around the paper, crumpling it.
She's throwing me out of her life like I mean nothing.
Yeah, well, I refuse to go so fucking easily.
Grabbing my car keys, letter in hand, I slam my way out of my house.

sixteen

INDIA

✥ LONDON, ENGLAND

THE DOORBELL RINGS just as I'm about to have a soak in the tub. On a sigh, I pull my robe on, tying it at the waist, and turn the running taps off.

Kit and Jett are away for the night. They've gone to watch Chelsea play Manchester United at Old Trafford, so they're staying overnight at a hotel, meaning I have the rare night to myself.

My plan was to relax in the bath with a glass of wine and feel sorry for myself over the whole Leandro thing.

I spoke to a colleague, Dr. Sanders, who I think will be perfectly suited to treat Leandro. He has great expertise in PTSD, and he agreed to take Leandro on as a patient. So, I had Sadie send out a letter to Leandro, detailing the termination of his treatment.

Did sending him that letter hurt?

Yes, it hurt like hell. But I know it was the right thing to do, the only thing to do.

Now, I just have to lick my wounds and move on.

I wonder if Leandro has received the letter yet. He should have.

A flash of thought goes through my mind. *What if he's at the door?*

That picks up my pace. I jog down the stairs.

Reaching the door, I peer through the peephole.

It's him.

A rush of fear and complete exhilaration run through me.

He rings the doorbell again.

Stepping back from the door, I make sure my robe is fastened properly. I take a deep breath, and then I turn the lock and open the door.

Holy God.

He's wearing racing overalls, hanging low at his waist, and a fitted black T-shirt is covering his amazing chest.

I have the sudden urge to pull him in here and tear that shirt from his body.

Of course, I don't, but my body reacts to him and the scenario playing on a loop in my mind. My nipples tighten, and my insides coil.

I cross my arms over my chest. "What are you doing here?"

He takes a step forward, his gaze dark, making me take a step back.

"I came to give you your fucking letter back." He crushes the paper in his hand, tossing it at my bare feet. "I don't accept it."

I lift my chin, staring him in the eyes. "You don't have a choice."

"No? We'll see about that."

He moves so fast that I barely get the chance to register it. Not that I would have done anything. He's in my house, the door shut, and I'm turned around and shoved up against the wall in seconds.

"Wha—" I don't get to finish that sentence because he slams his mouth down on mine.

I resist for about zero point one second. Then, I'm all hands in his hair, kissing him back like my very existence depends on it.

"Where are Jett and your brother?" His question is asked quickly and gruffly, against my lips.

I'm barely coherent enough to answer, but somehow, I manage to say, "Football match. Away game. Staying out overnight."

He makes a low growling sound in the back of his throat.

Then, he's kissing me again, harder, more aggressive. His hold on me tightens, and he thrusts his tongue in my mouth. The kiss is fueled with lust and anger.

I've never been kissed this way before.

And I love it.

God, he tastes good. And he smells good, too. A mixture of sweat and cars.

He smells exactly like a man should.

There are no words between us. Just hungry kissing, heavy breathing, and hot need.

His hand moves under my robe and trails up the outside of my thigh. As his fingers skim inward, I part my legs, letting him know that I want him there. When he finds me bare, he groans. His finger slides through my wetness.

He rests his forehead against mine. When I open my eyes, I find his on me, black and intense.

Then, he pushes his finger inside me. I let out a moan so loud that I should be embarrassed, but I'm not. I'm too far gone with him to care.

His other hand opens the belt of my robe. He pushes the silk aside, revealing my body to him. His eyes go to my bare breasts. He lets out a total sound of appreciation that I feel as much as the finger inside me. His hand comes up, cupping my breast. Squeezing, he pinches my hard nipple between his thumb and finger.

My eyes close on the pleasure as he fingers me. Inserting another, he gets rougher, the heel of his hand rhythmically pressing against my clit.

I need him inside me.

I go for his clothes. Gripping the overalls, I pull the zipper the rest of the way and push the material down his hips.

His impatience gets the better of him, and he takes over. He pulls his wallet from his pocket and takes out a condom. Holding it between his teeth, he toes off his driving shoes. Then, he shoves his overalls down, kicking them off. The running shorts he's wearing go and then his T-shirt.

Finally, he's naked before me. Every inch of him is perfect.

He's like a god in the purest sense of the word.

He removes the condom from between his teeth and tears the foil open.

I'm pretty sure I whimper with need.

He grins and then bites down on it, staring up at me through those long black lashes, and it might just be the sexiest thing I've ever seen.

I've never been this wet or this ready for a man in my life.

His hands go down to put the condom on, and my eyes immediately go with them. I stare unabashedly as he rolls the condom onto his impressive cock. And the girth.

Holy shit. I'm wondering if he'll even fit.

It's been a while since I've been with a man.

But I'm desperate for him, trembling with need, so he has to fit, no matter what.

Condom on, he presses me back against the wall, and his mouth finds mine again.

In all this time, we haven't said a single word to each other.

I feel like I need to say something, anything. "I ended things with Dan." My words come out in a breathy rush.

His eyes darken, but he says nothing. His hands go under my thighs, lifting me, and without hesitation, he slams inside me in one swift move.

"Leandro!" I cry out.

But there are no words from him, no reprieve, no time to adjust to his size, because he starts fucking me like it's all he's ever needed.

Like I'm all he wants.

He's stripped back to primal need, the urgency to fuck the only thing on his mind.

And I've never been so turned on in my whole life.

I wrap my legs around his waist. My fingernails score over his back. He groans and starts fucking me harder, nailing me to the wall. His mouth never leaving mine, he kisses me with an intense passion.

I've never been taken like this before, so, raw and intense and deep. He's fucking me with an almost madness, and I want him just as fiercely.

In this moment, I feel like I belong to him, and him alone.

I can feel myself starting to rise toward climax as his cock hits that deep part of me, his hips slamming mercilessly against my clit.

"Leandro..." I moan. "I'm going to...come..."

Finally, he speaks, "Yes. Come, babe. Squeeze my cock with your tight little pussy."

Pulling out to the tip, he slams into me, hard. That, and the sound of his voice, his words, send me free-falling over the edge, and I'm screaming to him and God and anyone else who might be listening.

"Fuck...India..." he grunts. *"Porra, estou gozando..."*

His head falls into the crook of my neck as I feel his cock pulsing inside me.

The sound of his mother language leaving his mouth while he's coming inside me nearly sends me over the edge again.

He stays there, head on my shoulder, holding me tight, as both our bodies twitch with aftershocks.

Then, we're just silent, two sweaty bodies connected by our most vital parts, while our hearts pound against our chests, and we try to catch our breaths.

I'm falling for him.

I can't.

I can't do this. I have too much to lose.

My job...I not only love my job, but I've worked damn hard, sacrificed so much, to get to where I am. And I need my income. I have a son to care for, bills to pay.

Reality leaves me feeling cold. "Leandro..."

"Don't..." He lifts his head, staring me straight in the eyes. "Don't ruin this, India."

I swallow against the pain in my chest, knowing what I have to do. "I have to. I'm sorry." I place my hand against his chest, gently pushing him away.

"Jesus Christ..." he growls, his eyes closing.

Then, he snaps his eyes back open and lets me down to my feet, slipping out of me. The loss of him inside me affects me deeper than I expected. Hurting, holding back the tears, I wrap my robe around myself and tie the belt, and I watch as he angrily pulls his clothes back on.

"You need to leave," I tell him in a whisper of a voice.

Seventeen

LEANDRO

✠ LONDON, ENGLAND

UN-FUCKING-BELIEVABLE!

She wants me to leave.

Normally, that would have me feeling relieved. Not that it's ever happened before. Women usually beg me to stay.

But not her, the one I want, and she wants me gone.

"Leave? Are you fucking kidding me?" I all but yell.

She shakes her head. Tears shimmering in her eyes, she looks like she's about to cry.

Seeing her like this...it hurts and confuses the fuck out of me.

If pushing me away is hurting her, then why is she doing it at all?

"India...why are you doing this?"

I reach for her, but she moves away from my touch.

My hand curls into a fist, coming back to my side.

"I have to."

My anger and frustration get the better of me. "You have to? Why? Explain this to me because I just don't fucking get it! You clearly want me, but you're telling me to leave? And don't you dare fucking say it's because you're my therapist. You no longer are, remember?" I jab my finger in the direction of the crumpled letter on the floor.

"I might not be your therapist anymore, but I was. That matters."

"To whom?"

"To the Health and Care Professions Council and...to me. You were my patient. I treated you. That doesn't just go away because of a letter. If people find out that I'm sleeping with a former patient, I'll be done for. If the HCPC gets ahold of that information, I'll lose my license to practice."

Controlling my frustration, I try to soften my voice as I ask, "How long would it take for this to be okay—you and me?"

"Never."

My anger flares right back up. "This is fucking bullshit!" I growl.

"No, it's the truth. I abused my power. I've become what I despise." A tear slides down her cheek. She brushes it away. "I'm a doctor, a therapist...who just had sex with a person I was treating."

"Jesus, India." I rub my head in frustration. "I am not some fucking kid who didn't know what he was doing. I am a grown man and I know exactly what I am doing, and what I want. And what I want is *you*."

I wrap my hands around her arms, not letting her move away. I stare into her face until she's forced to look back at me.

"I want you," I repeat. "Not just for tonight. I want to be with you. I want an *us*."

"I can't—"

"Listen—"

"No. Listen to me."

She tries to pull away, but I don't let go. If I let her go, I know I won't get her back.

"You might be a grown man and in control, but when I met you, you were in a bad place, and in some ways, you're still healing. I had an influence on you, on your recovery."

I stare deep into her eyes. "People influence one another every second of every day. That doesn't mean they can't be together."

"But those people didn't take an oath like I did."

My body is rigid with frustration. It's like talking to a wall. She won't hear me.

"So, by becoming a doctor, that means you're also a fucking nun?"

"No, but it means I can't fuck my patients!" she snaps.

I drop my hands from her arms. Her hands cover her face. I watch her, listening to her shallow breaths.

Slowly, she lowers her hands from her face and looks at me. I can see her words in her eyes before she says them, and my stomach twists.

"I'm sorry, Leandro, but this was a mistake." Her words are whispered, but I feel like she just screamed them at me. "I took advantage of you. I'm so, so sorry." Her hand slides over her stomach, tears filling her eyes.

In this moment, I feel like I'm missing something, but I'm so blinded by my anger that I can't see clearly enough to see past it. "You didn't take advantage of me!" I explode.

"You confided in me. I know how you use sex as an escape from your problems."

Her words instantly make me feel dirty, worthless. I hate that she can make me feel that way.

I grit my teeth and speak, "Used to—past tense, India, and you, above anyone, know this. Having sex with you was because I wanted to…because I want you."

"No, you think you want me, but you don't really. You just have a reliance on me."

"Bullshit!"

"It's not. It's the truth. You just can't see it yet. But with time, you will."

"Stop talking to me like I'm a fucking child, India! I didn't come to you for therapy because I was suicidal or not in control of my own mind. I came for your help because I needed to get back in a fucking car."

"You had—*have* PTSD. You were drinking and using sex as a way to cope. You were in a bad place."

"Not as bad as you think."

"You're painting a different picture in your mind because of what you think you want."

I pull at my hair in frustration. "I know exactly how I feel, not because of a patient-therapist attachment. I wanted you from the moment I saw you—before I even knew you. And, yes, you've helped me, but you haven't gotten in my head and twisted things around. I want you because I want *you*. And for no other reason." I cup her cheek with my other hand. "I want you," I repeat softly.

Closing her eyes, she takes a shuddering breath.

For a moment, I think I have her until she opens her eyes, and I see how shut off she is.

"I'm sorry, Leandro. In time, you'll see that I'm right. Ending this is right."

I've lost her.

The feeling is like a bullet to the chest.

"You're fucking wrong, and with time, you'll see that." I step back away from her, turning away.

"The kart..." she starts, pulling me back.

I stay there but don't turn around. I can't look at her. It'll hurt too much. My chest feels like it's bleeding out from the hole she just put in it. "Do what you want with it. Sell it, and give the money to charity. I don't fucking care."

"I'm so sorry," she whispers from behind me.

"Yeah, I'm sure you are." Sarcasm drips from my words.

I yank the door open and then stop. I pull a card from my wallet and toss it on the hall table. "If Jett still wants to get into karting, give this guy a call. He'll help get Jett started."

I risk a look at her.

She's crying. "I'm sor—"

"Yeah, I got it the first time. Have a nice fucking life, Dr. Harris." And I slam my way out of her house and her life.

SEVEN MONTHS LATER....

eighteen

INDIA

✦ LONDON, ENGLAND

I'D LIKE TO SAY I'VE MOVED ON FROM LEANDRO, but the truth is, it's like I'm still standing in my hallway, watching him leave.

The ending I play through my mind is the version where I chase after him, tell him I've changed my mind, that I want him.

The reality is, I'm sitting in my office after my day has ended, alone and missing him.

For days after he left my house, I wanted to speak to him. But each time I picked up my phone to call him, rationality would get the better of me, knowing I could lose everything if I went after what I wanted.

Then, time slipped by, and before I knew it, it had been weeks, bleeding into months, and there was no going back for me.

He'd moved on.

Even though it was hell—not seeing him, not speaking to him—it had to be this way.

But even still, I torture myself with him.

I do my usual ritual where I tell myself not to go online and search today's news for him. I relent for a few days, thinking how strong I am, and then I crack, just like I'm going to today.

I bring the screen on my MacBook to life. Bringing up the search engine, I type in *Leandro Silva*. The screen fills with stories of him and the races he won this past year since he returned to Formula 1.

I feel an undeserved sense of pride when I see the pictures of him crossing the finish line and when he's on the podium, holding the trophy. I might have helped him to a point, but he took himself the rest of the way.

I am happy for him. Happy that he's racing. That he has his life back the way he wanted it. He has it back in every way it was, if the press is anything to go by.

Leandro's name has been linked with several women since the racing season started, and there are pictures of him with women.

Each one hurts as much as the next.

He's moved on. That's what I knew he would do.

I knew that his attachment to me was purely because of the closeness we'd built during his treatment and what he felt for me was gratitude.

Still, it hurts badly to know I was right, especially when I can't seem to move past him.

I filter the page to read recent news stories.

Nothing new since the last time I checked a few days ago. Just the same pictures of him arriving back home for the British Grand Prix, which starts next weekend.

Staring at the pictures, I trace my finger over his face, like the Internet stalker I've become.

Not that he wasn't handsome before—because, of course, he was—but in these pictures, he looks amazing. There's a lightness in his expression, which wasn't there before. I'm guessing it's because of his return to racing.

He looks beautiful.

Leaning back in my chair, I close my eyes, trying to ease the ache of missing him.

Will this ever stop?

I thought I'd be past it now. Maybe if I stopped torturing myself with news of him, then maybe I'd be able to move on.

Sitting up, I shut down the screen.

My phone lights up with Jett's name.

"Hey, honey," I answer.

"You still at work, Mum?"

"Yeah. I'm just finishing up, and then I'm heading home."

"Well, just letting you know that I'm at the track with Uncle Kit and Carter. We're gonna grab something to eat here. We won't be home too late."

Dinner for one. Takeout and a bottle of wine it is.

"Okay, be safe and have fun."

"Will do. See you later, Mum."

"Bye, honey." I put the phone down on my desk and let my head follow it with a thud.

I'm turning into a total sad case Friday night, I'm childfree, and the best I can do is takeout and a bottle of wine.

I berate myself for this every week, too, yet I still do the same thing.

There's a knock on my door.

I lift my head from my desk. "Come in."

It'll be Sophie, my new assistant. She's been with me for a month now. Sadie left to go traveling with her boyfriend.

"I'm heading off for the night." Sophie crosses the room. "Here's the mail. I forgot to give it to you earlier."

"Thanks." I take it from her hand.

"The top letter was hand-delivered."

"Hand-delivered? What do you mean, hand-delivered?"

"A man came in earlier. He asked me to make sure that you got the letter."

"What did he look like?" I turn the letter over in my hand. My name is handwritten on the front.

"Black hair. Really good-looking." She grins.

My heart starts to race.

"And he had a foreign accent. I think it was—"

"Brazilian?"

"Yeah." She clicks her fingers. "Do you know him?"

"Yes…I do."

My hands are trembling, and I can't stop staring at the letter in my hands.

"Okay, well, I'm gonna head off. Have a good weekend, Dr. Harris," she says, retreating.

"Yeah, you, too," I utter, distracted.

The second the door closes, I slide my finger under the fold of the envelope and open it. My mouth is dry, fingers trembling. I pull out the contents of the envelope.

Tickets. Two of them to the Prix at Silverstone next week. Full VIP weekend passes.

And a folded piece of paper.

I open it, reading the same handwriting.

TICKETS FOR JETT, AS PROMISED. I HOPE TO SEE YOU THERE, TOO.

L.

My heart free-falls through my body.

He brought the tickets here. Hand-delivered them. But didn't ask to see me.

Of course he didn't.

The last time we saw each other, I was ending us before we had barely begun.

Maybe he wants to see me. Hope lifts my heart even though it's wrong to feel it because nothing has really changed. Only time between us. I was still his therapist.

I hope to see you there.

Or maybe he doesn't want to see me, and he's just being the good guy that I know he is and giving Jett the tickets he promised.

My heart sags back down.

I miss him though. Like I've never missed anyone in my life.

I need to see him. For what reason, I don't know. I don't really know what I'm doing. I just know I can't go on feeling like this.

And if he doesn't want to see me, then it gives me a foundation to start moving on from him because I've not found a way to move on in the last seven months.

But I guess there's only one way to find out if he does want to see me.

So, it looks like I'm going to the British Grand Prix.

nineteen

LEANDRO

✈ NORTHAMPTON, ENGLAND

THEY'RE HERE.

She's here...India.

It's been seven months since I last saw her, and now, we're in the same building.

I can feel her nearness like a vibration throughout my body, systematically making me feel alive and terrifying the fuck out of me.

She's here. I got her here, and now, I'm afraid to face her.

A million reasons not to go see her run through my mind.

I asked the guy doing the VIP tour to text me and let me know when India and Jett arrived.

I received that text an hour ago, and I still haven't had the nerve to go see her.

I'm telling myself that I'm needed in the garage. Truth is, it's practice sessions, and one of the test drivers has my car out on the track.

I'm just standing here, watching the screens, as he takes my car around.

I could go see India now.

Only, I don't know if she wants to see me. Sure, she's here, but Jett is obsessed with Formula 1, so of course, she'd bring him.

She was the one who ended us. Well, not that there actually ever was an *us*, because she never gave it a chance to get that far.

Granted, after I left, I didn't try to go back. I walked out of her house, and I shut down.

I haven't seen or spoken to India since I left her standing in her hallway.

Afterwards, I was hurt, frustrated and seriously pissed off, and instead of going home, I went straight to Lissa headquarters, got my Formula 1 car ready, climbed in her, and took her out on our test track.

My anger at India got me past that final stage of my fear. So, I threw myself back into racing, so, I didn't have to think about her. It only worked when I was in my car. Every other waking moment was controlled with thoughts of her.

I have everything back that I wanted after the accident. I still have my fears, but they don't control me like they used to. But, now, without India in my life, it feels just as empty as it did before.

It's like the universe is playing a fucking sick joke on me.

My racing was taken away from me, and then I'm given her. I get my racing back, and I lose her.

Well, not that I ever really had her.

But what I did have with her, the way I feel about India...

I can't get over her.

I have tried. Hard. I thought that being back on the track and racing would help.

It hasn't.

I've stayed out of the country, away from her. After I left for Melbourne at the start of March for the first race of the season, I just flew from race to race, not coming home, hoping the distance would help.

It didn't.

I thought putting myself back out there with women would help.

It didn't.

I knew I was done for when one of the hottest models around kissed me, and I felt nothing but this weird sense of guilt that I was somehow betraying India by kissing another woman.

Yes, I know how lame that sounds. But it is the way it is.

So, I've stayed away from all women even though I'm continuously linked with them.

If I speak to a woman and pose for a photograph with her, the next day, it will be in the press, saying that I am either dating or fucking her. The press has been aggressively intrusive in my life since I came back to the circuit. I guess it is to be expected after my accident, then absence, and now my return.

But a sick part of me hopes that India sees those pictures of me with women and that they bother her.

I hope they hurt her.

I know that makes me a bastard, but I don't care.

Now, I am back for Silverstone, and I thought I would be okay with being here, in the same country as her.

But what do I do?

A few days after I've been back, I find myself driving to her office and hand-delivering the tickets for the Prix that I promised to Jett last year, in the half hope that I might see India.

But I didn't see her.

It took all of my strength just to walk into her office, and I was too chicken to ask to see her, so, I just left the tickets with her receptionist, and ran out of there like the little pussy I am.

God, I am such a fucking loser.

I just need to man the fuck up and face her. She has probably moved on by now anyway.

The thought of her with another man makes rage flood my veins. I clench my fists, gritting my jaw.

I just need to see her. I need to know either way.

Seeing her will either help me move on or make me feel worse, if that is possible. But I need to do something because, clearly, what I have been doing for the last seven months isn't working.

The thing is, I am pretty sure I'm in love with her.

I always thought that love was something that wouldn't ever happen to me. Sure, I've had girlfriends, who I cared for, but love…not even close. Not once.

Not until her.

And that has to mean something, right? I can't be alone in the way I feel. She has to feel it too. Feel something for me at least.

If I see her, then, I'll know if she still feels something for me.

The barrier with India was never the way she felt for me. It was always about her goddamn ethics.

Yeah, well, I haven't been her patient for seven months now. And I know what she said about time not mattering, but it does.

Time gives clarity and perspective.

I just have to hope that time and space has given her just that and that she realizes she actually wants me.

A guy can hope, right?

I know where she'll be right now—at the talk that Quinn Moore is giving. Quinn is a retired racing driver. As part of the tour, a revered driver gives VIPs a talk about Formula 1. Jett will love it.

Yes, I know the itinerary of the day. My loser self knows no bounds.

I was always going to see her, no matter how much I had been delaying.

Backing away from the screens where I've been watching my test driver take my car around the track, I tell Patrick, one of my guys, "I'll be back in ten."

Then, I head out of the garage, my destination India.

twenty

INDIA

✈ NORTHAMPTON, ENGLAND

JETT AND I ARE HERE AT SILVERSTONE. We arrived an hour ago. As we found out on arrival, part of the VIP ticket that Leandro sent includes a speech from some retired driver I'd never heard of before, a tour around the garages, watching the practice sessions, and then dinner. We'll come back tomorrow for qualifying sessions. Then, Sunday is race day.

And I'm glad I had the forethought to book a hotel room for Jett and me to save me from driving the three-hour round-trip for the next three days.

I can relax and enjoy some time with my boy and not worry about Leandro Silva.

Well, I'm going to worry about him, only a little bit.

The thought of seeing him again makes my stomach roil with nerves.

I'm sure he'll be busy with prepping for qualifying tomorrow, so maybe I won't see him at all. I ignore the little stab in my heart that I feel at that thought.

I glance at Jett as the speaker yammers on about things I have no clue about. Jett looks enthralled and happy, and that's what counts. He was beyond excited when I told him that Leandro had sent the tickets as promised. I really need to thank him for them. I should get him a thank-you card.

Yeah, because that wouldn't be lame at all, India.

I guess if I see him this weekend, then I'll thank him. And if not, then I'll send a thank-you note to his house.

And I won't be heartbroken at not seeing him.

Total lie.

The speaker is rounding up, thankfully.

"So, we'll go on a tour of the garages now," our guide tells us.

Along with Jett, I get to my feet, and we follow everyone out of the room.

That's when I see him leaning against the wall, farther down from us, trying to go unnoticed. But I notice him.

Even under the ball cap, I see it's him.

He lifts his gaze, and when my eyes meet with his, I feel a jolt in the center of my chest.

Seeing him on TV or in photos online is nothing compared to seeing him in the flesh, being so close to him yet still so far.

My mind is assaulted with images of us together that one time, him moving inside me.

"Mum, Leandro is over there." Jett tugs on my arm and starts moving in his direction.

Glancing around, thankfully, no one from our group seems to have noticed Leandro standing there, and they are moving away to go on the tour of the garages.

"Hey, Jett." Leandro does a manly handshake with him. "How are you doing? You having fun so far?"

"Yeah, it's great. Thank you so much for the tickets."

"No problem." He lifts his eyes to mine as I come to stand beside Jett. "India."

Hearing his voice say my name…the memory assault starts again.

"Hello, Leandro." I smile, but it feels awkward and clumsy. I'm burning up from the outside in while standing here with him.

"How are you?" he asks.

"I'm good." I lift my shoulder. "You look to be doing great." I smile again, this one genuine.

"Yeah, I guess." He removes the cap, and after running his hand through his hair, he places it back on his head. Then, he pushes his hands into the pockets of his overalls. "So, I just thought I'd come see you both." He's looking at Jett now, not me. "And look...I wanted to ask if you both would like to have dinner with me tonight?" On the last part of his invitation, his eyes lift to mine.

My heart starts to beat double time. I part my dry lips to speak, but Jett beats me to it.

"Of course we would!" Jett says brightly.

I laugh lightly, very much loving my son's forwardness in this moment.

A chuckle escapes Leandro. His eyes lighten, but there's still the question in them.

He wants to hear my acceptance.

"Yes, we would love to have dinner with you. Thank you," I say calmly even though my insides are going nuts.

"I'm staying at Whittlebury Hall," Leandro tells me. "Astons Restaurant there is really nice. We could have dinner there, or I could take you somewhere else?"

"We're staying at Whittlebury, too, so Astons will be perfect," I say.

We were lucky to get a room at Whittlebury Hall that close to the Prix, but we managed to get a cancellation. Seems luck was on my side with Leandro staying there, too. A thrill passes through me at the knowledge.

"Great. So, I will reserve us a table. Say seven thirty?"

"Seven thirty is perfect."

"Should I pick you up from your room or—"

"We'll meet you at the restaurant." I smile.

"Okay. So, I will see you both tonight then." He glances at Jett and then me. "I should get back to the garage." He thumbs over his shoulder. Then, he seems to realize something. His eyes move to look past me, and he gestures to the now empty hall behind me. "You have lost your group. Do you know where you are going from here?"

Biting my lip, I shake my head.

"No worries. I will get you both back to them."

He smiles at me, and my insides turn to girlie goo. And I can't help my feeling of sheer excitement at the prospect of dinner tonight.

twenty-one

LEANDRO

✚ NORTHAMPTON, ENGLAND

OKAY...BE COOL. It is just dinner.

And Jett will be with us, so it is not like I can put the moves on India and fuck this up.

Nothing too soon with India. I need to take my time.

I know she wants me still. I could see it in her eyes. In the way that her body reacts naturally to me. Like she is tethered to me, her body naturally gravitates my way.

But she is gun-shy. I just need to show her that we are right together.

And I will do that with a little push and pull.

The elevator is waiting on my floor, so I go straight in and press the button for the lobby.

I smooth a hand down my shirt. I'm nervous as fuck. Sweating like a little bitch.

The elevator stops on the next floor down. The door slides opens, and there stands India.

My body responds in the only way it can when the most beautiful woman in the world is standing before me in come-fuck-me heels and red lips. Her dress is black and hits a few inches above the knees, showing those golden long legs of hers. Her hair is down and tousled around her shoulders, looking exactly as I imagine it would when spread out on my pillow.

Jesus. I'm pretty sure she's trying to kill me with those red heels and lips like fire to match.

She looks fucking stunning.

And I haven't breathed, and I have also spent an inordinate amount of time staring at her.

Good start.

"Leandro...hi." She presses those bee-stung lips of hers together, and my cock twitches in my pants.

"Hi," I say, like the lame fuck I am, trying to distract myself from my impending boner.

But she is kind of looking nervous herself. She is fidgeting, and she is still standing outside the elevator.

Be cool, Silva. You got this.

"Were you getting in the elevator?" I ask, my voice sounds hoarse.

She glances down the hall, like she is considering making an escape.

"I was, but, well, Jett's running late. He's still in the shower, and I didn't want you to be waiting for us down there, so I was coming first, and Jett was going to follow down, but as you're here, I guess...I don't know." She lets out a little laugh and runs her hand through her hair.

She's definitely nervous from being alone with me. It gives me a rise.

"Why don't we go down together and wait in the bar for Jett?"

She glances down the hall again and then looks back to me. "Okay."

She smiles at me, and the way it makes me feel...it is like her smile was made solely for me. And if I weren't already sure that I was in love with her, then I would know it in this moment.

I place a hand against the door to stop it from closing, and she slides in past me.

The scent of her perfume, a heady mix of citrus and floral, fills my senses. It serves as a memory of being inside her. It is like pure fucking torture. Having her here yet still so far away.

The door slides closed, and the lift starts its slow descent.

"India—"

"So—"

Our eyes connect, and we both laugh.

"You first," I say.

"No, you." A smile tugs on her lips.

I keep my eyes on her as I say, "I was just going to say that you look beautiful."

"Thank you." A blush rises on her cheeks.

I just can't fucking help myself. I reach out and touch her face with my fingertips.

The way I feel about her…it is not like anything I have ever known. It is all consuming—the unrelenting need to be with her, make her mine, brand myself into her skin because she sure as hell is branded into mine.

Her breath catches in her throat. She swallows audibly.

I see the tremble in her body. Her eyes are on my lips.

Then, I don't think. I just act.

I kiss her.

I kiss her for every day I have been away from her. For every single moment I have needed to kiss her and not being able to. I am taking everything I can from her because I don't know how long this moment will last. How long she will let me have her. I just need her to know how much I want her. How much I have missed her.

So much for taking my time with her. But then again, I have never been good with waiting.

My patience these last seven months, and my lack of patience now, is a testament to how much I want her.

Backing her against the wall, loving the feel of her fingers gripping my shirt, I blindly reach for the elevator buttons. Eyes quickly leaving her, I find the emergency stop button and press it.

"I have missed you," I say low against her mouth.

"I've missed you, too," she whispers.

Hearing those words from her mouth…that is when I lose my shit.

I devour her mouth, like she is the force I need to survive. I am starting to wonder if she actually is.

Her hands slide up my chest, nails scratching up my neck, curling into the hair at the nape of my head. I lick the inside of her mouth, loving the little moans of gratification in her throat. Pressing harder against her, I slide my leg between hers. She presses against me, squirming with need.

I am blinded by lust. Blinded by my complete need for her that I don't care where we are. I just know that I need to be inside her.

So you can imagine my absolute fucking disappointment when my hand reaches her thigh, my fingers skimming that soft skin of hers, and I feel her hand on mine, stopping me.

"I want nothing more than this, with you, right now," she pants against my mouth. "But Jett will be coming down soon, and he'll worry if we're not there."

I squeeze my eyes shut, pressing my forehead to hers.

She is right.

"Okay." I breathe heavily, still desperate for her. "Just give me a minute to calm down."

She presses her smiling lips against mine again.

"Not helping," I grumble.

She giggles, and I fucking love the sound.

With Superman strength, I somehow manage to move away from her. I press my back against the wall opposite her. Seeing her lipstick smeared around her mouth, knowing I did that, gives me utter satisfaction.

"You might want to fix your lipstick." I grin.

Getting her compact from her purse and opening it, she grimaces at her reflection and then starts to fix her lipstick. She puts her compact away and walks toward me. I can't take my eyes off of her.

"You have lipstick on your mouth." Reaching her hand up, she wipes it away with a tissue.

Her touch makes my heart pound in my chest.

"Ready?" She takes a step back and flicks a glance down to my now semihard cock.

I raise an eyebrow. "Kind of."

She lets out a light laugh as she reaches out and presses the button, starting the elevator.

"India…" I rasp her name over my tongue. "Just so you know, this isn't over, not by a fucking long shot." I gesture between us. "I intend to finish that kiss."

She bites down on the corner of those freshly painted lips. "I look forward to it."

twenty-two

INDIA

✚ LONDON, ENGLAND

"THIS ISN'T OVER, NOT BY A FUCKING LONG SHOT. I intend to finish that kiss."

Okay, well, that's what he said, but I haven't seen anything since.

No more kissing.

He literally hasn't laid a hand on me since that night in the elevator, and that was two days ago.

If I didn't believe my own sanity, I'd almost think the elevator kiss never happened.

Immediately after we were at dinner with Jett, Leandro saw us back to our room like a perfect gentleman. Then, we had breakfast with him on Saturday morning.

But we didn't see Leandro at all after that, except for when he was in his car on the track, qualifying. He qualified lower, at sixth, which was surprising for him—not that I know much about Formula 1, except for that it's long but kind of exciting. But I've been trying to keep up, and Jett's been guiding me through.

I could imagine that Leandro wasn't happy about qualifying so low.

Even still, it was a real privilege to watch him out there, knowing that I had a helping hand in getting him back in a car. I'm trying not to think too hard on the fact that I used to be his therapist because it reminds me that, no matter how I feel for him, in so many ways, we are impossible.

Even still, that kiss has been driving me to distraction. I want more. I want him.

The rational side of my brain isn't in play at the moment. Every time I have a rational thought about what a bad idea pursuing anything with him is, memories of that kiss come back, running through my head like his hands did over my skin, and I'm right back to being irrational, wanting him.

Saturday night, Jett and I had plans, and Leandro was at some sponsor function, so we didn't see him then.

Now, it's Sunday, and we're in the stands, watching the race. The atmosphere is amazing.

Leandro is in the top three. Apparently, he and this other driver, Hernandez, are fighting for second place, with Carrick Ryan holding first place.

I know Leandro and Carrick are friends, but I can still see their competitive rivalry on the track.

I'm just keeping my fingers crossed for Leandro, hoping he pulls it out of the bag and achieves at least second place. But I know with him, nothing short of first will be good enough.

Jett is having the time of his life this weekend, and I can see it on his face now, how much he enjoys Formula 1.

"You want that to be you one day?" I ask him over the sounds of the crowd. "Because if you do," I continue as he turns to look at me, "I just want you to know that I'd support you all the way."

"Who wouldn't want to be a Formula One driver?" He grins.

"Me." I laugh.

"It's an expensive sport though, Mum." He looks back out as the cars whiz by on the track.

"I'd make it work."

"Like, really expensive," he presses.

"If it was what you really wanted, then I'd find a way."

"I'll see how I get on with karting. I haven't even entered a competition yet. Just learning at the moment."

"I know, but I just want you to know that if it's what you see yourself doing in the future, then I'll support you."

"I already know that, Mum." He leans over and plants a kiss on my cheek. "Last couple of laps now," he informs me.

"And how's Leandro doing now?" I ask.

"Looking like third place." He grimaces.

After the last lap, the flag comes down, and Leandro takes third place.

Seeing him up there on the big screen, climbing out of his car and looking frustrated, makes me wish I were there to console him.

"Sucks," Jett comments. "But he wasn't on top form today. You could tell from his driving."

"Yeah," I agree even though I have no clue what I'm agreeing to.

"So, what's the plan?" he asks me. "Are we seeing Leandro before we leave?"

I shake my head. Leandro didn't ask to see us before we went back home. "He'll be busy, I imagine, doing press stuff."

"So, we're heading home then?"

"Yeah."

We already checked out of the hotel earlier, and our bags are in the car. So, it's out to the car and home.

With a despondent feeling in my gut—not knowing when I'll see Leandro again, if ever—Jett and I make our way out to the car park.

"When I come in here and you're nursing a bottle of wine, I know it's not good." Kit sits across from me, takes the bottle of red, and swigs from it.

"It's my first glass, and I'm only halfway through. I wouldn't call it nursing."

"You've got a face like a smacked arse. After a weekend at Silverstone, I expected more of a happy face. Jett's done nothing but talk about it since you got back."

"He had a great time."

"He did. Told me all about your dinner date with Leandro."

"Hardly a date. Jett was with us. Speaking of, where is he?"

"In his room, on the phone. I think it's with a girl."

"What? He has a girlfriend?" I sit up straighter.

Kit shrugs. "He hasn't said, but I'm sensing all the trademarks of a budding romance."

"What trademarks?"

"He's been talking about one girl in particular a lot lately—Anna."

"How do I miss this stuff?" I face-plant the table, feeling like the worst mother in the world.

"You don't miss anything. You're his mother. He's not going to talk about girls with you."

"I guess," I utter, my words muffled by the table.

"So, what's going on with you and Silva then?" Kit asks.

I lift my head and shrug. "Honestly, I don't know. We haven't seen or spoken to one another in seven months."

Kit knows all about the night—not the gritty details, of course. Just that we slept together, and then I kicked him out.

"Then, he's there, waiting for us after we get out of the Formula One talk thingy. Invites us to dinner. Kisses me in the elevator. Tells me it isn't over. Has breakfast with us the next morning, like nothing happened, and then…nada."

"Hang on. Back up. He kissed you?"

"Yep." I take a large swig of wine. "Jett was messing around, getting ready, and I went down to meet Leandro, so we wouldn't be late. He was in the elevator, and I got in. He kissed me, like toe-curling-rip-our-clothes-off kiss. Then, I stopped it because we were in an elevator, and I didn't want Jett to wonder where we were. Then, Leandro said, and I quote, 'This isn't over, not by a fucking long shot. I intend to finish that kiss.' Then, nothing since."

Kit is looking at me with a grimace. "That was way too much information for me to hear about my sister."

"Sorry." I wince, knowing how much I get grossed out hearing about his love life.

"So, Silva hasn't made a move since then?"

"Nope."

"He's waiting you out."

"Huh?"

"The last time you guys were together, before this kiss, you pushed him away and stayed away for seven months. He's the one who initiated contact with you via the Prix tickets. Then, he kissed you again. He's waiting for you to make the next move. He wants to know that it's not all one-sided."

I ponder that for a minute with another mouthful of wine. "You really think so?"

"Yep. Look, do you love this guy?"

That catches me off guard.

Do I love Leandro?

I've thought about this a lot, more so these last few days, and I'm pretty sure I do. Only...saying it aloud will make it real. And really, if I'm going to admit it to anyone, it should be Leandro.

Lifting my shoulders, I shrug.

"I'll take that as a yes. Look, I haven't seen you this way about anyone—ever. And I get your hang-ups, Indy, and I wouldn't say to do anything that would jeopardize your career. You know that. But I think you're safe here. It's been seven months since you last treated him. You're clearly in love with this guy. I want you to be happy. You haven't been happy for seven months. Since he came back into your life, you've been happy."

"I have been happy."

"Bullshit. Sure, you're happy when you're with Jett and me. But there's something missing for you, and that something is clearly him. On that note, after just sounding like a fucking advice columnist, I'm going to go get my man card back. I'm going to drink beer and watch the racing highlights, seeing as though I didn't get to watch it at Silverstone," he says pointedly.

I stick my tongue out at him.

Thirty years old, and my brother can still reduce me to a teenager.

He stands, not before taking another swig from my wine bottle.

"Kit…" I stop him with my words. "What do you think I should do?"

"I think you should man the fuck up and talk to him. Tell him how you feel."

"You mean, woman up," I call after him.

I hear his resounding chuckle. "Just go fucking see him, Indy. I'll stay home with Jett."

I stare down into my wine, thinking over Kit's words.

Seeing Leandro again this weekend, spending time with him…kissing him, I know that I can't go without him anymore. I can't spend another seven months without seeing him.

I can't go another day.

I need to see him now.

twenty-three

LEANDRO

✚ LONDON, ENGLAND

"FOR FUCK'S SAKE," I growl at the sound of the doorbell.

If it's Carrick coming to gloat about his win, then he can fuck off.

I was just about to call India. I didn't get a chance to see her at the track after the race. I had press obligations, and then I got pulled into a meeting, so my bosses could complain about me coming in third and figure out why I had lost.

I am pissed that I lost.

But I know why I did.

It had nothing to do with the car. It was running perfectly.

It was because of India. I was distracted with thoughts of her.

With India in my head for the past seven months, missing her was a distraction in itself, but it was a hell of a lot easier to find my focus when she wasn't near me. Having her at Silverstone, knowing she was watching me race, seeing her again, breathing in her smell, tasting her…

Jesus that kiss.

I had forgotten how amazing she tasted, how she felt against my body, and in my hands.

I haven't been able to stop thinking about that damn kiss. I am pretty sure I've spent the whole weekend hard.

I could barely concentrate enough to race.

I have been dreaming about being back inside her for seven months, and I really need to finish what I started. Hence, the reason I was going to call her. I had considered stopping by her place on my way home but decided against it. I thought I would come home and call her instead. Test the water and see where her mind is.

Sure, I want to fuck her again. But I want more with her. I don't want to rush her and end up pushing her away again.

I consider ignoring the door, but then the bell goes again. Getting up from the sofa, I head for the front door. Without checking the peephole, I pull the door open.

The air leaves my lungs in a rush, and all my blood flows directly to my cock. "India."

To say her being here is unexpected would be putting it mildly, but I am very fucking happy that she is.

"Hi." She is nervously wringing her hands.

My eyes go to them and then back to her face. "Are you okay?"

"Yes. No. I'm not sure."

"Is Jett okay?" I take a step closer to her.

Her blues blink at me in surprise, and then her gaze softens. "He's fine. I just...I don't know what I'm doing here."

She shakes her head, her eyes meeting mine.

"Yes, you do. Tell me why you came here, India," I urge softly.

"I'm starting to think this is our thing, turning up at each other's houses and talking complete crap." She shakily runs her hand through her hair, biting her lip.

I say nothing. I want her to tell me why she is here, and I hope to fucking God it is for the reason I think it is.

"I..." She bites her lip again, and it is beyond distracting. "I missed you. I deeply regret how things ended between us, but seeing you this weekend...the kiss in the elevator…I don't want to go another seven months without seeing you again, and…telling you how I feel…about you."

"And how do you feel?" My words are a whisper.

My heart is beating a mile a minute in my chest, but I don't miss the look of fear in her eyes. It makes me worry that I'm going to lose her, that she is going to back out from telling me what she came here to say. India is always gun-shy, so I don't hesitate to lay my feelings out for her.

"Because I know for sure how I feel about you." I step forward, and my hand circles her wrist, pulling her to me. "I love you. I am so fucking in love with you that I am blind to anything else. Being without you these past seven months has been agony. I was pretty sure I was in love with you when I walked out of your house after we had sex, but seeing you this weekend, being with you again, I know for sure. I'm in deep, and I don't want to get out. I want to get deeper in with you. I want you in my life…to be my life."

"I…" Her lips part, the word breathing from her, her eyes filling with tears.

"Say it," I gently coax.

She closes her eyes and then opens them, and I see all her feelings for me written there even if worry is etched into her features.

"I'm in love with you, Leandro. God, so much. I know it's wrong, and I shouldn't feel like this about an ex-patient, but I do and—"

I cut off the rest of her words with my lips.

"Nothing about this feels wrong," I breathe against her mouth. "It couldn't be more fucking right."

Her arms come around my neck, fingers curling into my hair. "I love you," she whispers.

Her words are like an aphrodisiac. My hands go straight to her ass, and I pick her up, loving the feel of her legs going around my waist. Bringing her into my house, I kick the door shut and carry her straight upstairs to my bedroom. We are kissing hungrily, and pulling at each other's clothes as we move.

God, she tastes so fucking good.

I just need to get her in my bed and pliable under my hands, screaming out my name. Then, I will bury myself so deep inside her that she will feel me in every part of her body, and nothing else will matter.

I'm taking my time with her. No rushing this.

Reaching my bedroom, I walk through the open doorway. She drops her handbag to the floor, right before I lay her down on my bed. Then, I just stand and stare at her, taking her in.

"What?" she says shyly.

"You are maddeningly beautiful, do you know that?"

She shakes her head, her cheeks flushing. I love how easily I can get to her.

I lean over her, taking her face in my hands. "Well, you are. You drive me to distraction." I brush my mouth over hers. "I can't think of anything but you."

I kiss her once more, and then leaning back, I start to unbutton her shirt. When it's open, I brush the fabric aside, revealing her bra to me.

Pink, silky, perfect.

I press a kiss to the top of her breast, and then I run my tongue to the dip in her cleavage. She grabs my head, a moan falling from her lips.

Rising up, I bring her with me. I remove her shirt and then my own before taking her bra off. Leaning in, I take her breast in my mouth, sucking on her nipple, and her hips jerk against me.

Kissing my way up her chest, I take her mouth with mine again. I am trying to go slow, take my time, but it is getting really fucking hard, and when I feel her hand press against my cock, through the fabric of my jeans, I nearly lose my shit.

Her jeans are off in seconds, and my own follow immediately after.

I fall onto her, and we're in a tangle of limbs and lips. I can't kiss or touch enough of her. It's like sheer desperation, an addiction, needing more and more, not sure when I will hit the point of enough.

But, something tells me, with India, there will never be enough.

Pressing my hand to the mattress, I lift myself from her, allowing me to slide my hand down her stomach. My fingers skim the top of her panties.

"Yes," falls from her lips in a breathy whisper.

I push my hand under the fabric, finding her wet. "Fuck." I groan, my head falling to her chest as I run my finger through her slickness.

Then, down over her clit, I lift my head to stare in her eyes as I push my finger inside her. She's tight, her insides gripping me like a vise. I start to finger her, pressing the heel of my hand against her clit, and then I slip in another finger.

I need to taste her.

"I want you on my mouth," I roughly tell her, kissing her still. I remove my fingers from inside her and slide my hand around her back. I flip us over until she is lying on top of me. "Sit on my face, baby. I want to feel that sweet little pussy of yours riding my face before I fuck you."

Rising up onto her knees, she stares down at me. Then, she stands on the bed, putting a leg on either side of me. She slides her panties down her legs, taking them off. Then, she moves over my face, lowering to her knees.

No hesitation or shyness. I fucking love that.

I grab the backs of her thighs, pulling her to my mouth where I want her.

The first touch of my tongue on her clit, she moans loudly. Falling forward, she grips my headboard with her hands.

She tastes fucking amazing. I could stay here all day with her on my face.

She starts to rotate her hips against me while I lick at her pussy.

"That's it, baby. Fuck my mouth."

"Oh God," she moans.

"Not God, babe. *Me.*"

I push my tongue inside her, and she cries out.

I want to give her more. I want to feel all of her.

I want to make her come so fucking hard that she will remember it for days after.

I slide my hand around her ass. Then, I run my finger through her slickness while my tongue licks her clit.

I don't know whether India is into anal, but there is only one way to find out. I move my wet finger over her tight puckered hole and gently press against it.

Her whole body stiffens, so I ease my finger off.

"You want me to stop?"

There's a brief pause, before she speaks, "I haven't ever…"

"Then, we won't do it."

"No…" She stares down at me. "I mean, yes. I think…I want to. Just be gentle."

"Always, babe."

My tongue goes back to her clit. Making soft strokes over it, I gently move the tip of my finger over her hole. I feel her lose herself to the sensation. Gathering some more wetness from her pussy, I use it to push the tip of my finger into her asshole.

I feel the orgasm tear through her as she screams out my name. I've never heard a more erotic sound.

When her orgasm starts to subside, I slide out from underneath her. Kneeling behind her, I press my chest against her trembling back. My arm coming around her waist, I pull her back to sit on my lap. My cock is rock-hard and pressed up against her ass.

She tilts her face back to look at me.

"Are you okay?" I ask.

Her eyes go to my lips. "I'm better than okay."

I kiss her, swiping my tongue over hers, letting her taste herself on me.

"You taste so fucking good," I tell her.

"I want to taste you," she says.

I nearly come all over her ass. "You don't have to."

"I want to." She bites down on her lip, drawing my attention to her mouth.

"Do you have your lipstick with you?" I ask.

She raises her brow. "Why?"

"Because…" I nip her lower lip with my teeth. "Since the moment I saw you wearing that red lipstick of yours, I have had this image stuck in my head of you sucking me off with your lipstick smeared all over my cock."

Her breath catches, her eyes flaring with desire. "It's in my bag."

Sliding her off of me, I grab her bag from the floor and pass it to her. She fishes her lipstick out and reapplies it without using a mirror.

"Impressive." I grin.

"It's just one of my many talents."

I'm pretty sure my dick just got harder. I'm at the point of being in pain, and my balls are so blue that it's not even funny.

"You have all your women put on lipstick for you?" she asks.

I take hold of her chin with my hand, staring into her eyes. "No. Only you. And there has been no one since you, if you were wondering that also."

I see surprise flicker through her eyes. It doesn't make me feel great. But, then, my reputation does precede me.

"You haven't slept with *anyone* since me?" The disbelief in her voice annoys me.

"No." I remove my hand from her chin, but continue to pin her with my stare.

"But, all of those pictures of you with women in the press…"

"They were just that—pictures. Have you fucked anyone since me?" I turn the tables on her, but I am not really sure if I want to hear the answer to this question.

Her eyes flare with indignation. "No." She juts her chin out.

"Good. Now, get down on your knees, and suck my cock."

I am a bossy bastard in the bedroom, but she doesn't seem to mind.

A smile lights her eyes, as she tilts her head to the side. "You could say please."

I slide my fingers into her hair, bringing her face closer to mine. "Sorry. India, get down on your knees and suck my cock, *please*."

She gives me a haughty look. "Better." Then, she slides off the bed, to her feet.

I follow her movement, putting my feet on the floor, sitting on the edge of the bed.

She lowers to her knees, and I have never seen anything more beautiful than the sight of her kneeling before me, those big blue eyes blinking up at me. My fingers slide into her hair, threading through the strands, and I guide her head down to my cock. The second her lips touch my cock, I know this will all be over way too soon if I don't control myself.

"Fuck, yes," I groan.

My fingers tighten in her hair as she slides her mouth down my cock, taking me throat deep.

"Shit. Jesus, that's it, baby," I hiss. "Take it all."

She is fucking amazing. A doctor who gives head like a porn star. I can feel the head of my cock hitting the back of her throat.

I brush her hair aside, watching her suck me off. "The sight of you, like this with your lips on my cock, is even better than I imagined."

My hips start to move as she flattens her tongue over my cock, taking me deep each time.

"That's it, baby. You suck me so good." I can feel myself starting to lose control.

I'm going to come. I need to stop her. But it just feels so fucking good.

She hollows her cheeks, sucking me hard, and a shot of pre-cum shoots from my cock.

"Ah, India, baby...you have to stop. I will come if you don't." I tug gently on her hair.

She lets my cock from her mouth with a pop. Sitting back on her heels, her lips are smeared red, and her lipstick is all over my cock, her hair tousled from my hands in it.

Fucking beautiful.

"I thought that was the idea." She runs a finger down my cock, and he jerks.

"Next time. Right now, I need to fuck you." Hands under her arms, I haul her to her feet and lift her onto the bed.

I get a condom from the drawer of my bedside table. I have it on in seconds, and I am between her welcoming thighs, my dick pressed up against her hot wet pussy.

She raises her arms above her head, pushing her breasts up to me. "I need you inside me," she whispers.

"Maddening," I growl.

I lean forward, taking her breast into my mouth. I graze my teeth over her nipple, making her hips buck upward.

"Fuck me, Leandro! Now!" she cries out.

"Say please."

Her eyes flash to mine.

I grin at her.

"*Please*, fuck me," she says through gritted teeth.

I slam inside her without hesitation.

"Oh God," she whimpers.

"Jesus, India…" I stare down at her, feeling lost in this moment. "Being inside you…I have never felt anything like you before. I am never going without you again."

"Never," she whispers, her eyes fixed on mine.

Holding her stare, I slowly pull out of her and then slam back inside.

Very quickly, it gets out of control, and we're fucking each other like rabid animals, kissing and biting and licking. Her nails rake at my skin while I fuck her hard, and I love it.

"Fuck, India, tell me you are close because I'm going to come."

Her hands go to my ass. Nails scoring my skin, she tries to press me harder against her. "I'm close. Keep doing…that…and I'll…ah, fuck…I'm coming!" she screams.

The feel of her tightening around me has me spinning out of control, and I am right there with her. "Fuck…India!" I growl, jerking my hips against hers. I come harder than I ever have before in my life.

And it is not just because I haven't had sex in so long. It is because of her. Everything feels different with her.

She's my game changer. My one.

I let my head fall into that sweet spot where her neck ends and her shoulder begins, and I press a soft kiss there. Her arms come around my neck, holding me, fingers pushing through my hair. I stay there a long moment, brushing gentle kisses over her skin.

I guess I am waiting for her to change her mind or push me away, but it doesn't come.

Lifting my head, I brush her hair from her face. I stare down at her, and I love the way she smiles at me.

"That was…wow." Her smile changes to a grin.

"I would call it better than wow. More like fucking amazing."

"Life-altering sex?"

"Definitely." I kiss her again. "Let me just clean up."

Leaving her, I go to the bathroom, get rid of the condom, and wash up. I wet a cloth in warm water and take it back to the bedroom with me. She is still exactly where I left her.

I press the cloth between her legs, cleaning her, as I watch her watch me with what looks like fascination and surprise.

Has no one cared for her in this way before?

It both angers and pleases me.

I toss the cloth back in the direction of the bathroom and climb back onto the bed with her. I wrap my body around hers.

"Stay the night," I whisper into her ear.

She turns her face to mine, and I see something in her eyes.

I already know what she is going to say before she says it.

"I can't stay."

twenty-four

INDIA

✣ LONDON, ENGLAND

I SEE HIS EXPRESSION DROP as soon as the words have left my mouth, so I'm quick to explain myself, "It's not what you think. It's Jett. I never stay out overnight. And I want to speak to him first about you and me before we start doing sleepovers."

"So, there will be sleepovers?" He runs his finger down my arm, a salacious look in his eyes.

"If you're lucky." I grin.

"I'm feeling pretty damn lucky right now."

A soft smile claims my grin. "Me, too."

"But?"

"Why do you think there's a but?" I frown.

He moves onto his back, his hand going behind his head. I'm momentarily distracted by the flex of his muscles in his bicep. He has great arms.

"Because I have gotten pretty good at reading you."

Exhaling a breath, I place my hand flat on his chest and rest my chin on it. "I'm just worried."

"About?" His brow lifts.

"A few things…" I stare into his eyes. "I'm worried about Jett getting attached to you." I bite my lower lip with my teeth.

"And that is a bad thing? Why?" His eyebrows pull together.

"Because if we don't work out for whatever reason, I don't want him getting hurt. That's why I've never introduced him to any men I've dated before—not that there's been many and not that we've exactly dated yet—"

"Which we need to rectify very soon."

That pulls my thoughts in a different direction. "You want to take me out on a date?" A smile edges my lips.

"Yes, and soon." Leaning his head down, he kisses the tip of my nose before resting his head back on the pillow. "You have nothing to fear, India. I won't hurt Jett or you. I promise. I think Jett is a great kid, and I can't wait to get to know him better." His chest rises, lifting me with it, as he takes a deep breath. "I have never been in love before, India, so believe me, I am not taking our relationship lightly."

"You've never been in love?" I eye him skeptically. "Ever?"

"No."

"How is that possible?"

I know I've never been in love before him, but Leandro has been around a lot more women than I have men. I just can't believe he's never fallen in love with one of them before.

He shrugs. "I waited for it to happen. It never did. Now, I know why."

My mouth dries. Licking my lips, I ask, "Why?"

His eyes darken with emotions. He traces his index finger over my cheek, tucking my hair behind my ear. "Because I was waiting for you."

Can your heart dance in your chest? Because mine currently feels like it is.

"I was waiting for you, too." Resting up on my elbow, I touch my hand to his face.

"You have been in love before…with Jett's father?"

"No." I strongly shake my head. "I was young and naive. I thought I was in love, but I had no clue what that truly felt like." I fix my eyes on him. "Now, I know. The way I feel about you...I've never felt anything like it before. That's why I'm willing to risk everything on us."

His fingers slide into my hair. Pulling my mouth down to his, he gently kisses me. "I love that we are each other's firsts."

I smile against his lips. "Me, too," I whisper. "But..."

"There's that damn *but* again," he growls over my lips.

Moving my head back so I can look in his eyes, I say, "I'm sorry, but while we're on the subject of Jett's father, I think you need to know something about him."

A dark shadow passes over his features. "I'm listening."

I swallow down past my nervous. "Jett's father is in prison."

That gets his attention. "Okay. What is he in prison for?"

I feel like I need to give Leandro all my focus when I say this, so I sit up beside him. Tucking my legs around my bum, I pull the cover around me in modesty. Leandro immediately pulls the cover down.

"I feel naked."

"You are. Naked or not, there is nothing you need to hide from me or can't tell me."

I feel wide open. Like he can see through to the very soul of me.

I nervously lick my lips. "Jett's father, Paul, is in prison for statutory rape, rape, and sexual assault."

His eyes widen, and anger envelops his features. He sits up, putting his back against the headboard. His eyes close together tightly. His jaw clenching, he pinches the bridge of his nose. "Did he...rape you?"

I touch my hand to his face, my thumb smoothing over the fingers pinching his nose, until he lowers his hand and opens his eyes.

"He didn't rape me. But I was the statutory rape part of his sentence." I take a fortifying breath. "I was fifteen when we started sleeping together. Paul was thirty." My gaze lowers. "When Kit and I were babies, we were abandoned, left in the doorway of an old factory building, where we were found by the caretaker. Kit's name came from the man who found us. My name came from the building—India House. It's in Manchester, where we're from originally."

"Jesus, India. I am so sorry that happened to you and Kit." His hand curls around mine, squeezing.

"It's fine. I found my peace with it long ago. I had Kit. He's the best brother a girl could wish for. But, back then, Kit and I were difficult to care for. We were both angry kids, Kit more so than me. He was always getting in trouble—mostly from defending me. I was a hell-raiser when I was younger."

"I don't see that in you." He smiles.

"I'm different now. I had to change when I became a mother. I became responsible. But back then, I didn't care about anyone, apart from Kit. So, we never settled anywhere, bouncing from foster home to foster home. It was hard enough to be placed and then add in the fact that there was the two of us together. If they ever tried to split us up, we'd just run away and come back to each other, so they finally stopped trying. Then, we started getting older, and people don't want troublesome teenagers. Eventually, we ended up in a foster home for wayward kids. We were there when Paul started working as one of the caregivers."

"He was your caregiver? Jesus fucking Christ," he grinds out, thumping his head back against the headboard, his hand tightening around mine.

"I was young and impressionable. He spent a lot of time with me, listened to me, made me believe he really cared about me. Back then, I didn't know he was grooming me. I was fifteen, and I just wanted to be loved. I didn't realize I was looking for it in the wrong place." I squeeze Leandro's hand, which still has a firm hold of mine. "I'd been sleeping with Paul for about two years when I found out I was pregnant with Jett. When I went to tell him"—I suck in a breath at the memory that still gets to me, even now—"I found him in bed with someone else. She was a girl who was new to the home we lived in. She was fourteen, a year younger than I was when he started sleeping with me."

Leandro lets out a sound of pain. "Fuck, India."

"This is bad I know. I'm sorry."

He sits up and grabs my face with his hands. "Don't ever be sorry. I am just angry that this happened to you."

"Me, too, but I can't regret it because for all of Paul's faults, he did give me Jett." Tears touch my eyes, surprising me. It's been a really long time since I cried over my past. "When I found Paul with that girl, I rang Kit and told him everything. He lost his shit. He kicked the crap out of Paul."

"I like your brother already."

"When it comes to me and Jett, he's fiercely protective."

"As he should be."

"Someone called the cops when the fight spilled out into Paul's building. Kit was arrested. Thankfully, he didn't do any jail time for it, but he messed Paul up pretty bad. To save Kit, I told the police why Kit had lost his crap with Paul—who Paul was to us, about me and him, my pregnancy, and the underage girl I found in Paul's bed. I needed to protect Kit the way he'd protected me his whole life. Paul was arrested. Somehow, the press got wind of it…and that's when it got worse." I close my eyes against the onslaught of memories. "I wasn't the first underage girl who Paul had slept with, and clearly, I hadn't been the last. He had a thing for young girls. More started to come forward. Some said they had been sexually abused by Paul. That he had even raped some of them. It went to trial. I was one of the main witnesses. He got sentenced to fifteen years in prison for statutory rape, rape and sexual abuse."

"Jett knows all of this?"

"Yes. I haven't kept who his father is from him."

"Has Jett ever met him?"

"No."

"And he's still in prison?"

"Yes. After he went to prison, I received compensation from the government for what had happened to me. It wasn't a lot, but back then, it was to me. Kit and I left Manchester and moved here to London. I used the money I received to buy the house we live in and to put me through school. I wanted to start fresh here and give Jett a better life than I'd ever had."

"You are amazing, do you know that?"

"Not really."

"You are," he states emphatically. "And your reluctance to be with me makes a whole lot more sense now."

"I didn't want to be like him. I wouldn't want to take advantage of someone in my care."

"I was never in your care, babe. And you never once took advantage. If anyone did, I took advantage of you." A sexy smile appears on his lips.

"So, I was thinking that maybe we should keep our relationship on the down-low for now."

With the darkening of his eyes, I know that he doesn't agree. "Because of Jett's father?"

"Because of who you are. Your public profile. For Jett. I don't want anything coming out into the papers that could hurt him. And also my career. I was your therapist. If the Health and Care Professions Council find that out, my career will be over."

"How will they find out? The only people who know won't say anything—well, on my side for sure. What about your side?"

"Kit knows." I wince. "After we kissed that first time, I was a mess." I meet his eyes. "He guessed. But you can trust Kit. He would never say anything."

"It's fine, India." He takes my hand again, squeezing it.

"And Sadie, my old receptionist, of course knows you were a patient, but she is bound by a confidentiality agreement that I make all my receptionists sign."

"So, we're covered."

"I guess. But what about Jett? I don't want him in the public eye because we're together."

"I'll protect him. I will have my lawyer and publicist stop the press from publishing any pictures of him. I don't want to hide us, babe. I have you, and I want the world to know that you're mine. You and Jett are both my family now."

"Family?"

"Mmhmm...you have a problem with that?"

"No problem at all. And you do realize that we've just made Jett's dream come true—you and me being together? He's going to be over the moon. He'll also expect to come to every race you do."

"I would be offended if he didn't come." He smiles. "Jett can come wherever with me. So long as his hot mother comes along, too."

"And she will, as long as work permits it."

"Can you take a break from work at all? I have to leave for Hungary in a few weeks. As it is school break, I would love it if you and Jett would come with me."

"I'm not going to be able to say no in this, am I?"

"No, babe, you're not."

"I should be able to juggle things around a bit, and if necessary, I can always get someone in to cover my patients while I'm away."

"So, you will come?"

"I'll ask Jett, but I know what his answer will be. So, yes, we'll come."

"Good." He rolls me onto my back and kisses me hard on the mouth.

"Your work takes you away a lot?" I blink up at him.

"It does. But we will figure it out. We will make it work."

"We'd better because I'm risking my job for you." I poke his side with my finger.

"Hey!" He laughs, grabbing my hand, stopping me. "I am the only one who gets to poke anyone around here."

I raise my eyebrow. "You have a dirty mind."

"Oh, babe, you have no idea."

A shiver runs through me, curling my toes. "Then, you'll have to enlighten me."

"I plan on it." He shifts, pressing his very apparent erection up against me.

"Now?"

"That is what you do to me. I could go all night with you."

"You're insatiable."

"Because you are irresistible."

He brushes his mouth over mine, grazing my lower lip with his teeth. I kiss him back, running my fingers through his hair. I touch the scar on his scalp, the scar his hair hides from the rest of the world.

I press my hand to his face. "I wish I'd been there for you after the accident."

"I wouldn't have wanted you there...to see me that way."

His eyes close on a long blink before slowly opening to meet mine. I see it all there in his eyes—the memories that still hurt him now. And I regret brining it up.

"I was a mess."

"I've already seen you at your worst, Leandro." My hand slides around his neck.

"No, you haven't." He shakes his head. "What you saw was a frustrated man, battling his demons with alcohol and women."

I wince at the mention of his past indiscretions.

"I'm sorry," he whispers, brushing his nose along my cheek.

"Don't be. You're not saying anything I didn't already know. Just hearing it was hard back then. Now, it's…just harder."

"It is in the past."

"I know." I run my finger over his scar again. "I'm glad I'm your future."

"Me, too." He brings his lips back to mine, brushing them over mine. "How long can you stay before you have to get back home?"

"I'm okay for a few hours."

I trail my fingers through his hair and down his back. I lightly score my nails over his skin, causing him to groan with pleasure.

"Good, because for these next few hours, I am going to bury myself deep inside you, making you come so fucking hard and so often that you will never want to leave."

"Less talking, more showing," I murmur, lost to him again.

"Oh, I am going to show you." He chuckles darkly. "Right fucking now."

He takes my mouth in a lush deep kiss. Then, kneeing my legs apart, he presses his hard cock up against my wet heat and suddenly thrusts inside me.

"Leandro!" I cry out, instantly breathless.

Stilling inside me, he stares down at me with those all-encompassing dark eyes of his. "Mine," he says low with meaning. "You are mine, India, and I am never letting you go again."

I rouse, feeling Leandro's warm solid body wrapped around me. With the sun on my face, I feel an ache between my legs, which can only come from having amazing sex.

Hang on. I can feel the sun on my face. *What time is it?*

My eyes flash open to see the dawn light shining through his open blinds that he never got around to closing. I scan for a clock and see one on his bedside table. It's six a.m.

"Shit!" I sit up, Leandro's arm still banded around me. "We fell asleep." I shake his shoulder. "I have to go."

"Hmm…what?" He blinks those beautiful eyes of his open, not loosening his hold on me.

I tug on his arm. "You need to let me up. We fell asleep. I have to get home."

My heart is thudding in my chest. It's early, so Jett will still be sleeping, but I can't believe I fell asleep.

Worst mother ever!

Out of bed, I run around his room, pick up my clothes, and dress as I go.

I catch sight of him, and he's sitting up in bed, watching me with amusement.

"What?" I say.

"Nothing. You look beautiful."

"I look terrible." I run a hand over my messed up hair.

He gets out of bed and comes over to me. He's still naked and so hot. "Beautiful." He softly kisses me.

"So are you. And you're seriously tempting while you're pressed up against me in the buff…but I've got to go," I grumble against his lips.

He gives a low chuckle, and I feel it rumble through his chest to mine. "You can go, as long as you let me see you tonight. I want to take my girl out on a date."

I tilt my head back, looking into his eyes. "Sounds wonderful."

"It will be." He kisses me again. Hand cupping the back of my head, he slips his tongue in my mouth. His other hand finds my bum and squeezes, pressing his morning wood against my hip.

Another few minutes wouldn't hurt, would it? We could—

No, I have to go.

I give an internal groan and say again, "I really need to go."

He lets out a groan of disappointment. "Fine. Go," he says good-naturedly, then, slaps my behind with his hand, as he releases me.

I gather up my shoes and handbag and make my way downstairs. Leandro is soon behind me, now wearing a pair of boxer shorts.

Shame. I like him naked.

When I'm by the front door, I slip my feet into my shoes. "I'm going to tell Jett about us today."

"Good."

"He'll be fine, of course, because...well, you're *you*." I gesture at him.

He chuckles. "Jett has got good taste, like his mother."

Smiling, I shake my head at him. "I was thinking it might be good for him to spend some time around you. Maybe dinner at our place one night this week? Then, you can meet Kit, too."

"Sounds great." He leans in and kisses me again, threading his fingers through my hair.

I find myself pressed up against the door as the kiss quickly turns heated.

"You really have to go right now?" he breathes against my lips.

"I really have to go," I say wistfully.

He takes a deep breath and steps back from me. Dark eyes bore into mine. "Tonight, you are mine. I am taking you out, and then, later I am bringing you back here and fucking you until neither of us can walk."

Excitement ripples low in my belly. "Can't wait." I reach back for the handle and pull the door open.

"I will pick you up at seven thirty."

"What should I wear?"

"As little as possible."

Laughing, I step out the door. "And by that, you mean, no underwear, right?" I give him a sexy look, lifting my eyebrow.

"That is definitely what I mean." He leans against the doorframe, arms folded over that amazing chest of his.

He watches me get in my car, and he lifts a hand as I pull away. I blow him a kiss.

I really hate leaving him, but I'm a mother first and foremost—and currently failing by falling asleep. I can't believe I did that. I guess that shows how much Leandro wore me out and how comfortable I feel with him.

God, the sex. I've never had sex like it before.

Maybe this is what it's like to have sex with someone you love, but I think a lot has to do with him. The man is a god in bed.

I'm making good time getting home as the roads are quiet with it being so early. Fifteen minutes later, I'm pulling into my driveway. Turning the engine off, I get out and ease my car door shut.

I quietly unlock the front door before letting myself in. The house is silent. Everyone's still sleeping.

Thank God.

I put my bag down in the hall and head to the kitchen to make some coffee. Then, I'm going to take a shower. I smell like sex. And Leandro.

I momentarily considering revising the shower, as I like smelling like Leandro, but I'm not that gross.

I walk into the kitchen and nearly have a heart attack when I see Jett sitting at the table, eating cereal and looking at his phone.

"What are you doing up?" I choke out the words.

His eyes lift to me. I watch him take in my appearance. "Why are you wearing the same clothes you were wearing yesterday? Did you just get home?" His brows rise in question.

"N-no, I-I, um...I..."

"Mum, are you stuttering?"

"No," I fire out defensively. "I'm wearing yesterday's clothes because..." *Shit! Why can't I lie on the spot?* "Because I really like this shirt."

"Okay...well, just so you know, your favorite shirt is buttoned up wrong."

"What?" I look down to see that I did indeed button up my shirt incorrectly in in my haste to leave Leandro's house. I start redoing the buttons correctly.

"So, you stayed at Leandro's last night?"

My face floods with embarrassment. "Yes. No! I mean, no." God, I hate it when he fires a question at me when I'm distracted.

"You know, Mum, lying to your only son is a terrible thing to do. I'm pretty sure that lies between a mother and child are the beginning of a potential downfall. I mean, you lie, and I could feel hurt and rejected. I might rebel. Start hanging out with the wrong kind of people. Smoke. Do drugs. Who knows where it'll end?"

Shaking my head, fighting a smile, I sit down in the chair opposite him. "Nicely played. When did you get this smart?"

"I've always been this smart. I learned from my super smart, very pretty mama."

"You're on a roll this morning." I laugh, feeling scarily impressed. "Okay, truth. I was going to speak to you today, but I guess now is as good a time as any. Yes, I was with Leandro last night, and I'm sorry I lied and said I wasn't."

"I freaking knew it! So, is he your boyfriend? How long has this been going on? Does this mean I can go to the Prix whenever I want?"

"Whoa. Slow down there." I lift a hand, halting his rapid-fire questions. "First, let me apologize. I went to Leandro's to talk last night. And after talking, I was tired, and I fell asleep. I'm sorry I stayed out all night because I shouldn't have." I had to white lie a little then because there is no way I am telling my twelve-year-old son that Leandro and I had sex, and that's why I fell asleep. Hell will freeze over first before that happens.

"Uncle Kit was here, it's no big deal. It's not like I was alone."

"I know, and you never would be. But it's not something I do, staying out. And in the future, if I plan on staying out all night, you will know beforehand. Okay?"

"Okay." He digs his spoon into his cereal, puts it in his mouth, and starts crunching.

"And to answer your other question, yes, Leandro and I are together."

"Awesome! So, can I get more tickets to the Prix?"

Smiling, I shake my head. Got to love my kid's priorities, and tenacity.

"Depending on where, because we're talking about overseas here, but I'm sure Leandro would get you tickets to go, so long as it's not in school time and I can afford the time off work to take you. He has actually invited us to Hungary." I hear the words leaving my mouth before I properly think them through. Even though this would be an amazing trip, I was going to hang off on telling Jett for a little while.

"You being serious?"

"Hmm." I press my lips together, hating my big mouth.

"Oh my God, this is awesome! It's going to be amazing! Do you think he will let us watch from the garage?"

"Um, I don't know. Maybe."

"I'm sure he will. Oh my god, it's gonna be fantastic! Freaking Hungary! I cannot wait to tell my friends!"

"Okay, well, let's not get too excited."

"Why wouldn't I?" His brow furrows in confusion.

"I don't know." I shrug helplessly. So, I opt for a subject change. "Anyway, why are you up so early?"

A sly grin appears on his face. "I wanted to catch you coming in."

My jaw drops open. "You knew I was out last night?"

"Of course I knew. I heard you and Uncle Kit talking in here last night. I have ears like a bat. And for future reference, I can pretty much hear everything you and Uncle Kit talk about in this kitchen." He points his finger up to the ceiling. "Your voices carry straight up to my room."

"Oh God," I groan. Putting my arms on the table, I drop my head into them, thinking of the conversations I've had with Kit recently.

I hear Jett laugh, and then get up from the table. A few seconds later, he pats my shoulder with his hand. I lift my head to look up at him.

"I'm glad you're happy, Mum. And not that you're not pretty because, of course, you are, but seriously well done for scoring a Formula One driver. I couldn't be prouder. Overnight, you've just made me the most popular kid in school. All I need now is for Uncle Kit to bring home a Victoria's Secret model, and my life will be set. You want me to make you a coffee?"

"Um, who are you and what have you done with my baby boy?" I stare at him in shock.

"Your baby boy is almost a teenager."

"Ugh, don't I know it?" I grumble, dropping my head back down again. "And that's a yes to the coffee."

"I'll make you it now." He chuckles.

Twenty-five

LEANDRO

✢ LONDON, ENGLAND

"SO, WHERE ARE WE GOING?"

I just picked India up for our date, and we are on our way after some serious scrutiny from her brother, Kit, who seems like a good guy, and also some words from Jett—mainly that, even though he thinks I am awesome and I am rich and famous, if I hurt his mother in any way, he will kick my ass. He said he has never met anyone his mother has dated before, so him knowing about me is a big thing for her, and that must mean she likes me a lot. I assured him that I like his mother a lot, too.

I am crazy about her.

I missed her like crazy when she left my place this morning. Afterward, I went back up to bed. All I could smell on my sheets and pillows was her. It just made me wish even more that she were still there, so I could bury myself deep inside her again.

I have never felt so lost yet so completely fucking found than I do when I'm inside her.

Being with India is where I was always meant to be. Inside her and beside her.

I always used to wonder what being in love meant, what it would feel like. Now, I know.

"I thought you would want low-key, and I want privacy with you. So, I'm taking you to dinner at my restaurant."

"You have a restaurant?"

I note the surprise in her voice.

"Mmhmm. I bought it a few years ago. It was my favorite place to eat. They do the best Brazilian food in London. The place was going to close due to some financial difficulties. I really like the owner, and I didn't want to lose my favorite place to eat, so I bought it. I invested some money in renovating it and then advertising. Now, it's doing really well. Victor still runs it for me, and I mostly keep out of the business side of things."

"You're a sweetheart."

I give her a look. "Leandro Silva, a sweetheart? No fucking way. Business savvy. Best racing driver ever. Hot as fuck, definitely."

She laughs, and the sound pulls at my heart.

I reach over and take hold of her hand. I press a kiss to her soft skin. She curls her fingers around my hand, and I hold it resting on my thigh.

"Have you tried Brazilian food before?"

"No. Will I like it?"

"You like meat?"

She grins, biting her bottom lip, and I know exactly what she is thinking. I love the dirty in her mind. She looks so classy and wholesome on the outside, but underneath all that, she likes it rough and dirty.

"Will there be sausage?"

I let out a dark chuckle. "No, but I can provide the sausage later—when we get back to my place."

"Definitely." She runs her tongue along her lower lip, and my cock nearly explodes.

"So, maybe while we're at the restaurant, you can teach me about those Brazilian phrases you say when I have that sausage in my mouth."

Holy fuck.

"You are so fucking sexy." I let go of her hand and glide my fingers up her bare arm. When I reach her shoulder, I push my fingers into her hair, tiling her face my way. "After dinner, I am taking you straight back to my place, getting you naked, and fucking you into next week."

"I can't wait." Her offered smile is sexy as hell.

It's not long before I am pulling up to my restaurant. It took all my strength not to spin the car around and take her straight to my place. But I want to give her a proper date. I don't want her to think that I am just all about fucking her even though that is all I think about when I'm with her and not with her. But I want more from her. I want it all, and I want her to know that, too.

"Eduardo's," she reads the restaurant sign.

"My father. I renamed the restaurant after him."

Turning off the engine, I climb out of the car and move fast around it to open her door.

I take her hand as she gets out. "Thank you. I can't remember the last time a man opened a car door for me. Actually, I think it was…never." She giggles.

"Well, get used to it because you're with me now. I am always going to open your doors."

Leaning in, I press a gentle kiss on her lips, loving the soft moan she makes.

As I move back, she rubs her thumb over my lips. "Lipstick."

"Have I told you how much I love your red lips?"

"You told me quite a few times last night." A spark of mischief enters her eyes, and it has my cock sitting up and paying attention,

"You know, I could have met you here. Save you driving out to my place and then back on yourself." She's referring to the fact that we're in Mayfair, a few minutes from my house.

"No way would I ever have you meet me out. We are on a date, and I pick my girl up for our dates."

"I like it when you call me that."

"My girl?" I stop at the door.

"Mmhmm."

"Well, you are."

The smile she gives me leaves me feeling a little breathless.

I open the door, letting India through first. The smell of this place always reminds me of home.

"Mr. Silva, good evening. I have your table ready for you."

"Thank you, Miguel."

I follow Miguel to the table I requested, which is a booth in the back. The restaurant is busy tonight, but the positioning of this booth gives us total privacy. Just what I want with India.

India slides into the booth. Instead of sitting opposite her, I take the seat next to her. I plan on having my hands on her a lot this evening.

When we're seated, we order our drinks, and Miguel leaves us with the menus. I don't need to open mine. I know everything on this menu.

India removes her jacket, and I am greeted with an amazing view of her cleavage from the plunging neckline of her dress. My cock starts to harden. She opens her menu, leaning forward to read it, and I can see straight down her dress.

"What's best to eat here?" she asks without looking at me.

"Everything. But I'm only hungry for one thing right now—you."

Her eyes lift to mine.

"You look seriously hot in that dress."

"I'm glad you like it."

"I more than like it."

She bites her lip, and my cock jerks. Her lip biting really does it for me.

"Are you ready to order?" Miguel appears back at the table with our drinks.

I have to contain my growl of annoyance at the interruption.

"Do you want me to order for us both?" I ask India.

"Sure."

I quickly place our order with Miguel, so he can fuck off and leave us alone.

"This place is amazing." She picks her wine up, taking a sip.

"Thank you."

"I can't believe you own a restaurant and that I didn't even know about it." Smiling, she shakes her head. "I thought I knew a lot about you, but I feel like there's still so much for me to learn."

"Ask me anything. I'll answer. You know that." I give her a look, referring to our sessions, where I wasn't exactly shy on divulging information.

"Any more businesses that I don't know about?"

"No. Just the one."

"How old were you when you started racing cars?"

I shrug. "Young. A teenager."

"First race you won?"

"Well, aside from the illegal street racing I used to do..." I see her eyes flash with danger. "A junior rally championship back home in Brazil when I was fourteen."

"So, you were a bad boy when you were younger?"

"I'm still bad now." I grin.

She rests her elbow on the table, chin in her hand. "I bet being the hot racing bad boy got you a lot of girls."

"I did all right." I give a lazy shrug.

"First serious girlfriend?"

"Larissa Garcia."

"How old were you when you lost your virginity?"

"Sixteen."

"With Larissa?"

"No. With Larissa's older sister, Marisa. She was eighteen."

"You're kidding?" She lets out a shocked-sounding laugh.

"No. It was why Larissa and I broke up. I was a bit of a shit when I was a kid." I chuckle, pulling a face.

"And as an adult." She raises a brow in reference to my conquests, which she knows all about from our therapy sessions. The only downside of dating my therapist.

My playful mood takes a quick nosedive.

"That's who I was. I am not that man anymore."

"I know," she says softly, her hand touching my face. "I'm sorry, I shouldn't have said that."

I bring my eyes to hers. "No, you weren't wrong. I just want you to know, that guy before…he is in the past. You are my future."

The happiness that shines in her eyes makes my heart beat faster.

"You're my future, too." She leans in and kisses my lips. "I love you, Leandro." Her words whisper over my skin, heightening my need for her.

I take over the kiss, my hand in her hair, tilting her head back so that I can kiss her deeper. My other hand grips her hip, pulling her closer to me. She makes a mewling sound in the back of her throat, her fingers curling into the fabric of my shirt.

I break off from the kiss, breathing heavily, as I stare into her dilated eyes. "You want to know something else about me?"

She nods.

"I get off on making my beautiful girlfriend come in public places." I move my hand down to her thigh, and slip my fingers under the hem of her dress.

Her eyes widen, but she doesn't falter, doesn't look away from me.

"Could we be seen?" she whispers, sounding breathless.

"Only if someone comes over."

Excitement flares in her eyes. Then, her legs part in invitation. A shiver of pleasure ripples down my back, heading straight for my cock.

I angle my body toward her so that if someone does come over, all they'd see is my back. I slide my hand up the inside of her thigh. My fingers meet with silk panties that are damp already.

"You are wet for me," I whisper. Leaning in, I press my lips to her throat.

"Always."

I run the tip of my finger over her panties. She squirms against my hand. Wanting to feel her, I push the fabric aside and slip a finger inside her. She moans a little too loud, so I capture her mouth with mine.

"Hush. No sound, babe. I'm going to fuck you with my fingers and make you come all over my hand, and you can't make a sound."

My eyes stare into hers as she whispers, "I'll be quiet. Please make me come. I need this...*you*."

On a growl, I start fucking her with my fingers, rubbing my thumb over her clit, loving the way she clamps around me so greedily.

I am so fucking turned on. I am either going to come in my pants or bend her over this table and fuck the hell out of her with everyone watching.

"Oh God..." she whispers, trembling against me. "I'm so close."

"That's it, India. Come for me. Show me what I do to you."

Her eyes stare deep into mine, and I feel her orgasm erupt through her as she tightens around my fingers. Total bliss covers her face as her body shudders with her release. When she's done, she falls against me.

I slip my fingers out, putting her panties back in place. "You okay?"

"I'm better than okay." She lifts her head, eyes on me. "That was amazing."

Her face is flushed from the orgasm, her lips swollen from my kiss.

"It was definitely something." God, I need to be inside her so fucking bad. I don't know if I can make it through this dinner.

"I can't believe we just did that." She gives me a shy look.

I find it amusing, considering that, a minute ago, she had my fingers inside her while she came around them, and now she's embarrassed.

"Believe it, babe, because we will be doing that often. I intend on making you come everywhere I can."

I put the fingers that were just inside her in my mouth and suck her from me.

Desire reignites in her eyes. "How long will dinner take?"

"Why?"

"Because I want to get back to your place as soon as possible, so I can return the favor." Her eyes flicker in the direction of my cock, which is straining against my zipper.

I thought she would never fucking ask. "We can get the food to go?"

Her eyes come back to mine, an undeniable heat in them. "Let's do it."

twenty-six

INDIA

✣ LONDON, ENGLAND

"SO MUCH FOR DINNER." I laugh lightly as we walk through Leandro's front door, the food containers in my hand.

"Hey, don't blame me. You were the one who suggested it."

"I know. I'm not complaining." I sashay in front of him moving down the hall, heading for the kitchen. "Just wondering if we'll make it through a date before checking out early and coming back here to have sex."

"We're going to have sex?"

I turn to see him standing in the doorway. A smirk on his sexy face.

Turning away, I put the containers on the breakfast island. "We could just eat if you'd like?"

"Fuck, no." His chest hits my back, pinning my front to the island. He brushes my hair aside and presses his lips to my neck. "I have been desperate to be back inside you ever since you left this morning." He skims his fingers up the outside of my thigh, lifting my dress. "Let's get rid of these."

His lips brush over my ear, making me shudder, as his fingers curl into the elastic of my knickers. He tugs them down.

Letting them fall down my legs, I step out of them before kicking them aside.

He hitches my dress over my waist. "You have an amazing ass, India."

I glance down at him as he lowers to his knees. He presses a kiss to my bottom, skimming his teeth over my skin, making me shudder. Then, he slides a finger through my folds, and I whimper an unintelligible sound.

"Chest flat to the countertop and spread your legs, India."

Without hesitation, I do as he asked. I know my quick compliance turns him on.

His hands palm my bum cheeks, spreading them. I feel his breath blow over me, and then his hot tongue touches my clit, making my knees nearly give out on me.

"Leandro!" I cry out, gripping the far edge of the counter with my fingertips.

He doesn't let up. He pushes his tongue inside me, fucking me with it, and then slides it back to my clit, swirling it around.

Then, he's leaving me. He gets to his feet. Arm around my waist, he straightens me up and turns me to face him. "I want you naked. Now."

He drags my dress over my head. My bra is next to go. I'm naked, except for my heels, while he's still fully clothed.

He lifts me, setting me on the island. His body against mine, the cotton of his shirt brushes my hard nipples and the roughness of his trousers rubs against my clit, arousing me further, as he leads me into the wettest, hottest kiss I have ever had.

Then, he suddenly breaks the kiss, leaving me panting.

"Don't move." He walks over to his refrigerator, taking off his cuff links. He tosses them on the counter and removes his shirt, giving me the sight of his gorgeous body.

Holy fuck he's stunning.

I can't believe how lucky I got with Leandro. He could have any woman he wants, yet, for some reason he wants me.

I watch as he opens the door to the freezer and pulls out a tray of ice cubes. I tilt my head with interest. He brings the tray back with him. Then, he turns it over and empties the contents on the countertop beside me.

Some of the ice cubes slide toward me, touching my thigh, chilling me.

Picking up a single ice cube, Leandro brings it to my breast and runs it over my nipple, making me shiver.

Removing it from me, he leans down and closes his mouth around the same nipple, and sucks hard. *Holy fuck that feels good.* The contrast of cold and hot sends desire lancing through me.

His mouth leaves my breast, and he places the ice cube back on my body, taking it on a journey between my breasts and down my stomach, his tongue following the trails of water south.

When he reaches my hipbone, he straightens and tosses the used ice cube on the counter. He picks up a fresh one.

Dark eyes on mine, he places it in his mouth, holding it between his lips, and then he drops to his knees, pushes my thighs apart, and puts his mouth on me.

"Oh my god!" I scream out.

The cold against my heated swollen clit is like nothing I have ever felt before.

I just need…more of him. More of this.

"You like that, baby?"

"God, yes. Don't stop." I grab his hair, trying to bring his mouth back to where I need it.

His chuckle is dark and erotic. I hear the crack of the ice cube in his mouth as he bites it. Then, his mouth is back on me, and he slides the pad of his tongue, which is covered in ice, up my clit.

My eyes roll back in my head. "Holy fuck." My arms give out their support, and I fall back on the counter while Leandro continues to toy with my clit. He slides a finger inside me, and starts to fuck me with it, as he continues his merciless ice play on my clit. Then, I feel him wetting another finger on my pussy, and that one moves to my bum hole, and begins teasing it.

"Yes," I breathe out, letting him know I want him there.

I have never let anyone touch me there before Leandro. I can't believe how much I like him doing it. It just feels so darkly erotic and hot, and it makes me come like I never knew possible.

He groans against me, then, slips his finger inside my bum.

Fucking both my holes, he sucks my clit into his mouth, grazing his teeth over it, and I'm done for.

I go off like a rocket. Screaming my way through the most intense orgasm I have ever experienced, my body convulses, my muscles locking up tight.

I'm still coming down from the high when I hear his zipper being lowered.

I struggle up onto my elbows, looking at him, seeing an undisguised animalistic look of raw need on his face.

His need for me.

"Are you on the pill?" he asks me.

"Yes."

"I'm clean. My last checkup was right before the first time we had sex, and you know there has been no one since. I want to fuck you without a condom. I want to feel your tight pussy around me while I come inside you."

Jesus. I love how he talks so blatantly about sex.

"I want that, too."

His gaze softens on me momentarily, and then that hungry look flares back in his eyes. Hands curled around the backs of my thighs, he pulls me forward until my bum is on the edge of the island.

He takes his cock in his hand and rubs it up and down my center, teasing me.

"Leandro, please." I push against him, digging the heels of my shoes into his bum, trying to put him where I want him. I'm desperate to have him inside me.

In response, he takes hold of my legs. Sliding his hands to my feet, he removes both of my shoes, letting them drop to the floor.

He places my feet on counter edge. "Patience," he tells me, his voice so low it makes me shiver.

"I want you inside me." I look him in the eyes. "I thought you wanted me, too?"

"You know I do." He presses the head of his cock against my entrance. "But I am the one in control here, India." His accent has gotten thicker, turning me on further.

"So, be in control, and just fuck me."

He lets out a dark laugh, throwing his head back. Then, his eyes are back on mine. Pinning me with his heated stare, he slams inside me, giving me what I want, and need.

"Yes!" I cry out at the feel of him, so big and thick, filling me.

"Fuck," he growls, stilling inside me. "You feel unbelievable, India. So tight and hot. Fucking amazing."

His hands slide up my stomach. He takes my breasts in his hands, his thumbs brushing over my nipples, sending a bolt of lust straight to my clit. I squirm against him, needing the friction.

Moving his hands from my breasts, his large hands cup my face. His thumbs press against my throat. "I want your eyes on me the whole time."

He pulls out of me and very slowly pushes back in.

Then, he leans over me, his chest pressed against mine, his cock nestled deep inside me. Without looking away from my eyes he kisses me. "I fucking love you," he says against my lips. "And I love fucking you."

"I love you. And I love being fucked by you, too, baby."

His eyes flash at my term of endearment.

Keeping hold of my face with one hand, his other presses to the counter beside me, and he fucks me there on his breakfast island until we're both hot and sweaty and coming hard.

twenty-seven

LEANDRO

BUDAPEST, HUNGARY

INDIA AND I HAVE BEEN OFFICIALLY TOGETHER for a few weeks, and it has been the best time of my life.

There hasn't been a day where I haven't seen her even if only to have lunch with her. I want to be sure not to take too much of her time away from Jett. But it is damn hard not being with her.

We have been out a few times with Jett to the cinema and bowling, and we went up to his karting track one day.

Honestly, the kid is awesome. He's totally stealing my heart.

I have never spent much time around kids before, but Jett is smart beyond his years. He absolutely adores his mother. And he races really well.

I am getting on great with Kit, too, which is good, as he and India are really close.

We are in Budapest for this leg of the season. Jett, Kit, and India are with me.

I have managed to keep India out of the press since we started dating, but now that she is here with me, it is impossible. I'm staring down at the news on my iPad, and there is a picture of India and me that was taken yesterday at a sponsor event. She is detailed as my mystery blonde. I stifle a laugh at the term. But India being a mystery to the press won't last long. When they realize she's staying here with me and that she has a son, they will look into exactly who she is.

"Is that us?"

I didn't hear her come up behind me.

I glance over my shoulder at her. She's wearing my T-shirt. Her hair is all tousled from sleep and from when my hands were wrapped up in it when I was pounding inside her from behind. She looks fucking beautiful.

And she's all mine.

"Yes. But they don't know who you are yet, so we have still got a little more time of privacy."

"It was bound to happen at some point, and at least they posted a nice picture of me." She takes the seat opposite me, resting her bare feet up on the chair between my legs.

I put the iPad down on the table. "Are there any bad pictures of you? Because I highly doubt it."

"Ones of when I was pregnant with Jett and I'd bloated to the size of a house."

"I bet you looked beautiful while you were pregnant."

"I really didn't." She laughs.

I slide my hand over the top of her foot, taking hold of it. She lets out a sigh of pleasure as I run the pad of my thumb along the arch in her heel.

"I'll show you some photos of pregnant me when we get home, and you'll soon change your mind."

She ends with a giggle, and I just shake my head in disagreement. I will never see India as anything less than beautiful.

"God that feels good," she comments on my foot rubbing skills.

"I am to please. And speaking of pleasing, I ordered breakfast for us." I nod at the food on the table. "Are Jett and Kit up yet? Do you think they'll want to eat with us?"

"Without a doubt, they're still sleeping. And I'm pretty sure Kit said he was going to order food for them both."

I originally had the two-bedroom suite booked for India, Jett, and me to stay in and a separate one-bedroom suite for Kit. But then Jett said he wanted to stay with Kit, so they've ended up in the two bedroom, and India and I have the one bedroom. I can't say I'm disappointed with the sleeping arrangements. It means I get unfettered access to India, and she can make as much noise as she wants while I fuck her.

"They are coming to watch testing today though, right?"

She rests her head back, smiling at me. "Like they'd miss it."

"Good."

"And what are we doing tonight?"

"I thought we could all go out for a quiet dinner. Then, I need to get an early night, rest up for qualifying."

"Sounds perfect." Sitting up, her foot slips from my hand.

I watch as she comes over and straddles my lap. My hands go to her hips.

"Does that early night involve me at all?"

"All of my early nights involve you. I drive better after I've fucked you."

"You haven't driven since we've had sex," she says.

"Yes, I have. Aside from practice for this upcoming race, I have driven in ten Prixs since we had sex the first time when I fucked you against the wall in your hallway, remember?"

Her cheeks flush red. "I remember."

I push away the painful thought of those ten races I spent without her.

I have her now. That is all that matters.

"And my wins and overall points have been higher than ever before." My hands slip under my T-shirt that she's wearing. Feeling her soft skin beneath my hands, my cock starts to harden in my boxers. "I would say fucking you is my new pre-race luck ritual."

"Hmm...is that so?" She raises a brow.

"Definitely. And I think I could do with some pre-race ritualizing right about now."

Standing with her, she starts giggling, wrapping her arms around my neck. I carry her through to the bedroom and deposit her on the bed, and then I spend the next hour showing just how much good luck she really does bring me.

twenty-eight

INDIA

BUDAPEST, HUNGARY

I'M IN LEANDRO'S TEAM GARAGE, standing between Kit and Jett, watching on the screen while Leandro fights to take first place in qualifying.

It's such a different atmosphere, being here in the garage than it was watching in the stands at Silverstone. The vibe is intense as his team is on edge, wanting him to achieve pole position.

"He's gonna do it, Mum!" Jett says excitedly from beside me.

I love hearing the happiness in his voice. He is totally in his element here. And Leandro has been amazing with him, including him and Kit in everything—showing them around, introducing them to all the drivers from the opposing teams. They also spent some time with Carrick over in Rybell's garage.

Dinner with Andi and Carrick was fabulous last night. They brought along a few friends with them. Andi's friend Petra works on Carrick's team, and Kit seemed pretty interested in talking to her for most of the night. I also met one of Carrick's mechanics, Ben, and Andi's Uncle John. Of course I've heard all about these people in Andi's sessions with me, so it was nice to put faces to the names.

Carrick and Andi have been really cool about Leandro and me being together even though they know I was his therapist. I did feel slightly anxious at the thought of spending time with them, worried what they would think about me, but Leandro assured me that they were really happy for the both of us.

Knowing that put me at ease a little, but I didn't feel truly relaxed until I spent time with them and realized they didn't care about how Leandro and I met at all. They genuinely seemed happy that we were together.

My phone vibrates in the back pocket of my jeans.

I wonder who that could be. The only people who ever call me are here with me. And all my patient calls are being handled by Amanda, the therapist I brought in to cover me while I'm here in Hungary.

I slide my phone from my back pocket.

The number I see is one I haven't seen in a long while. And I immediately get the worst sense of foreboding.

"I'm just going to take this call." I lift my vibrating phone up to Kit, who briefly glances at me in acknowledgment before looking back to the television screen.

I move quickly through the garage. Slipping out the door, I connect the call. "Russell?"

Russell is the defense attorney who tried the case against Paul, which put him in prison.

"India. Hi. I'm sorry to call on a weekend, but I only just got the call myself, and I thought you would want to know."

"What call?" My lips tremble slightly.

He sighs lightly. "Paul had a parole hearing yesterday. I didn't know. Apparently, the paperwork was sent to me, but I never received it. I'm so sorry, India, but it's been granted."

A ripple of fear runs down my spine. "He's out," I nearly choke on the words.

"Not yet. He'll be released this Tuesday."

A few days. My breath leaves me in a rush. I press my hand to my forehead, trying to calm my spinning thoughts. "But I thought I had a few more years before he got out."

"So did I. I really didn't think his parole would be granted. I thought he would serve his full term, especially after failed escape attempts in prison and…the letters he sent to you. The threats."

The memory of receiving them. Seeing those words. The hatred he spewed.

The feelings of hurt and betrayal and anger at him and myself attack me, leaving me winded.

"First thing on Monday, I'm putting in for an emergency restraining order for you and Jett," Russell tells me.

"You think he'll come looking for us? Is Jett at risk?" Panic seizes me, and I start to quickly think of ways for us to escape Paul. Leaving the country springs to mind.

He wasn't a violent man before he went to prison, but I saw in ink the hatred he feels for me, thinking I stole his life from him, and prison can change even the mildest of men.

The Paul leaving prison in a few days is a man I don't know.

"I don't think so. Paul is being released on electronic tag and curfew. He won't be allowed to leave the Manchester area. I can't see him risking going back to prison after trying for so long to be released that he would violate those conditions to come to London. And he doesn't know where you are. But still, it's better to have a restraining order in place than not."

I know how easy it is to find people, and my name isn't exactly a run-of-the-mill name. Maybe I should have changed it, so he could never find us.

Hindsight is a great thing.

"Okay."

"It's going to be okay, India. We always knew this day would come. It's just happening a little sooner than we expected."

"You're right. I know."

"Since Paul's parole has been granted, maybe he's a different man now. Maybe he's let the hatred toward you go."

"Do you believe that?"

"I want to, for your sake. I'm getting the parole documents sent over to me today, so I can see what terms allowed his release. I do think this is going to be okay."

"If there is anything in there—a desire on his part to meet Jett—"

"He knows he's not allowed to, but yes, if there's anything, I'll let you know immediately."

"Thank you."

"Does Kit still live with you?"

"Yes."

"And do you have a good security system on your house?"

"We have a standard alarm."

"Maybe it's time to upgrade."

"You're not making me feel better about this, Russell." I let out a humorless laugh.

"Sorry. Even though I believe you'll be fine, I'm just trying to offer ways to make you feel safer about this."

"I know, and I appreciate it." I blow out a breath, running my fingers through my hair.

I hear the roar of the engines, and it brings my thoughts to Leandro. Who he is. Where I am.

"I'm seeing someone," I tell Russell. "It's new, but he's in the public eye."

"Does being with him put you and Jett in the public eye?"

"It will. We've been photographed together already. Not Jett, but I'm sure it won't be long before they get my name and Jett's. Do you think that could be a problem?"

There's a pause while he thinks. His silence unnerves me.

"If Paul has truly changed, then no, it shouldn't be a problem. But it will tell him exactly where you are and how you're living your life. The media will give him unfettered access to you and Jett. My advice is to stay out of the press as much as possible upon Paul's release. And we'll see how things go from there."

"Thanks, Russell, for everything. And thank you for letting me know."

"No problem. I'll keep you updated as I know things…and I really am sorry, India."

"Yeah, me, too."

I hang up with Russell and lean back against the wall, pressing my head against the bricks. I can't believe he's getting out now. I always knew this day would come, but I thought I had a few more years, that Jett would be a bit older.

How the hell am I going to tell Jett that his father is free?

I cover my face with my hand. Sliding it up into my hair, I tug on it with frustration.

"There you are!" Jett's voice hits me.

I look up to see him standing in the doorway to the garage.

His happy expression drops, and he takes a step toward me, letting the door close behind him. "Mum, are you okay?"

I clear my face of all emotions and paste on a bright smile. "I'm fine."

"Who was that on the phone?" He nods at the phone, which my fingers are tightly gripped around.

"Just a patient." I slide my phone back into my pocket, trying to relax the tense muscles in my body.

I can see the skeptical look on his face. I can't tell him now. Not here. I need time to think this through. Figure it out.

"How's Leandro doing?" I nod toward the garage, going for a subject change.

A big smile spreads over his face. "He's starting first tomorrow."

A genuine smile briefly pushes up through my fake one. "That's great news."

"He's gonna win tomorrow, no doubt."

"He sure is."

"You coming back in? He'll be back in the garage soon."

"I'm coming now." I push off the wall, trying to shake off the fear weighing heavily on my shoulders.

twenty-nine

LEANDRO

✢ LONDON, ENGLAND

INDIA HAS BEEN DISTRACTED FOR DAYS. She was fine before qualifying, but since then, there has been a distance with her. She seems preoccupied.

Even when we make love, it's like a part of her isn't even there with me, and I don't like it. I really don't like it.

I was supposed to be heading straight to Italy with the team after leaving Budapest, but I changed my plans and flew back to London with India. I wasn't going to leave her while she was like this. I have only got a few days before I have to fly out to Italy, and I intend on finding out what the hell is going on with her before then.

We got home yesterday, and she went into work today. Didn't meet me for lunch. She made up some bullshit excuse about being too busy.

This is the first time I'm seeing her since we returned, and we are at her place right now. Jett is upstairs, Kit's out on a date, and India and I are watching a movie together, but once again, I might as well be sitting here alone.

Well, I have her here with me now, and I am going nowhere until she tells me what is going on with her.

"Are you going to tell me anytime soon? Or do I just have to start fucking guessing?" My words come out a little harsher than intended.

She slides her eyes to mine. There's a flare of anger in them. "Tell you what?"

I pick up the remote control and turn off the TV. "Tell me what it is that is bothering you."

Her expression clears. "Nothing is bothering me."

For fuck's sake!

"I won the Belgium Prix on Sunday."

She gives me a look of confusion. "I know. I was there."

"Physically, yes. Mentally, no. You checked out on me the day before. Jesus, India, your lack of enthusiasm at my win after the first race you have been to since we got together—so it was pretty fucking important to me to have you there to witness it—and all I got was a congratulations and a pat on the shoulder."

"Jesus, I'm sorry I didn't give the required amount of attention!" she bites. "What did you want me to do? Stick my tongue down your throat. Strip my clothes off and screw you right there and then? I'm sorry, but that would have been inappropriate—you know, with my kid and the rest of the racing population being there!"

"Are you yelling at me?" I say to her.

Seriously, there's something wrong with me because I get majorly turned on when she gets mad. Seeing her all fired up has my cock as hard as nails. Well, pretty much anything she does has my cock hard, but her anger is a definite aphrodisiac to me.

"Bloody well sounds like it, doesn't it?" Her brow is all puckered into a frown.

She looks hot as fuck.

"I really want to fuck you right now," I tell her in all seriousness.

Her eyes swing my way, wide and blazing. "Are you being serious?"

"I never kid about fucking you."

"Jesus! You're really pissing me off," she huffs.

She makes to get up from the sofa, but I catch her arm, stopping her, and I pull her onto me. She makes a sound of protest but doesn't actually try to get up.

"And you're really turning me on," I say to her.

Pausing she stares down at me. "I'm really mad at you right now, Leandro," she grumbles, her voice less angry than before.

"Yes, well, I'm kind of mad at you, too, India. But I'm still hot as fuck for you." I slide my hands to her ass giving it a squeeze.

She narrows her eyes at me. "We're not having sex."

"Not right now we aren't, but as soon as Jett is asleep, I'm tying you to your bed and fucking the hell out of you."

She shudders beneath my touch. I love that she can't resist me, just like I can't resist her.

"And if I have to torture the truth out of you by delaying your orgasm, then I will. But I would much rather you tell me what it is that's bothering you, so we can fix it, and I can spend my time in bed giving you multiple orgasms."

Her head drops to my shoulder, and she lets out a sad sounding sigh. It sets me on edge.

"Talk to me, babe."

She lifts her eyes to mine. I see fear move through them, and then her eyes fill with tears.

I sit up straighter, taking her face in my hands. "Jesus, India, you're really starting to scare me."

Her eyes flick in the direction of the closed living room door and then back to me. She exhales, then, begins talking in a quiet voice, "Paul, Jett's father, was released from prison today. While you were on the track on Saturday, I got a call on Saturday from Russell, the defense attorney who tried the case against Paul. The case I was a key witness for. The reason he went to prison."

"You are not the reason that motherfucker went to prison. *He* is the reason."

"Paul blamed me for him going to prison."

"India, he went to prison because he's a pedophile. He was having sex with teenage girls. He got you pregnant while you were still a teenager, for fuck's sake."

She cringes. Distress crosses her features, and a tear runs from her eye. It makes me feel like callous bastard.

I catch her falling tear, wiping it away with my thumb. "I'm sorry, babe. I shouldn't have said that."

"No, you're right. Just hearing it makes me feel like a victim."

"You were a victim, but now you're a survivor." I curl her hair around my hand. "You are a fucking miracle. You're the strongest person I have ever known, India. Where you came from to where you are now…most people would have given up, but you didn't. You fought hard to give your son the best life possible. You should be proud of yourself."

A soft look enters her eyes. "I kind of love you, you know." She runs her fingers into my hair.

"I kind of love you, too. A whole lot." I lean close and press my lips to hers.

Moving away, I lean my head back against the sofa. "Paul getting out of prison—what does this mean for us?"

I see her smile when I say *us*. Then, she shrugs. "He'll be living in Manchester, where he's from. He'll be on electronic tag and curfew, so he won't be able to come here even if he wanted to. But Russell has had a restraining order put in place for Jett and me."

"Has Paul ever threatened you?"

Her eyes lower. "Yes. A long time ago. Right after he went to prison, he sent me threatening letters."

Pure undiluted rage burns through me. That fucker goes anywhere near India and Jett and I will kill him myself.

"I'm getting security for you and Jett for when I'm not here." I hate that I have to leave soon, knowing that bastard is out there free to do as he pleases.

"What? No, it's not necessary." She shakes her head. "I don't think he'll bother us. I haven't heard from him since the letters. And he's been trying for parole for a long time, and now that he's out, I'm sure he won't want to jeopardize it."

"Has Paul ever asked to see Jett?"

"No. I think he attributes Jett to him going to prison. I'm pretty sure he thinks if I had never got pregnant, then he would never have been found out."

Anger and frustration and worry for her and Jett are pulsing through my veins.

"Please, just let me put some security guys on you to keep you safe."

"It's not necessary, Leandro." She presses her hand to my cheek. "I'll be fine. But okay, for Jett, yes, that would be a good idea. Just to be safe."

"I fucking hate that I have to go to Belgium." I sigh. "I really don't want to leave you. Why don't you and Jett come with me?"

"We can't. I have to get back to work. I have patients depending on me. I've already taken time off. I can't take any more." She blows out a breath, looking a little lost.

"I won't go to Belgium, then."

She looks at me, aghast, dropping her hand from my face. "No," she states emphatically. "You have to go. You're contracted, and this is important to you. It's your first season back since the accident."

I cup her face in my hands. "*You* are more important to me."

"I'll be fine." Leaning close, she presses a kiss to my forehead. "Kit's here." Then, a kiss to the tip of my nose. "Please, don't worry."

I hate feeling trapped and conflicted. I really don't want to leave her while that fucking bastard is out on the streets, but I am contractually obligated to go to Belgium. I just wish she would come with me.

I start to speak, but she cuts me off with her lips, kissing me passionately.

I know her game, but I'm helpless to the feel of her delicate tongue in my mouth, her tight body against mine.

"This isn't over," I murmur under her lips, my hands reaching for her ass.

"I don't doubt it," she whispers. Then, she deepens the kiss, grinding herself against my erection.

I can work on her later, talk her into coming with me.

Because there is no way I feel comfortable with leaving her here without me.

And if she won't come, then I will, without a doubt, have security detail assigned to her and Jett, until I can get back to them. Then, I will figure out what the fuck I am going to do for the rest of the races because I'm sure as hell not leaving her for extended periods of time while her jailbird of an ex is on the loose.

thirty

INDIA

✚ LONDON, ENGLAND

"HE'S DRIVING ME NUTS!" I hiss down the phone at Leandro. "He's everywhere I go. I can't even pee in peace without him standing outside the door. I feel like I'm back to the days when Jett was a toddler, and he used to follow me everywhere—bathroom included!"

Leandro laughs that deep rich laugh of his.

"It's not funny!" I bite.

"I know, babe, but Andre is only doing his job."

"A job that I don't want him to be doing. I told you that getting a security guy for Jett was a great idea, but I don't need one." I point a finger at myself as if he could see me. "And I have patients coming in while he's sitting out in the waiting room, and he's scaring the life out of them. He's bad for my business. I work on privacy here, Leandro."

"Okay, I'll tell him to sit outside your building in his car. Would that be better?"

"Much. Thank you. I do appreciate you looking out for me," I add so not to sound like an ungrateful bitch, even though I didn't want the security for myself. "It's just weird, having him shadowing me."

"I just want you to be safe, India. You and Jett both."

Jett doesn't know that Paul is out of prison. I thought long and hard whether to tell him or not, and both Leandro and Kit agreed with me that the best thing would be to keep it from Jett for now. I don't want to disrupt his life unnecessarily at the moment. He thinks we have the security because of Leandro's fame. Honestly, he loves having a bodyguard. I think he thinks he's a celebrity now.

"We're fine. It's been over a week since Paul got out of prison, and he's made no attempt to contact me."

"Well, I am not taking any chances, so Andre and his team stay put until I get back."

"How's it going there?" I ask, changing the subject.

"Good. The car is performing well, so it's just going to be down to me."

"You'll do amazing like you always do, and we'll be watching all weekend, cheering you on."

"I really wish you were here." His voice lowers. "I miss you so fucking much. I hate being away from you."

"Me, too."

"When I get back, we're spending a full day in bed."

I feel a tingling between my thighs. I went years with minimal amounts of sex, but since being with Leandro, I've gotten used to having it every day, multiple times, and now, my body is struggling to go without him. "Sounds awesome."

"It will be. I'm going to strip you naked, and kiss and lick every inch of your hot body. Lavish my full attention on every single part of you. Then, when I'm done worshipping you, I'm going to sit you on my face and have you come all over my tongue. And when I'm done licking up all your juices, I'm going to fuck your mouth with my cock, then, I'm going to fuck your gorgeous tits, right before bending you over and taking you from behind while I fuck your ass with my fingers."

"Jesus, Leandro." I shudder.

"Are you wet for me, India?" His voice has gone dark and sultry.

"Yes," I breathe.

"I'm hard, babe. So fucking hard. Touch yourself for me."

I'm just reaching my hand down when the buzzer in my office goes off, telling me I have a patient.

I let out a groan. "Shit. I have a patient. Can we put this on ice until later?"

"Sure. But I might have to go jack off in my room before I go back to the garage. Otherwise, I'm going to be sporting a boner all day."

"Sorry." I giggle.

"You will be when I see you next," he growls.

"I love you."

"Love you, too."

"Speak to you tonight?"

"I'll call you when I'm done at the track."

Reluctantly, I hang up and dial through to Sophie to let her know to let my next patient in.

My working day is done. I lock up my office and head down to the car where Andre is waiting to drive me home.

As I exit the building, I have the strangest sensation ripple down my spine.

Like I'm being watched.

I've been feeling it these past few days, but I'm putting it down to anxiety. The fact that Paul hasn't made any form of contact has actually left me unnerved and a tad paranoid.

As I approach the car, Andre already has the door open and waiting for me.

"Thank you." I smile at him.

For all that his presence annoys me in a way, he is a really nice man.

He rounds the car and gets in, shifting the car with his large frame.

"Good day?" he asks as he starts the engine.

"Long. I'm ready to get home and relax."

"Jonah will be taking over from me in half an hour, so you'll see his car sitting outside," Andre tells me as he walks me to my door. "Usual protocol. Anything suspicious, press the panic alarm."

"I'll be fine," I assure him.

The security guys rotate on shift. Leandro wanted Jett and me to have twenty-four-hour security.

I unlock my door, and I'm surprised when the alarm beeps at me. "That's strange. The alarm is on."

"Did Jett not tell you that Kit took him to the karting track? Simon is with them. He'll drop them off when they're done, and Jonas will cover you both until morning when I take back over with you, and Simon with Jett."

"No, he didn't tell me."

Clearly, my security guy knows more about my son's movements than I do.

"Thanks, Andre."

I close the door and kick off my heels. As I wander into the kitchen to pour a glass of wine, I see a note tacked to the fridge from Jett and Kit.

GONE TO THE TRACK. WE'LL BRING PIZZA HOME.

LOVE, J & K

I pour myself a glass of wine, grab my phone, and go upstairs to take a bath.

The book lying in the center of my bed stops me in my tracks.

Red Dragon.

It was the book that Paul gave me. It was his favorite book. He had highlighted his favorite passages in it.

For some reason, I kept it for all these years. I guess maybe a part of me—the part that wanted to believe he wasn't all bad, remember the times he'd been good to me—held on to that book. Now, it's here, lying on my bed.

I never kept it on the bookshelf in the living room as I didn't want Jett to ever find and question it.

It was in the box in my wardrobe with all the newspaper articles from the trial.

My hand trembles as I put my wine down on my bedside table.

Why would this be here?

Did Jett maybe find it and begin reading it?

I go to my wardrobe and pull out the box it was in. Laying it on the bed, I open it. Aside from the book being out, everything else is still there, as I left it.

I stare at the book.

Could this have been…

No. I would have known if Paul were here in London. His tag would have alerted the police to him leaving Manchester. Russell would have called me.

It can't be him.

It must have been Jett or maybe Kit. Maybe Kit was looking for something and just left it there by mistake.

But, Kit doesn't know I kept Paul's book.

I pick up my wine and take a fortifying sip, then, put it back down.

Using my phone, I dial Kit's number.

"Hey," he greets me.

"Hey. How's karting?"

"Good. Jett's kicking ass out there at the moment. Did you get our note?"

"I did."

"We won't be much longer, and then we'll be heading home. What do you want on your pizza?"

"The usual, chicken and ham...Kit, were you in my room earlier?"

"No. Why?"

"It's nothing. There was just a book on my bed, and I'm fairly certain I didn't leave it there."

"Maybe it was Jett?"

"Yeah...maybe."

"Indy...are you okay?"

"Yeah, I'm fine. Just a long day, is all."

"Okay, well, we'll be home soon."

I hang up with Kit and stare at the book still sitting there, mocking me.

Reaching over, I pick it up. My hand is trembling again.

I look down at it, tracing my finger over the cover. Then, I drop it back in the box and put the lid on. Getting to my feet, I put the box back in my wardrobe, and close the door on it, and my past.

thirty-one

LEANDRO

■ STAVELOT, BELGIUM

"I'M CONSIDERING RETIRING NEXT YEAR. Making this my last season."

"I'm sorry, what?" Carrick shakes his head as he sits forward in his seat. "I'm not sure I heard you correctly. Did you just say you're considering retiring?"

"I am more than considering. And please keep your voice down. Ears." I gesture at the people around us.

We're in the hotel bar. Carrick is bored because Andi has gone for a night out with Petra, so I'm his date for the night. I would really rather not be here. A couple of women are at the bar, and one of them has been eye-fucking me since I arrived ten minutes ago. Brunette with big tits. The type of woman I would have fucked without a second thought—before India.

Now, I have no interest in other women. I only see India.

"You're the first person I am talking to about this, so keep it to yourself—meaning tell no one, including Andi—because nothing is definite yet."

"You haven't talked to India about this?"

"No." I shake my head.

"Well, while I'm honored I'm the first you're telling, can I ask, why the fuck are you considering it?"

"Because…" I shrug.

"Oh, well, that explains it." He throws a hand up, letting it fall back to his lap. "You just got your career back, and now, you're *considering* throwing it away."

"I'm not throwing it away." I frown at him. "I am thirty-one years old. This is the last year on my contract. Sure, it's up for renewal, but I am not sure I want that. I have been behind the wheel of a car since I can remember. I nearly lost my life for the fucking love of it. But things are different now. I'm different. I thought coming back would be everything, but it's not. Of course, I still love racing. Just not in the same way. And now I have found something I love more."

"India?"

"Mmhmm."

"But India's not asking you to quit, is she?" He raises a brow in question.

"No, she's not. She would never do that. But come on, Carrick, you know what this life is like. We're on the road nine months out of the year. I will hardly see her. I hardly see her as it is. And it's not like it is with you and Andi. She travels with you. India can't do that."

"So, hire India to work for you. You're clearly having another mental break, and you could do with a staged intervention from a professional."

I give him the middle finger. "Look, even if I did make up some imaginary job and somehow got India to give her career up to come and work for me—which I would never do because I'm not that much of a selfish bastard—she has Jett. He has school. She needs to be in London, and I need to be there with her."

Carrick slumps back in his chair and takes a sip of his beer. "You're really serious then?"

"Yes, I'm really serious." I start to pick at the label on my bottle.

"Just...don't make any rash decisions. Talk to India first, see what she thinks."

"I'll discuss it with her when I get back home."

"Good. God, it'll be weird without you around. It was strange last year when you weren't on the track, bugging the fuck out of me, getting in my way."

"Love you, too, Ryan." I smirk at him.

"Yeah, well, don't expect me to give you a pity win for this championship, so you can go out on a high."

"Ha! Like you need to. I'm kicking your ass, and you know it."

"Fuck you, Silva. I'm gonna kick your arse on Sunday. My car's performing like a dream. And I have the best mechanic on my side."

"Yes, you do." I have to agree with that. Andi is one of the best mechanics around. There was a time, just before my accident, when I was considering how to poach her from him.

"Don't worry though. If you do retire, I'll make sure you're remembered for being a great driver. Second to me of course."

Laughing at him, I take a sip of my beer.

"So, what will you do, if you do decide to go?" Carrick asks with genuine curiosity.

"I don't know." I rest my bottle on my thigh. "I'll have to do something though, or I will go out of my mind with boredom while India is at work."

"You could always take up drinking and whoring around like you did last year."

"You're a prick."

"I know." He smirks. "But, in all seriousness, you know my dad gave his job up when I was younger, so he could be there full-time for my career."

"And what does that have to do with me retiring?"

"Well, Jett is showing a real interest in karting, and the kid's really good. He's got real natural talent. You could help him hone it, get him racing, entering competitions, building his reputation. That'd keep your retired arse busy. I know my racing kept my dad busy. Still does. And at least you'd still be a part of the racing circuit, so I'd get to see your ugly face around."

"I suppose I could. But it would depend on that being what Jett wants."

"A racing-obsessed kid getting the chance for Leandro Silva to coach him. Yeah, I'm sure he'd turn it down." He chuckles.

I'm pondering Carrick's suggestion when a throat clears beside me. I turn my head, and my eyes meet with a huge pair of tits. I mean, they're literally in my face.

I tilt my head back to find the chick who's been eye-fucking me from the bar now standing over me.

"You're Leandro Silva, right?"

She sounds English. She must be here for the race. She clearly knows who I am. Surprised she hasn't clocked Carrick though.

"I am." I give her a congenial smile so not to come off as a bastard. I still have a public profile to keep up.

"Could I have my picture taken with you?"

"Sure." I hold back the sigh I feel. The last thing I want is to have my picture taken with a chick who is probably aiming to get in my pants.

"Bev!" she calls to her friend at the bar. "Come take the pic for me."

Her friend comes wobbling over on her high heels, clearly well on her way to being drunk. She gives me the eye as she takes the camera from Big Boobs next to me.

Big Boobs puts her arm around my waist, sliding in close to me. "My name's Andrea," she says, trying to sound sexy.

All it does is make me cringe. "Nice to meet you, Andrea." I give her a friendly smile. "Are you a racing fan?"

"No, my boyfriend is. He's a big fan. His company got him tickets for the race, so he and his best mate are watching. They brought me and Bev along with them for the weekend."

"Sounds nice." I look ahead, ready to have my picture taken so I can get back to my beer.

"Not really, but my weekend's been made, meeting you."

I flash her a smile, and then my eyes look forward again. Her friend is taking for-fucking-ever to take the picture.

"So, my boyfriend is out at dinner, schmoozing some clients for his company while he's here." She leans in, whispering in my ear, "Meaning my hotel room is empty for the next few hours. You wanna come up and fuck? I give amazing blow jobs, and I really want to suck your cock. I bet it's massive." Her hand grabs my cock through my jeans.

"What the fuck?" I grab her hand to remove it from my junk and spin my face to her.

I don't get a chance to say anything else. The next thing I know, she's landing a kiss on me.

I jerk my head back, pushing away from her. "Jesus! What the fuck is wrong with you? Seriously, not happening." I lift my hands, backing away from her. "I have a girlfriend."

"So?" She shrugs. "I won't tell her if you don't."

"Did you not hear me the first time? *Not fucking happening.*"

"Your loss." She shrugs. "What about your friend?" She looks at Carrick. "I wasn't kidding about my blow-job skills. I'm amazing."

Carrick sputters out a laugh. Lifting his hand, he says, "I'm sure you are, and I'd tell you I'm married—happily—but clearly, that wouldn't matter to you. So, I'll tell you, you're definitely not my type. No, thanks, and we'll leave it at that."

"Andrea, I got some really good pics!" Her friend beams at her, handing her the phone back.

My eyes flash to it.

Oh no. "Did you take a picture of her kissing me?"

"Um, yeah, of course I did." The friend gives me a dumb look.

"It's a good one, too." Andrea turns the screen to me, showing me the picture.

Jesus Christ. It couldn't look more incriminating than if she were straddling me. Her hand is on my junk, her mouth on mine.

For fuck's sake.

"You need to delete that picture. Now."

Hearing the pissed off tone in my voice, Carrick gets up from his seat, coming to stand beside me.

"No way am I deleting it!" Andrea laughs. "This one is going in my personal spank bank, and I'm putting it up on Facebook. The amount of likes I'll get with this will be awesome. I'll be a fucking celeb among my mates."

"Are you for fucking real?" I move toward her, but Carrick catches my arm, pulling me back. "I have a fucking girlfriend. And you have a boyfriend!"

"He won't care." She shrugs the words off. "If he even notices, then he'll be impressed that I managed to get a kiss from you. You're his hero. He loves watching you race. You're the reason we're here."

This woman is crazy. "You're insane. You and your fucking boyfriend. Now, delete the fucking picture."

"No." She lifts her chin in a defiant manner before putting her phone in her clutch.

I grind my teeth in frustration. "I'm not asking you. I'm telling you. Delete that fucking picture."

She lets out a laugh. "You can't make me. Actually…" She taps her finger to her lips. "A pic like this and you having a girlfriend. I bet I could make a mint, selling it to a tabloid."

I actually growl.

"Let her sell it," Carrick says from beside me. "All that matters is India knows the truth. Tell her what happened, so she expects to see it. I was here. I can vouch for you."

Ignoring Carrick, I step toward Andrea, and she takes a step back.

"Delete the fucking picture," I repeat in a low, menacing voice.

"Fuck you." She turns on her heel and starts to walk away from me.

"You're a fucking bitch!" I yell to her back, losing my cool.

Stopping, she turns back, a smug smile spreading across her face. "You've just doubled the money I'll get with that comment." She wafts a hand at the people who are watching our exchange. "You're my witness, right, Bev?" She nudges her friend.

"Yeah." Bev lifts her chin. "I heard everything. How he tried to hit on you and then called you a bitch when you turned him down."

What the actual fuck?

I shouldn't be shocked, but I am. I guess I've gotten used to being around India and how much of a good person she is that I'd forgotten what fucking bastards people could be.

"And you"—I point a finger at Bev—"you're a fucking cunt. Use that to quadruple your money, you pair of soulless bitches!"

Andrea gives me the middle finger, and then they're both walking away.

"Nicely played." Carrick's hand lands square on my shoulder. "I thought you handled that really well. I specifically love the soulless bitches line."

"Fuck off," I grunt, shrugging off his hand.

He laughs, loudly. "It's a good thing you are retiring. Keep this kind of shit up, and you wouldn't have a fucking career left. Come on, old man. Let's finish our beer, and then you can call India and tell her what happened."

thirty-two

INDIA

✛ LONDON, ENGLAND

I'M RELAXING IN MY BATH, sipping on my wine, Adam Levine telling me "It Was Always You." Well, not me specifically, but a girl can dream, right?

Then, my phone starts going crazy. When I say crazy, I mean, a quick succession of texts come through, and my phone starts ringing at the same time.

I reach a hand out of the tub, quickly drying it on the towel hanging on the rail by my head, and grab my phone off the floor.

I don't recognize the number, but it's a local area code, so I connect the call. "Hello?"

"Am I speaking with Dr. Harris?"

"You are. Who is this?"

"My name is Sally, and I'm an operator at Safer Security, your alarm provider. I'm calling to let you know that the alarm at your office has gone off. I've temporarily disabled it from my end, and the police have been notified and are on their way to check it out."

"You're kidding?" I sit up, the water sloshing all around me. "Was the office broken into?"

"I don't know the situation yet. But if you want to wait, I can call you back once the police have notified us."

"No." I stand up, stepping out of the bath. "You say the police are going now. I'll head there myself. Thank you for calling me."

"All part of the service, Dr. Harris. Please call me once the police have assessed the situation. I can have the alarm enabled at my end, and I would advise setting a new code."

"I will. Thanks." I hang up and grab a towel from the railing, wrapping it around myself.

I don't believe this.

I glance down at my phone, seeing the texts are from Leandro. Four of them.

> *Trying to call you, but for some reason, it's not connecting.*
>
> *Ring me when you get this text.*
>
> *P.S. I love you.*
>
> *A lot. XX*

That puts a temporary smile on my face, and then I remember that my office might have been broken into.

I'll text him back once I know what's going on at my office.

I quickly dress in jeans and a T-shirt, leaving my hair tied up, and I jog down the stairs.

I've just reached the bottom step when Kit and Jett come in through the front door, pizza boxes in hand.

"Hey, Mum. What's up?" Jett asks at my expression.

"I just got a call from the alarm company. My office alarm has been going off. I'm heading there now."

"You're kidding," Jett says.

"Wish I was." I sigh.

"Do you want me to come with you?" Kit asks.

"No, it's fine. The police will be there."

"The police?" Kit frowns.

"It's the alarm company's standard policy when the alarm goes off. You stay here with Jett."

"Well, take Jonah with you, just to be safe."

"No. I'd rather Jonah stay here and watch over Jett."

"I'm fine," Jett says.

"I'll watch over Jett." Kit gives me a pointed look. "You take Jonah."

"Okay," I concede, not having the energy to argue with Kit. I slip my feet into my ballet flats, pull on my coat, and put my phone in the pocket. "I'll see you both soon. Save me some pizza."

I let myself out into the cool night air and walk toward Jonah's car. He gets out at my approach.

"There's a problem at my office, the alarm is going off, so I need to head there now. Kit is staying here with Jett."

"Okay. I'll drive you."

On the drive to my office, I ponder calling Leandro, but I decide to wait until I know what's going on at my office.

I see the police car outside my building. Jonah parks up behind it. I get out, and Jonah follows me. I approach the female police officer who is standing by the car.

"I'm Dr. Harris. This is my office building," I tell her. "Safer Security called me about the alarm going off."

"I'm afraid your office has been broken into, Dr. Harris."

"Why would anyone break into my office? It's not like I have valuables. Only my iMac. Oh, shit! Has my iMac been stolen? It has all my patient details on there."

"I didn't see a computer when I was in your office, Dr. Harris. I'm afraid the place has been left in a bit of a mess. We've got someone coming now to fingerprint. But you can go in and look, see what's missing, so long as you don't touch anything."

"Okay, I'll do that now. I'm sorry. I didn't catch your name?"

"I'm Police Constable Fellows. My colleague PC Hunter is in your office."

I follow behind PC Fellows up to my office, Jonah close behind me. Who I'm assuming is PC Hunter, is in the reception of my office. It looks untouched, except for Sophie's iMac, which is missing.

"Hunter, this is Dr. Harris. This is her office. I've said that she can look around, see what's missing, so long as she doesn't touch anything."

"Of course," he says.

Stepping past PC Hunter, I walk through my office door, which I always lock after I leave for the day. By the looks of the smashed wood, it was kicked open. I gasp, upon entering my office. The whole place has been trashed—furniture upturned, my bookcase pulled over, papers and books everywhere.

My iMac is nowhere to be seen.

Fuck.

"Anything missing?"

I turn to the voice of PC Fellows, who is standing in the doorway.

"My receptionist's iMac from out there." I point behind her. "And my iMac in here." I let out a deep sigh. "It has all of my patients' details on it. They're confidential. The files are password-protected, but still…" I trail off, worried about my patients' details and treatment files being potentially read by someone else.

"I wouldn't worry. It'll surely be wiped and fenced pretty quickly. That's how these things usually work."

"I won't get it back?"

"I doubt it." She gives me a resigned look. "It's strange though. When we see smash-and-grabs like this, they don't usually take the time to trash the place. They just take what they can and go, especially when an alarm is going off. Probably a junkie, who was high."

I let out a shuddering breath. "I just can't believe this." I shake my head, disbelieving the mess around me. "I guess I had better call my insurance company."

"I am sorry, Dr. Harris."

I walk back out of my office with PC Fellows. Jonah is still in reception, waiting for me, PC Hunter is nowhere to be seen.

"I'll be right outside," PC Fellows tells me, exiting the room.

"Anything missing?" Jonah asks me.

"From what I can tell, just my iMac and my receptionist's. Oh, and my office has been trashed, too."

"Trashed?" He frowns.

"Yeah. Furniture upturned, books and papers everywhere. Looks like a tornado blew through the place."

His brows pull tight together. "I'm going to make a call, make sure Paul is still in Manchester."

"What? You don't think it could be him? The policewoman said she thought it was just a smash-and-grab."

"Since when do smash-and-grabbers spend time trashing the place? I'll call, make sure he's still there." He pulls his phone from his jacket pocket and makes the call. "It's Jonah. I need you to check an electronic tag for me. Paul Connelly. Manchester. Yeah. Call me back." He slips his phone back in his pocket. "We'll know in a few minutes if he's still there."

"Okay." I start to nervously twist my fingers.

It seems like forever before Jonah's phone rings.

"Yeah? He's still there." He meets my eye. "Good. Thanks." He hangs up the phone. "He's still in Manchester at home. This wasn't him."

"Thank God." I sigh in relief.

"I'm gonna call Andre, let him know what's happened. You might want to call Leandro. Andre will call him right after he speaks to me—he has to report everything to him—so you might want to beat Andre to it."

"I'll call him now."

Thirty-Three

LEANDRO

■ STAVELOT, BELGIUM

"I'M CATCHING THE FIRST FLIGHT BACK." I climb out of bed and grab my jeans off the chair, pulling them on.

"No, stay where you are." India's stern voice comes down the line.

"You've been fucking robbed, India. I'm coming home."

"My office was burgled. I wasn't in any danger. I was at home when it happened."

"Your office is broken into, and the fucking pedophile cunt who threatened you recently got out of prison. Coincidence? I don't think so. I am coming home. And it's nonnegotiable, India."

"It is a coincidence. Jonah had Paul's electronic tag checked. He's still in Manchester in his house. Leandro"—she drops the tone in her voice to softer—"you need to stay in Belgium. You have a race to do."

"I couldn't give a fuck about my race right now," I snap.

"You might not, but your team will. And the sponsors and all the fans who bought tickets to come watch the race—they all give a fuck. The burglary has nothing to do with Paul. The police think it was just a junkie looking for things to sell."

"Fuck!" I drag my hand through my hair, rubbing at my scalp, feeling helpless and frustrated, and hating it. "Who the hell robs a therapist? It's not like you have anything of value in your office."

"The police think he might have seen the sign on my door, seen the word *doctor*, and probably thought that I had prescription drugs on site."

"Fucking scum," I growl. Taking a pause, I breathe deep, trying to calm down. I pinch the bridge of my nose. "Are you okay?" I ask her.

"I'm fine, baby. Don't worry."

"I am going to worry because I'm here while you are there, and I feel fucking helpless. I hate that I'm not there with you, to help you."

"Just hearing your voice helps me. And I got your texts earlier. They came through at the same time as when the alarm company called, but I came straight to the office. I'm sorry I didn't get a chance to reply."

I cringe, remembering why I had text her. "Don't worry about that. Where are you right now? Are you okay to talk? There is something you need to know. The reason I text earlier…God, it's been a shit night all around."

"I'm sitting in Jonah's car. He's in my building, on the phone with Andre. What's wrong, Leandro?"

I can hear the worry in her voice loud and clear.

"It's nothing for you to worry about…and I am really sorry to land this on you when you are already dealing with the burglary, but I don't want to not tell you, and then the pictures appear in the news, and you see them."

"Pictures?" Her voice goes cold. "What pictures?"

I let out a sigh. "I was in the hotel bar with Carrick earlier, having a beer. A woman came over, asked to have her picture taken with me. So, I said yes because I have to do shit like that, and to cut a long story short—and this is going to sound bad, India, so hear me out first—this woman propositioned me while her friend took pictures of us, and…she grabbed my crotch. As I tried to get her hand off of me, I turned my face in her direction in shock, and she…kissed me." I wince at what I'm telling her. "Her friend caught the whole fucking debacle on camera…and I…kind of lost my temper. She was threatening to sell the photos to the press." I'm quick to add, "So, I might have called her a soulless bitch and her friend a fucking cunt."

When I finish, there's just absolute silence on the end of the phone. I close my eyes against it, worried about what's going through her mind.

"India…babe, are you still there?"

She exhales. "I'm here."

Relief. "Are you…okay?"

"Just processing."

"I am sorry."

"It's not your fault that some lunatic woman violated you. I'm actually pretty fucking angry. If a guy did that to a woman, he'd be arrested for assault."

A smile pushes up my lips. "I fucking love you, a real lot, India Harris."

"I love you a whole lot, too, Leandro Silva."

"When my season is over, I'm taking you and Jett on a long vacation where there are no junkie burglars or psycho crotch-grabbing women."

"Sounds like heaven."

"It will be, babe. I promise."

"I should go." She sighs. "I need to call my insurance company, and someone is coming to fingerprint my office. I have to wait until they're done, so I can call the alarm company, and they can reset the alarm. Not that there's much point as there's nothing left to steal."

"Leave it. Go home, and sort the alarm out in the morning. Like you said, there is nothing left to steal."

"Yeah…I might do that."

"I'll have to call Sophie first thing, let her know. We need to cancel my patients for Monday, as I can't see the office being in any sort of shape by then. I'll need to get some new furniture and computers. God, my head's hurting from just thinking about it. Ugh, tomorrow is going to suck monkey balls."

"Suck monkey balls?" I laugh.

"It's a saying…not a nice one. In fact I have no clue where I heard it from or why I even used it." She giggles, and the sound soothes me.

"I love that sound," I tell her. "You have the cutest laugh."

"And you have the sexiest voice. With your accent…" She trails off.

"Does my accent turn you on?" My cock sits up and pays attention.

"Maybe," she says coyly.

"Estou com saudades de você."

She moans softly. "Tell me what you said?"

"I said, I miss you."

"I miss you, too, so much. Say something else in Portuguese."

"Preciso muito te foder."

"What does that mean?" Her voice is breathy, making my cock harder.

I palm my dick through my jeans, really needing her touch though, not my own. "I said, I really need to fuck you."

She lets out a sexy giggle. "And I really need to be fucked by you."

I groan, squeezing my cock with my hand. "Ring me as soon as you get home. So, I can make you come with my voice."

"In Portuguese?" Her voice is gentle groan.

I close my eyes on the sound, imagining her here with me. "Anything you want, babe. I just need to hear you come."

"I love how you can fix any situation with sex."

"It's a gift."

"A gift that you're really good at. I'll call you as soon as I'm home in bed. I love you."

"Love you, too."

Disconnecting the call, I toss my phone on the bed and grab a bottle of water from my fridge, turning the sound back on the TV. There is no way I am sleeping right now. Not until I know she is home, safe.

And if I wasn't sure before about retiring, then I am now. I'm making this my last season, and after this year, I am never leaving India's side again.

Thirty-Four

INDIA

✛ LONDON, ENGLAND

My weekend officially sucked monkey balls, aside from Leandro winning the Prix in Belgium. I was worried he wouldn't, with the stress of everything, but that's been the only good thing to happen this weekend.

I spent all of Saturday morning canceling my Monday appointments while Sophie canceled my Tuesday appointments. I thought it best to give myself a good window to get the office back in shape.

Kit and Jett came to the office with me. Sophie met us there, and we all spent the rest of the Saturday sorting the office back up, putting it into some semblance of normality. We got to catch parts of Leandro's qualifying race on Jett's iPad, which he'd brought with him. That was good, as I'd have hated to completely miss it.

The office was dirty, covered in powder from the fingerprint guy. Honestly, it just felt unclean and violated. I wanted it scrubbed back to clean. So, I came back on Sunday and scrubbed the place until it was gleaming.

Afterward, I went to the local PC World and bought new iMacs for Sophie and for myself.

When I got home, I saw the pictures of Leandro and that woman in the news. Kit had gotten the local paper, and it was on the front page, the picture of him and her. At the bottom was a small picture of him and me that was taken in Hungary.

Of course, the press knows Leandro and I are together. They know my name, what I do for a living, and that I have a son, but they don't know anything more than that.

But this kind of story, claiming he's cheating on his girlfriend, is the kind of fodder the press lap up.

If I hadn't expected the picture, then I would have been devastated. The picture really does look convincing. I felt sick looking at it. I didn't even bother reading the story beneath the headline.

I trust Leandro, and I just hate that he's being exploited in this way.

The press was going for maximum impact, releasing the story on the morning of the Prix.

Leandro called me right before his race. I didn't say anything about the story or picture to him. I was assuming his team and manager would keep the story away from him until the race was over, so not to affect his concentration. I was right because he didn't mention it to me on the phone.

I was glad they hadn't because he won, and I know he might not have, had he seen that story first. It would have knocked his concentration.

He called not long after his race, and he was happy but pissed off, too. As soon as he'd finished the race, he was told about the story circulating, so he wouldn't be blindsided when he spoke to the press about his win.

And my phone hasn't stopped ringing since. Journalists want a quote from me. I gave them no comment by hanging up on them, and then I started ignoring all calls from numbers I didn't know.

Now, it's Monday morning, and Leandro will be home tonight. I can't wait. He just had some commitments he had to do this morning, some press interviews, and then he's flying home.

It feels like he's been away forever. Honestly, I don't know how I'm going to get used to him being away so much. It's a thousand times harder than I thought it would be.

My phone starts vibrating on the kitchen table with an unknown number. Sighing, I ignore it and get up from the table, pouring myself another coffee. As I sit back down, it starts vibrating again. I cancel the call and continue reading through some patient notes that I had managed to salvage from the mess in my office.

My phone starts vibrating again. Same number.

I cancel it again.

It rings back immediately.

Cancel.

Rings again.

It's almost becoming a game.

Getting angry with the incessant caller, annoyance takes over, and I answer the call, "Stop calling me. I'm not giving you a bloody quote, so just piss off, will you?"

I hear a deep chuckle come down the line. A chuckle followed by a voice...a voice that I recognize immediately.

"Still a firecracker I see."

A shudder runs down my spine. "P-Paul."

"It's been a long time, India. I've missed you."

I feel myself retreating back to the girl I used to be.

"W-why are you calling me? I have a restraining order. You aren't allowed to come near me."

"I'm not near you, India. I'm a few hundred miles away. It never stated that I couldn't call you."

"It did. You are not allowed to contact me in any way. No calls. Emails. Nothing."

He lets out another chuckle. "I must've overlooked that part."

"I'm ending this call now. And don't ever contact me again."

"Your office was broken into a few days ago, right? Terrible. You can't trust anyone nowadays."

My blood freezes cold. "H-how do you know that?"

"Because I was the one who broke in—well, not me, of course. I can't leave Manchester, thanks to that dastardly electronic tag. I had a friend help me out."

"I'm calling the police."

"Call them and tell them what? That you're in a relationship with a former patient."

I gasp. "I don't know what you're talking about."

"You know exactly what I'm talking about. Leandro Silva. He was your patient, and now, you're fucking him. Trust me, I of all people know that's not right, India. And Silva? You've really gone up in the world." He lets out a slow whistle.

"You have no clue what you're talking about."

"Sure I do. I have your laptop. It's all here, all the gory details on Silva's pathetic PTSD, your treatment for him. Funny though, I must have missed the part where it said part of your treatment was to fuck him better."

My whole body is cold. "You're despicable."

He laughs. "I saw pictures of you with him in the paper. God, India you look even more beautiful now than did thirteen years ago. But I did wonder how you'd managed to meet someone like Leandro Silva. I mean, it's not like you spin in the same circles. I wanted to know more about you. So, I had your place broken into. It was just my good luck that Silva was there on your laptop. All his pathetic story written in black and white for me to read. Because if I hadn't gotten anything from your office, then I was going to have your house done over properly until I found something, but I didn't really want to upset my son with a break-in like that."

"He's not your son!" I yell down the phone.

"He's mine, India, and don't you fucking forget it. My blood runs through his veins."

"Your blood might, but he's not yours, and he never will be."

He lets out a maddening laugh. "You've done well for yourself. I want to know all about you and Jett."

"How do you know his name?" I whisper. I never told him. I kept Jett far away from him.

"Come on, India. It wasn't hard to find out. He's into football and Formula One, right? Guess it helps that you're fucking a Formula One driver."

"Screw you," I bite.

He laughs again. "And you kept my book, the one I gave you. That really touched me, India."

I freeze still, my breath catching.

"Do you remember when I gave it to you? It was right after we'd made love for the first time at my place. We were lying in front of the fire, wrapped up in that blanket you loved. I wanted to give you something of mine that I treasured because you'd just given me something important."

"You mean, my virginity? The one you took when I was fifteen years old! I don't need a trip down memory fucking lane, Paul. How do you know about the book?"

"My friend found it in your little box of memories while he was snooping around your house. I told him to leave it on your bed. A little reminder of me. I really don't like being in a box, India. I've spent the last thirteen fucking years in a box!" He yells, losing his cool.

His anger has me recoiling away from the phone. I hear him blow out a breath.

"My time in prison…it was your fault, India. You owe me."

"I owe you nothing. You went to prison because you like to manipulate and groom vulnerable young girls into having sex with you."

"You were never vulnerable, and I sure as hell never groomed you. You were up for it. Couldn't get enough of me, if I remember rightly. Always begging me to have sex with you."

"You make me sick."

He gives a vile sounding laugh. "God, I have missed you, India."

"I haven't missed you. Honestly, I haven't thought of you since the day you were sentenced in court and I watched with relief as the police led you away. Now, tell me what you want because clearly you want something."

There's a slight pause before he says, "I want money."

It's my turn to laugh. "I don't have any, and even if I did, I wouldn't give it to you."

"Your boyfriend is loaded. Net worth around a hundred and fifty million, according to Google. I'm sure he can spare the money. It'll pocket change to him."

Leandro is worth a hundred and fifty million? Of course I knew he was rich, but I didn't realize he was *that* rich. We never talk about his money because it's not important. I don't want Leandro's money. I just want him.

"I am not asking him for money."

"You should because, even though you do pretty well with your therapy business, I'm sure that you don't have the kind of money I want, to spare, whereas your boyfriend does. If I don't get my money, then I'm sending your files straight to the Health and Care Professions Council along with the pictures of you and Silva together and a nice little letter telling them how you've been screwing your patient. You'll be up in front of the Council board faster than you can plead your innocence, and your practicing license will be snatched out of your pretty little hands. You know how the HCPC has zero tolerance for these kinds of things. You'll never be able to practice again, India. You'll be blacklisted. A therapist with no license. All those years of training and hard work, time away from our son, wasted. Then, I was thinking, just for the hell of it, I might leak the documents to the press. You know how they love a good scandal."

"Why are you doing this?" My voice breaks, betraying me.

"Why?" He sounds enraged. "Because you stole my fucking life from me, and now, I want payback!"

My eyes blur with tears. "How do I even know you have these documents? You could be lying."

"I'm not, and you know it. But if you don't believe me, then you can always come here and see for yourself. I would come to you, but obviously, I don't want to break my parole conditions."

"I'm not coming there," I state without hesitation. "You'll have to send them to me. Email them. I'm sure you have my email address."

He laughs dryly. "I do. I'll send them over in a few minutes. But, India, when you see these and know I'm telling the truth, don't for one minute think I'm bluffing. I will destroy your life the way you destroyed mine, if you don't give me five hundred grand."

"Five hundred thousand pounds," I nearly choke.

"It's a week's wages to your boyfriend. I'm sure he won't miss it. And the other condition is that when you have your proof I'm not lying and you have the money, you bring it here to me. I want to see you. And my son…I want to meet him."

"No." I slam my hand on the table. "That will never happen."

"I just want to meet him, India. Just once. I want to know what he's like. Then, I'll leave you both alone. I'll never contact you again."

"You're not getting anywhere near him."

"I'm not a monster, India."

"Says the man who's blackmailing me. I won't do it. Do what you want to me, but you're not getting near Jett."

"Then, you'll lose everything. Your career. Your reputation. You know how people love a juicy story about a bad person. Scandal is all the rage nowadays. A doctor taking advantage of her vulnerable patient. A patient who suffered with PTSD after an almost fatal accident…" He tsks. "It's bad, India. And I will make you look as despicable and seedy as you made me look for simply loving the wrong person. Seems you and I aren't so different after all."

And I'm suddenly that girl again. I'm staring into the past at the man who used to manipulate me into doing whatever he wanted by telling me he loved me.

A tear tracks its way down my cheek. "You never loved me, Paul." I brush the tear away with my hand.

"That's where you're wrong. I did love you. A hell of a lot. I still do in some fucked-up way. You're the mother of my child, India." His voice is soft. There's a brief pause before he says in a harsher voice, "I'll send you the documents that I have. Then, you have twenty-four hours to decide. If you're smart, like I know you are, you'll bring me the money and my son to meet me. If you don't, I'll destroy you. And by the time I'm done with you, India…even Silva won't want you."

thirty-five

LEANDRO

✢ LONDON, ENGLAND

My plane finally landed after a three-hour delay, being stuck in the goddamn airport in Belgium. It's nearing midnight, and I am finally in the car, leaving the airport and heading to India's house.

I'd texted her when I was still stuck in Belgium to tell her my plane was delayed, and as soon as I landed, I was coming straight to her place, but she didn't respond. When I was going through security at the airport, I decided to text her again, letting her know I had landed and I was on my way.

Still no response.

It's bugging the fuck out of me that she hasn't responded. Something doesn't feel right. I'm just about to call her when I receive a text from her.

I'm at your place. See you when you get here.

It's not the usual happy text I get from her and no kiss at the end, which she always does, but I'm still really fucking happy to know she's waiting at my house for me. Hopefully, in my bed, naked.

My cock stiffens at the thought.

God, I can't wait to get home and bury myself deep inside her. I'm going to fuck her all night, all over my house. There'll be no surface we won't have christened by the time I am finished with her.

"Change of plans." I lean forward, toward my driver. "I'm going straight home." Then, I rest back on the seat and close my eyes.

"You're home, Mr. Silva."

I feel the night air on my face and blink open my eyes to see the car door open and the driver's face.

"Shit. I must have fallen asleep." I rub my eyes.

"I'll get your case for you."

I climb out of the car. My driver hands me my case.

"Thanks," I say to him. Getting my wallet, I pull out a few fifties. "For coming out so late to pick me up."

"Thank you, but I can't accept it. Company policy, Mr. Silva. It's not worth my job."

"You're sure?"

"Yes. But thank you."

I shove the notes in my pocket with my wallet, and drag my suitcase to my front door. Key in the lock, I open it and dump my suitcase in the hallway.

"Honey, I'm home!" I call out, a smile on my face. I close and lock the door behind me.

"I'm in the kitchen."

Well, that is not the greeting I was hoping for. And her voice sounds monotone. It leaves an uncomfortable feeling in the pit of my stomach.

With a sense of foreboding, I remove my shoes and head to the kitchen.

India is seated at the breakfast island. She's staring into a glass of red wine in front of her.

"India?"

She lifts her head to look at me. Her eyes are red and puffy. She looks like she's been crying. "I came here because I need to talk to you, and I didn't want Jett overhearing what I have to tell you."

My mouth dries, my chest tightening. "And what do you have to tell me?"

"Paul...he rang me this morning."

"What?" I exclaim, stepping into the kitchen.

She turns on her stool to face me. Briefly closing her eyes, she blows out a breath, her hands curling on her lap. "He did the break-in at my office. Well, he had someone do it for him, one of his prison buddies I'm guessing. He has my laptop. Somehow, he got through the passwords and into my patients' files. He knows you were my patient, Leandro. He's blackmailing me. He wants me to give him five hundred thousand pounds, or he'll send your patient records and pictures of us together to the HCPC."

"Jesus." I rub my forehead with my fingers. Moving toward her, I sit on the stool beside her. "Please tell me you're kidding."

She lets out a humorless laugh as she brushes a tear from her cheek. It kills me to see her crying.

I am going to beat that life out of that fucker when I get my hands on him.

"I wish I were." She rubs her cheek with her wrist. "There's something else..." She worries her lower lip with her teeth before meeting my eyes. "He's threatening to sell the details of your PTSD to the press if I don't comply."

I let out a derisive snort. "And I would have my lawyer shove an injunction so far up their asses that it would be bleeding out of their noses. There is no way they would be able to print that shit because it would be coming from an illegal source. Don't fucking worry about that, babe."

"But I have to worry about Jett." She sniffs again. "Paul wants me to take the money to him in Manchester...and take Jett along with me, so he can meet him." Her jaw clenches in anger. "That's never going to happen. So, I'm sitting here, drinking your wine and mourning the loss of my career. Even if I had the money to pay him off, he's not getting anywhere near Jett."

I take her soft hands in mine, needing to touch her. "If he will agree to just take the money and not see Jett, then let's pay him."

"I don't have that kind of money."

"I do. Five hundred thousand pounds is nothing. It's a scratch on the surface of what I have."

"Five hundred thousand *is* a lot of money. I'm not taking your money, Leandro." She shakes her head, resolute.

"India." I give her a firm stare.

"No, Leandro. Even if Paul would agree to just taking the money and leaving Jett out of it, where would it end? He takes the money, and then after he's run out, he'll come back for more. I couldn't trust that he'd not keep copies of your patient transcripts." Her sad eyes meet with mine briefly, before sweeping to the floor. "I appreciate your offer, but this isn't your problem to fix. It's mine."

I frown at her. "I am going to try to not be offended by that last statement because you are upset and not thinking straight." Dropping her hand, I take hold of her chin, forcing her eyes up to mine. "But I am telling you this. You are mine. You and Jett are my family, now, and for the rest of fucking forever. So, that makes this my problem. That bastard is hurting you, so I'm going to fucking hurt him—badly."

"No," she gasps. "Please, Leandro, don't do anything stupid. I don't want you getting in trouble." She curls her hand around my wrist, her pleading eyes on mine.

"I'm really fucking angry, India." I drop my hand from her face, shoving it through my hair. "I feel helpless, and I don't like feeling helpless. And I definitely don't like pedophiliac motherfuckers blackmailing my girl. I'm at a loss here. You won't let me kick his ass. You won't let me pay him off. And you're going to lose your fucking job because of me. I need to have a sense of control here, and right now, I have none."

I want to lose my temper. I want to drive to Manchester and smash that motherfucker's face in.

Her eyes flash at me, shock in them. "This isn't happening because of you, Leandro. I can't believe you would even think that."

"Come on. If we weren't together, this wouldn't be happening to you." My hands are curling into fists on my thighs.

She slips off her stool. Standing between my legs, she rubs my hands, forcing me to relax them, then takes them in hers. "Then, Paul would have just found some other way to get at me. This isn't your fault. I am so happy, beyond happy, that we're together. I knew what I was doing, the risk I was taking by being with you, and I wouldn't do anything differently. I would choose you every single time. I love you too much to not be with you. I just wish I could have both, you and my career, but I guess life doesn't work that way."

"Babe…" I lower my head. "This is fucking killing me. I need to do something. I need to be able to help you."

One of her hands comes to my face, lifting it to hers. "I'm going to go to the police in the morning to tell them I'm being blackmailed. I need you to come with me. That's how you can help me."

Sighing, I say, "If you are sure that is how you want to handle this…"

"I'm sure." She looks at me, determined.

"Then, of course I will come with you."

She curls her fingers around my ear, brushing them into my hair. "After the police, I'm getting in touch with the HCPC and telling them about you and me, and I'll deal with the consequences from them. I will definitely need you to hold my hand on that one." She gives me a sad smile.

"Anything, babe. I will do anything for you." I slide my hands around her waist, pulling her closer. "But you'll lose your license to practice."

Tears well in her eyes, and she bites her lip. I know it is to stop herself from crying, and it breaks me.

"I don't know what I'm going to do. Being a therapist, helping people, is all I know. And I need to work to pay the bills. I mean, I have some savings, so we'll be okay for a while, but I'm going to have to find something else to do."

"I have plenty of money. You don't need to work. Let me take care of you and Jett."

"No." She shakes her head. "I'm not sponging off of you."

"Sponging?" I let out a frustrated laugh. "India, I love you. I am beyond in love with you. I am yours, wholly and completely. And you are mine." I take her face in my hands. "You and Jett are everything to me. There is no argument here. I'm taking care of you both."

"Leandro...I've worked my whole life, provided for my son. I wouldn't know how not to work."

"Then, you can find a job doing something else. Something you love. But take the time to figure that out. And until that time, I'm taking care of you, babe."

By the time she finds a job, I will have her and Jett living with me, and then I will hopefully have a ring on her finger, making her mine permanently, so she will never have to work again.

She leans in, resting her head in the crook of my neck. My wrap my arms tightly around her. Her breath is hot against my neck, turning me on. I know I shouldn't be horny right now, but I have been without her for too long. She smells and feels so fucking good pressed up against me.

She brushes a kiss to my skin and slowly trails more up my neck, over my jaw, until she reaches my mouth. She kisses me there. "Take me to bed," she whispers against my mouth. "I want to forget everything. I only want to think and feel you."

I swipe my tongue over her lower lip. "Babe, when I'm done with you, you won't even remember what year it is."

She smiles against my lips. "I adore you, Leandro Silva."

"And I adore you. Now, let's go upstairs, so I can show you exactly how much."

thirty-six

INDIA

▌▌MONZA, ITALY

I'M STARING AT LEANDRO lying next to me in bed, watching him sleep. His long black eyelashes fanning his skin. His hair all tousled and caressing his forehead. He looks beautiful.

Jett and I are with Leandro in Italy. We're staying in a stunning two-bedroom suite in Milan, just ten miles away from the Monza track. We've being relaxing for the last few days, just sightseeing and eating true Italian food.

Tomorrow, Leandro has qualifying. Jett loves attending all these races, traveling to all the different countries.

It's been a week since I went to the police station and told them that Paul was blackmailing me. Telling the whole story to the officers was horrible, and I could see the judging looks in their eyes when I told them that Leandro used to be my patient. But I guess I'm going to have to get used to those kinds of looks.

The HCPC wasn't any easier. It was worse. My practice license has been suspended, pending review. Even though I confessed to them about being in a relationship with a prior patient, I have to go through the official process. Leandro and I might have no longer been patient and therapist when we got together, but we shared a kiss while I still was treating him. That matters to the board.

And it matters to me.

Even though I love my job, I just don't feel the same way about it as I used to anymore. As devastating as it is to not be able to help people anymore, I know this is the right thing.

The only person I care about not thinking badly of me is Jett. And thank God, he doesn't. My son is wise beyond his years.

After I had been to the police and the HCPC, I sat Jett down and told him everything. About how Leandro and I met. About his father being released from prison. The break-in. Paul trying to blackmail me. I didn't want Jett finding out from anyone else.

And after I'd told him all of this, he said to me, "As long as you are okay and you're happy with Leandro, that's all that matters to me. The rest is just white noise."

I cried. How could I not? I knew right then, hugging my son, that everything would be okay. That everything would right itself, and that everything happens for a reason.

Paul was arrested and put back in prison for violating his parole, meaning he'll serve out the rest of his sentence. And he will stand trial for attempted blackmail and extortion. Once again, I'll be a witness at his trial. Ultimately, it's my word against his, in regard to the blackmail attempt. But my laptop and the documents about Leandro that Paul had printed out, were seized at his house.

The fact that, by coming forward, I had everything to lose and nothing to gain will show that I'm telling the truth. I'm hoping that he will be sentenced for it, adding a few more years to his jail term. I'm praying by the time Paul gets out, Jett will be a grown man, and hopefully, Paul will have the foresight to leave us all alone.

School is still out for the holidays, going back next week, and Leandro was having a hard time with the thought of leaving us even though Paul was back behind bars, so we came with him to Monza for this leg of the Prix.

I'm feeling relaxed and safe for the first time since Paul got out of prison. And I'm just relieved that everything is out in the open.

The press hasn't gotten wind of the story about Paul, or how Leandro and I met. Maybe they will. Maybe they won't. If they do, then we'll deal with it together.

"You're watching me sleep," he murmurs, surprising me, eyes still closed. His voice is rough with sleep, and sexy as hell.

"I might be." I curl into his side, hooking my leg over his hip and feeling his morning wood beneath my leg. "You just look so adorable when you sleep."

He opens one eye, peeking at me. "The last thing I am is adorable. You, on the other hand…" He opens his other eye as one hand skims down over my bum, curling around my thigh, under my pajama shorts, to touch my quickly dampening knickers with his fingertips.

I gasp at his featherlight touch. "Jett might be awake."

"Then, we'll be quiet." He gives me that sexy grin of his that instantly has me doing what he wants.

My response is to kiss him. His fingers slip inside my knickers, and he pushes one inside me.

"God," I breathe as he fingers me, rubbing my clit with his thumb. "I need to touch you." I push my hand into his pajama bottoms and palm his cock. Gripping it, I stroke it up and down. I love the hiss of air that escapes him at my touch.

The next thing I know, my shorts and knickers are being pulled down my legs, and I'm none too gently turned over, facing away from him.

"Part your legs," he whispers into my ear.

I do as he asks. I feel the head of his cock rubbing over my entrance, up to my clit, and back down again before he pushes inside me.

"Fuck," he groans in my ear. His hand slips under my pajama top, and he palms my breast, pinching my nipple.

A cry escapes me.

"Shh," he whispers, his other hand comes up to cover my mouth as he slowly moves in and out of me. "Do I need to gag you, babe? Or will you be a good girl?"

The thought of him gagging me excites me along with the feel of his hand against my mouth, but I shake my head. "I'll be good," I murmur against his hand.

Keeping his hand over my mouth, his other hand pinches my nipple again. I sink my teeth against his palm. He groans and starts fucking me harder. The sound of his flesh slapping against mine is such a turn-on.

"Rub your pussy, India. I want you to touch yourself."

I've never touched myself in front of him before, but the thought thrills me.

I press my fingers to my pussy, letting the tips of my fingers touch his cock as it thrusts in and out. Then, I start rubbing my clit.

"Fuck. Yeah, that's it," he says roughly in my ear. "Bring yourself off. I want you coming hard and squeezing my cock like a vise."

The rubbing of my clit increases. I'm turned on beyond rationale. I just need to come. Nothing but that matters right now.

I tilt my head back, watching back at him. His hand slips from my mouth and his fingers tangle in my hair. Gripping the strands, he pulls my mouth to his, and he kisses me deep and hard. With the feel of his tongue against mine, his cock inside me, and my fingers rubbing my clit, I come hard, moaning my orgasm into his mouth.

"Fuck..." he whisper-groans. "Your pussy feels so fucking tight around my cock."

He pumps into me a few more times, and then I feel his body tensing in preparation for his release.

"I'm coming, babe," he whispers. "I'm coming inside your hot tight pussy."

I watch his face as he comes down from his orgasm. I love the look of pleasure in his eyes and the love he feels for me that's all on display. I've never been loved before the way Leandro loves me. I didn't even know a love like this existed.

He kisses me again, staying inside me. "There is nothing better than waking up inside you."

I smile, but it's tinged with a little sadness. "I'll miss waking up with you when you're away for the races."

He gives me that heart-stopping smile of his. "Only until November, and then you will be waking up every morning with me inside you."

"When the season finishes."

"No. Every morning for the rest of forever." He takes a deep breath. "India, I'm making this season my last. I'm retiring from Formula One."

"What?" I exclaim, turning to face him, causing him to fall out of me.

"I think we've made a mess of the bedsheets." He chuckles, gesturing at the wet spot caused by my sudden movement.

"You're retiring?" I ignore his humor. "Is this because I lost my job because we're together, and you feel guilty because of that? Because, if it is, then, no, you can't do it. I won't let you."

He takes my face in his hands, brushing my hair from my face with his thumbs. "No. It's not because of that. I was already considering retiring before any of that happened. I hated being away from you when I was in Belgium. My contract is up this year. I came back and achieved what I had wanted to achieve. I fought my demons and got back on the track. But racing just doesn't give me the same feeling as it used to. I want to start my life with you and Jett. I don't want to be away from either of you for most of the year."

I feel a sense of warmth rush through me. "You're sure this is what you want?" I ask in a soft voice.

"Yes. One day soon, I'm going to marry you and fill your belly with lots of Silva babies."

"Lots?" I sputter.

He chuckles, eyes twinkling. "Of course. I'm thinking three, maybe four." He lifts his shoulder, nonchalant.

A strangled laugh escapes me, my eyes widening. "Three, maybe four? Slow down there, Mr. Virility. How do you know I even want more children?"

I do want more children. I couldn't think of anything better than having a baby with Leandro. Probably not four though. But I do love teasing him.

The expression on his face freezes. Then, as quickly as it froze, his expression relaxes. "Then, I would be fine as we are. Jett is mine, so—"

"What?" My breath catches in my throat.

"I said, Jett is mine." His voice softens, his fingertips running down my cheek. "As far as I am concerned, Jett is my son. I'm not trying to step on Kit's toes. I know he has raised Jett as his own. But I want to be Jett's dad, so long as he wants me to be."

My lips tremble, my eyes watering. "I'm pretty sure Jett would be okay with that. Kit, too."

He smiles, one corner of his lips lifting. "Good."

God, I love him. So much.

"And I do want to have more kids, just so you know." I smile gently.

He kisses me again. "We can get started making baby number one as soon as the season is over. We will just get in plenty of practice beforehand."

I press my hand to his chest, over his heart. "How did I get so lucky to have you love me, Leandro Silva?"

"I am the lucky one, babe. Believe me. My life was on a downward spiral to hell before I met you. You saved me in more ways than one. Loving you saved me." Covering my hand with his, he kisses me again, slow and deep, until he's moving inside me, making good on the baby-making practice he has planned for us.

epilogue

LEANDRO

THREE MONTHS LATER

YAS ISLAND, ABU DHABI

When I started racing, I knew this day would come, but I didn't think I would feel the way I do right now or finishing for the reason I am. I thought I would be racing until I was forced to stop by age, or death. Not leaving because it was simply time, and so I can begin my life with the woman I am in love with and her son, who I love equally as much. He is not just India's son. He is mine, too. The more time I spend with Jett, the further that kid burrows deeper into my heart, right along with his mom.

If someone had told me a few years ago that this right here would now be my life—in love with a beautiful woman and me now having a twelve-year-old son—I would have laughed in their face.

Now, I am beyond happy. I have found my place in the world. A place I didn't even know I was looking for until I found it.

Even knowing this is my final race and although traced with a little sadness, I'm just ready for it to be done, so I can get my family home and start the next chapter of my life with them.

Helmet on my head, I say the words I haven't uttered since right before the accident that changed everything. The race that I thought had almost ended my life, but instead, it led me straight to the best thing in my life, India.

"Being second is to be the first of the ones who lose," I whisper under my breath.

With one last look at India—with Jett on one side, my mother on her other—I mouth to her, *I love you.*

A stunning smile spreads across her face, and then she mouths the words right back to me, leaving my heart feeling full.

I climb into the cockpit. *Time to go.*

I run through the tire warm-up. Then, we are at the starting line. I'm on pole position from qualifying first yesterday. Now, I just need to win this race.

I'm not going to win the Prix. Carrick is just a little more up on points than me. But if I'm retiring, then I'm going out with a win.

Red…

Red…

The usual flicker of anxiety grips my chest. But I control it and then dispel it.

Red…

Red…

Red.

Go!

My car starts off, rapidly gaining speed, until I'm flying around the track. The voices in my ear are drowned out by my own focus on winning this race and getting back to my family.

My family.

"Yes!" I pump my fist into the air as I cross the finish line, coming in first.

My team comes running toward my car as I slow to a stop. I pull the steering wheel off, tossing it aside, and I climb out of the car. I tear my helmet off as I'm being hugged and patted by all the members of my team. The cheer of the crowd roars through my ears as my eyes search out India.

The instant my eyes meet hers, a sense of ease moves through me, making me smile even wider. I push through the crowd. Reaching her, I sweep her up into my arms. Her hands pressing against my face, I kiss her.

I kiss her with every ounce of love I feel for her.

Breaking from our kiss, panting, she quickly glances at the crowd of people in the stands, all cheering my win around us.

"Are you sure you want to leave all this behind?" She gives a gentle tilt of her chin in the direction of the stands.

My eyes do a quick sweep over her shoulder. I can see the banners with my name on them, some begging me not to retire. Then, I look back to my girl. "I'm more than sure."

She smiles wide and presses her lips to mine again, softly kissing me.

God, I fucking love her.

"Sorry to interrupt the love fest." Carrick's voice comes from behind me, and I feel the pat of his hand on my back. "But we have to take our places on the podium."

I reluctantly break away from India's lips.

"I'll wait here," she tells me.

Turning to Carrick, I slide my arm around India's waist. Andi comes over to Carrick, and he wraps his arm around her shoulders.

"You mean, the podium on which I'll be standing on first place."

A grin spreads across Carrick's face. "You know I totally let you win this one, right? I mean, it was the least I could do, with you retiring, and the fact that I had already won this year's Prix on points."

Laughing, I shake my head. "You're a prick, you know that?"

"Yeah, Andressa tells me all the time."

Andi slaps a hand to his stomach.

Jett comes over, standing beside me.

I drop my other arm over his shoulder. "You want to come up on the podium with me?" I ask Jett.

His face lights up bright with a smile. "For real?"

"For real." I smile at him. "You might as well have a taste of what it's like for when you are up there on your own one day, accepting your own trophy."

His smile gets wider, and I feel India's hand tighten on my waist. I remove my arm from Jett and turn my eyes to hers, seeing them filled with nothing but love and that watery look she gets in her eyes whenever I do something for Jett.

"I love you," she whispers.

I cup her cheek, pressing a soft kiss to her lips. "Love you, too, babe."

Releasing her, I take ahold of her hand and sling my arm back over Jett's shoulders. "Come on then, son. Let me show you what it's like to look down on Carrick Ryan."

Carrick discreetly gives me the middle finger. I let out a laugh, and with India's hand in mine and my arm around Jett, my family and I start the walk toward my last podium climb.

epilogue

INDIA

FIVE YEARS LATER

✠ NORTHAMPTON, ENGLAND

I'M STANDING IN THE TEAM GARAGE at Silverstone, watching Jett prepare for his first race. Leandro is with him.

My baby boy is seventeen and has signed with his first team, and he is debuting in the FIA Formula 3 European Championship. Leandro is his manager. They make quite the team.

"A little someone wanted you."

Turning at the sound of Kit's voice, I smile at the little girl wriggling in his arms.

"Mama!" Adriana holds her arm out to me.

"Hey, baby girl." I take her from Kit.

Adriana has her father's dark eyes and hair, and—of course, I'm biased—she's the most beautiful little girl in the world. She's just turned two. It took Leandro and me about a year to get pregnant, but we'd sure had fun trying.

"You okay with holding her?" Kit nods his chin at my pregnant belly.

I'm six months pregnant. We're having a boy.

"I'm fine for a few minutes." I press a kiss to Adriana's soft hair. "She is getting heavy though." I give her a gentle squeeze.

"She was getting fussy upstairs," Kit tells me. "You know how she wants to be in the midst of the action."

"Like her father, brother, and uncle."

Kit chuckles at that.

"Petra here yet?" I ask Kit.

"She's on her way."

Kit is settled down and married now to Petra, Andi's best friend. It took them a while to come together, and it was a messy long process, mostly because of my brother, but they got there in the end. They're happy together now. I'm really glad because Petra is good for him.

I am so happy that he found his someone.

I'm just hoping they give me a niece or nephew soon.

Adriana starts to tug on the cute little pink headphones covering her delicate ears.

"No, leave those on, Addy," I tell her.

"Did you ever think we'd be standing here, waiting for our boy to take his first step into the world of Formula racing?" Kit says from beside me.

I meet his eyes, smiling. "No. But I'm sure glad we are, if not a tad nervous."

"Yeah, me, too—on both counts." He exhales. "But he's right where he was always meant to be. As are you."

My life has changed beyond recognition since Leandro came into it. Not that it was bad before him because it wasn't, but the moment he came into it, he brought more color into all our lives.

After Leandro retired from Formula 1, we took some time to settle into our lives together, finding our groove with each other. We lived separately in the beginning, but more and more, Leandro started staying over at my place until he was practically living there.

It was the smoothest way to do the transition for us all. After all, it had been just the three of us for so long, and I didn't want Kit to feel pushed out in any way. I made sure to be careful of Kit's feelings, but the house was definitely getting too small with the four of us living together.

Then, when Leandro took me to his restaurant, the place where we'd had our brief first date, and he asked me to marry him after us being officially together for six months. To say I was surprised would be putting it mildly, but I was elated. Of course I wanted to say yes right there and then, but I was concerned about Jett and Kit and how they would react. Getting married would be a big change. Then, when Leandro saw my hesitation, he told me that he'd gotten their blessing before asking me. Once I knew that, nothing could stop me from saying yes.

After we were married, Leandro had another surprise for me. He had bought us a house in Buckinghamshire, a few miles from where Carrick and Andi live. I'd gotten quite close to Andi, which is strange considering how I first met her, but now, she and Petra are my closest friends.

Jett had helped Leandro pick the house out. But I was worried about Kit and where he would live. I didn't want him to think we were getting rid of him by getting married and moving into the new house. Because, to be honest, I wouldn't know how to live my life and not have Kit close by.

But Leandro was way ahead of me. He already had it all covered. It was like he had thought of what all my concerns would be and covered them, ensuring I would be happy.

He had bought another house for Kit to live in, less than a five-minute walk from ours. Even though Leandro could afford to buy the house for Kit without a second thought, Kit being Kit wouldn't accept it and said the only way he would live in the house was if he paid rent. Leandro reluctantly agreed.

Kit and Petra still live there now. And it finally became their house, when Leandro gave it to them as a wedding present. Leandro always gets his way in the end. I love that about him.

I am the luckiest girl in the world that I get to have the man I love and keep the family I love close to me, too.

So, I was a married woman, and Jett was thirteen and independent, hardly needing me for anything. I was starting to feel like a spare part. I had no job. My license, as expected, had been stripped from me at the hearing, which was held a few months after we'd gotten back from Leandro's Italian race. Although I'd expected that to be the case, it didn't make the knowledge hurt any less. I sold my practice to another therapist, hoping he would enjoy his time there as much as I had.

I was bereft, but I wasn't alone. Leandro was in the same position as me.

There was, of course, Jett's karting, which he had gotten really serious about at that point, to keep us busy-ish, but Leandro and I are workers. We'd both worked our whole lives, so we needed more.

Then, one day, after one of Jett's races, Leandro came home with a great idea. He'd heard of some land going up for sale a few miles from where we lived. He suggested we buy it and turn it into a karting track and also a kind of youth center. A place for kids who have nowhere to go to race and have fun. I immediately loved the idea, as it meant I could be helping people—kids who were just like Kit and I had been—lost with no real place to go. And it would also be a place where Jett could train.

So, Leandro put in a generous offer the next day. It was quickly snapped up, and six weeks later, the place was ours. It took a good few months to get it up and running, but Silva-Harris Karting officially opened its doors seven months after we'd put in the initial offer.

We charge no entry fee to the kids, and the money to run it comes through charity donations and fundraising, which I'm in charge of. When we put on races, we charge for the ticket entry. Of course, Leandro's name pulls people in, and we also call in favors from famous driver friends of

Leandro's. Namely, we get Carrick to come to as many races as we can when he's not off at the Prix. And Leandro also puts a lot of his own money into the center, but he—well, *we* can afford it.

It's amazing, running the center. Leandro helps train kids on the karts, and we have people working there, too. He's heavily involved with Kit's career now, and that takes up a lot of his time.

Kit helps out at the center when he can. But he's busy nowadays. He no longer models, but he acts. Film and TV. He's made quite a name for himself.

My brother, the famous actor—who'd have thought?

Adriana starts wriggling in my arms. She doesn't last long. She always wants to be off.

"Mama, want Dada, Jett Jett." She starts tugging on my hair.

"Okay, baby girl." I turn to Kit. "You coming?"

He gives me a nod, and we walk over to where Leandro and Jett are talking. Discussing race tactics, no doubt.

As soon as we reach Leandro, Adriana is reaching for him. "Dada!"

His face lights up at her. "Addy Baba."

He grins at her, taking her from my arms, and she squeals, grabbing at his hair as he blows a raspberry on her cheek.

I love watching them together. Something Jett never got to have with his father. But thank God he had Kit, and now, Leandro, too.

"Silly, Dada! Not Addy Baba!" she tells him off.

He laughs at her and then looks at me. "You doing okay, babe?" He presses a hand to my stomach, rubbing it.

"I'm good." I press my hand over his, smiling lovingly at him.

Then, I turn to Jett. He looks exactly as Kit did at that age. The age I found out that I was pregnant with him.

My boy is going to be breaking hearts all over the world soon, if he isn't already.

"How are you feeling about the race?" I ask him.

"Fine." He gives a lazy shrug. He has the teenager thing down pat.

"You're not nervous?"

He's usually fine at his karting races, but Formula 3 is a whole different ball game. If what Leandro says is anything to go by, he says Jett will be up to Formula 1 within three to four years. He's that good.

Jett glances at Leandro and then back to me. "Nah, I got this in the bag, Mum." He grins at me.

I love his confidence. He's always had confidence, but Leandro has rubbed off on him over the years, and now, he has it in spades. The ever-growing relationship between Leandro and Jett has been a joy to watch happen. A true privilege. They have a great bond. A father and son bond.

My son might not have his biological father in his life, but he has better. He has a wonderful uncle, who loves him like he's his own, and an amazing man who might have come into his life later but loves him like he's been there since the day he was born.

He has two men who would do anything for him.

After Leandro and I got married, Leandro told me that he wanted to become Jett's father in the legal sense, too, that he wanted to adopt him. After carefully approaching the subject with Jett, he told us he wanted that, too.

Leandro and I were so happy to make it legal, but we had a hurdle to jump, and I knew it wouldn't be easy. And sadly, it wasn't. Leandro couldn't legally adopt Jett because Paul refused to sign the papers. He didn't do it out of love for his son. He did it out of spite.

But it didn't matter. Leandro was his dad where it counted. Still, Jett never let it go, and he wanted to do something to show Leandro that he was his dad. So, we were colored surprised when Jett came home on his sixteenth birthday to tell us that he'd legally changed his name to Silva. Even though he had my maiden name and no link to Paul in that way, he wanted to show Leandro that he saw him as his dad and that we were a family in the fullest sense.

Aside from the day Adriana was born, it was the only other day I saw Leandro brought to tears. Of course, I cried, too.

The call comes through that the first race is soon to start.

I hug Jett. "I'll see you at the finish line," I tell him, cupping his cheek.

"I'll be the one crossing it first." He grins confidently.

"That you will. Love you, kiddo."

"Love you, too, Mum." He plants a kiss on my cheek, and he goes over to his car.

Leandro hands Adriana to me and goes with him.

Once Jett is set, Leandro comes back over to us.

He takes Adriana from my arms again and puts his arm around me, pulling me close.

"Jett's okay?" I ask.

He smiles at me. "He's fine, babe. Don't worry."

"You're not worried?"

"No, because I know how good he is. And I trained him, so you know…" He smirks. "I better get over to the desk, so I can talk our boy through this race." He nods in the direction of the bank of desks where Jett's team is watching on the screens, their earpieces in so that they can communicate with him.

"Okay."

He leans in close and kisses my lips. "I love you."

"Love you, too."

He presses a kiss to Adriana's neck, and she squeals happily.

"You okay?" Kit asks me, as I watch Leandro walk away.

"Yeah. But I'm really nervous now though."

"Jett's golden, Indy. He's got this in the bag."

"Yeah." I bring my eyes to him, giving him a light smile. "You're right."

The engines roar, and my body tenses up as I see the race about to begin on the screens before me.

And I think about my life then and now.

If someone had told that scared shitless pregnant seventeen-year-old girl that, in close to eighteen years' time, she'd be getting ready to watch that baby boy growing in her stomach take his first drive as a Formula 3 driver, she would have told them that they were crazy.

Or if someone had told me five years ago that I would be happily married and pregnant with my second child with that broken, angry Brazilian racing driver who'd just walked through my office door, I'd have definitely said they were insane.

Falling in love with Leandro wasn't part of my plan, and I know for sure that it wasn't his, but God, am I glad it happened.

We were wrong for each other but so right in the truest sense of the word.

Leandro and I were inevitable.

Life has twists and turns and sharp bends and throws all manner of hardship at you, but it's how you deal with it that counts.

If you stand up and be truthful, with yourself and others, everything will come out right.

Telling the truth about Leandro and me showed me that.

Yes, I might have lost my career over our relationship, but I don't regret it. Not for one single minute.

Leandro always tells me that I saved his life. But really, I think we saved each other. I was living but not to the fullest. Not until him. And now, we're both living to the max, together, as we were always meant to be. We had to endure the worst, to be able to find each other.

But it was those things we endured and faced separately that made us who we are together.

And I wouldn't have it any other way.

acknowledgments

I WILL TRY TO KEEP THIS AS BRIEF AS POSSIBLE. Firstly, I want to say thank you to everyone who bought, read, and loved *Revved*. This book is possible because of you guys.

As always, thank you to my family. My ever-patient husband and children, you three saved my life in more ways than you'll ever know.

Sali—"God has not taken them from us. He has hidden them in his heart, that they may be closer to ours." Author Unknown. #LiveLikeBenny

Trishy—My days are simply brighter with you in them. Disneyland next year!

Christine Estevez, my lifesaver and patient friend—One of these days, I will surprise you by having something ready on time! Thank you for being you.

My agent, Lauren Abramo—Your support and patience is truly appreciated. And I promise, I will finish that book for you now!

Zoë Lowdon—Your enthusiasm and love for *Revved* and Carrick truly touched my heart. Thank you for your awesomeness and for *Revved* Round Up!

A big thank you to India Partis, soon-to-be Kendall, for letting me borrow your name.

Huge thanks to Ulla Milla and Cleida Roy for the Portuguese translations.

And, as always, my biggest thanks goes to you for reading this. Three years ago, my life changed in a way I never imagined possible, and I have *you* to thank for that. My gratitude is limitless.

about the author

SAMANTHA TOWLE is a *New York Times*, *USA Today*, and *Wall Street Journal* bestselling author. She began her first novel in 2008 while on maternity leave. She completed the manuscript five months later and hasn't stopped writing since.

She is the author of contemporary romances, *The Mighty Storm*, *Wethering the Storm*, *Taming the Storm*, *Trouble*, and *Revved*. She has also written paranormal romances, *The Bringer* and The Alexandra Jones Series, all penned to tunes of The Killers, Kings of Leon, Adele, The Doors, Oasis, Fleetwood Mac, Lana Del Rey, and more of her favorite musicians.

A native of Hull and a graduate of Salford University, she lives with her husband, Craig, in East Yorkshire with their son and daughter.

CPSIA information can be obtained at www.ICGtesting.com
Printed in the USA
LVOW04s0042050815

448804LV00035B/1678/P